JOSIE COULD SEE THE REFLECTION OF HER ALARM clock. Any moment now. She held her breath, unable to peel her eyes away from the mirror, as the time hit 3:59.

The image blurred. Josie's reflection distorted as if she were staring at it through a pool of water. Ripples cascaded across the surface of the mirror, obscuring her reflection entirely, then dissipated. The image resharpened and Josie found that she was staring at her own face, her own eyes once more. Only the girl in the reflection had blond highlights, bright and shiny where Josie's hair was a duller blond, and the girl in the reflection wore a denim pencil skirt and a red gingham tank top, while Josie was in her shortie pajamas.

Not a reflection.

Josie stared at the girl. The girl stared back.

This was Jo. The girl from Josie's dreams.

GRETCHEN McNEIL

Balzer + Bray
An Imprint of HarperCollins Publishers

3:59

For my boys: John, Roy, and Wolfgang

Balzer + Bray is an imprint of HarperCollins Publishers.

3:59
Copyright © 2013 by Gretchen McNeil
All rights reserved. Printed in the United States of America.
No part of this book may be used or reproduced in any manner whatsoever
without written permission except in the case of brief quotations embodied
in critical articles and reviews. For information address HarperCollins
Children's Books, a division of HarperCollins Publishers, 195 Broadway, New
York, NY 10007.
www.epicreads.com

Library of Congress Cataloging-in-Publication Data
McNeil, Gretchen.
    3:59 / Gretchen McNeil. — First edition.
        pages cm
    Summary: Betrayed by the two persons she trusts the most, Josie jumps
at the chance to trade places with her twin in a parallel universe until Josie
becomes trapped in a dangerous world where shadowy creatures feed on
human flesh.
    ISBN 978-0-06-211882-0
    [1. Space and time — Fiction.   2. Interpersonal relations — Fiction.
3. Science fiction.   4. Horror stories.]   I. Title.   II. Title: Three fifty-nine.
PZ7.M478752Aah   2013   2013000231
[Fic]—dc23   CIP
                                                                      AC

Typography by Ray Shappell
14 15 16 17 18   LP RRDH   10 9 8 7 6 5 4 3 2 1
❖
First paperback edition, 2014

And moving through a mirror clear
That hangs before her all the year,
Shadows of the world appear.

—from "The Lady of Shalott"
by Alfred, Lord Tennyson

ONE

2:20 P.M.

JOSIE CROUCHED BEHIND THE PHOTON LASER module and aligned it with the beam splitter at the other end of the lab table. "Once we build the vacuum dome," she said, making a minor adjustment to the laser's trajectory, "this should work."

"Should?" Penelope said.

Josie glanced at her lab partner. "There's a reason no one's been able to prove the Penrose Interpretation."

Penelope snorted. "Because it's unprovable?"

"Thank you, Captain Obvious," Josie said, with an arch of her brow. "Would you also like to tell me why the sky is blue and the Earth is round?"

"Ha-ha." Penelope bumped Josie out of the way with her hip and took her place behind the laser. "I don't know how you talked me into doing *this* as our science-fair entry. What if it doesn't work? I'll never get into Stanford if I fail AP Physics."

"We're not going to fail." Josie looked around the room at the array of textbook experiments their classmates were working on:

balloons and static electricity, wave pools, concave mirrors. Total amateur hour, whereas she and Penelope were tackling Penrose's wave-collapse theory of quantum gravity. It was like bringing a major leaguer to a T-ball game. "Mr. Baines grades on a curve. We'll be fine."

"We'd better be." Penelope moved around the table. For the bazillionth time, she began carefully measuring out the positions of the one hundred or so mirrors they'd use in the experiment, noting their exact locations in her spiral notebook. Her straight black hair swished back and forth in front of her face as she scribbled furiously. "Are you sure you're not just doing this as an FU to your mom?"

Josie stiffened. "Of course not."

Penelope didn't look up. "I don't know. Seems like trying to prove an almost impossible theory that's in direct conflict with the hypothesis your mom's spent her entire career exploring is kind of a slap in the face."

It was, of course. Josie knew it. Penelope knew it. If Josie's mom had bothered to initiate an actual conversation with her daughter in the last six months, she'd probably know it too. But Josie wasn't about to admit that in fourth-period physics.

"I'm worried about the laser," she said, changing the subject. "I'm not sure it's strong enough."

Penelope calmly looked up at Josie with her almond-shaped eyes. A grin crept across her face. "We could always borrow the experimental laser your mom has up at her lab."

"No way," Josie said.

"Oh, come on! It's perfect."

Josie held firm. "We cannot use the hundred-kilovolt X-ray free-electron prototype from my mom's lab, okay? Get over it."

Penelope wasn't about to give up. "Maybe you could have your dad borrow it? For legitimate work purposes? And then if it just *happened* to end up in our demonstration the night of the science fair no one—"

"My dad moved out last weekend," Josie interrupted in a clipped tone.

She hadn't told anyone yet, except Nick, and only because he'd picked her up for a date ten minutes after Josie's dad had broken the news that he'd rented an apartment in Landover.

"Oh," Penelope said, her eyes wide. "Shit, I'm sorry."

"It's okay." It wasn't.

Penelope opened her mouth to say something, when the loudspeaker in the classroom crackled to life.

"Attention, students," said the voice of the school secretary. *"We have a special announcement."*

"What now?" Penelope groaned.

"Quiet down, everyone," Mr. Baines said. The murmur in the classroom dulled.

Josie checked her watch. A special announcement five minutes before the end of the school day? That was weird.

"Good afternoon, this is Principal Meyers. As some of you may have heard, another body was found in the woods west of Crain Highway this afternoon."

The classroom erupted into agitated whispers. "What?"

Penelope squeaked. "Another one?"

"Like the previous incidents, the victim was killed sometime between the hours of ten o'clock in the evening and four o'clock in the morning, from an apparent animal attack."

Josie arched an eyebrow. "Animal attack? In Bowie, Maryland?"

"Shh!" Penelope hissed.

"Therefore, students are asked to refrain from visiting the Patuxent River Watershed or other surrounding uninhabited areas after dark until the animal or . . ."

Principal Meyers paused and cleared his throat with that kind of dry, forced cough a kid makes when they're trying to convince Mom and Dad they're too sick to go to school.

"Until the animal," he continued, *"or other perpetrator responsible for the attacks is apprehended."*

"Other perpetrator?" Josie said. "What the hell does that mean?"

But Principal Meyers offered no response to Josie's question. The loudspeaker popped once, twice, and fell silent.

2:35 P.M.

THE END-OF-DAY BELL PEALED THROUGH THE classroom, jarring everyone into action.

"Don't forget," Mr. Baines shouted above the commotion of screeching chairs, backpack zippers, and the almost choral musicality of thirty cell phones all being powered on at once. "Final review of your projects tomorrow. Be prepared to defend your hypotheses."

"How can I think about my science project after that?" Penelope clutched Josie's backpack as they slowly filed out of the room. "Other perpetrator. See? I knew the police were covering up for a serial killer."

Josie half turned around. "Who said anything about a serial killer?"

"Sixteen dead bodies in six months, their gruesome, dismembered, and half-eaten remains left in the woods in the dead of night?" Penelope almost sounded excited as she described the murder scenes. "Please, this is classic serial-killer territory."

Josie laughed. "Okay, CSI."

"Fine, don't believe me." Penelope trotted alongside her in the crowded hallway. "But it fits. The pattern, the escalation. And now we've had two murders in the last week alone." She paused and dropped her voice. "I'm sure this animal-attack crap is just a cover-up so the population won't panic and descend into martial law."

Ah, that was the Penelope Josie had known for years. The lovable conspiracy theorist who spent most of her free time combing antigovernment blogs and with each passing day became increasingly convinced that Big Brother was watching her. "Pen, you're blowing this way out of proportion."

"No, I'm not," Penelope said, sounding hurt. "I never blow anything out of proportion."

Josie planted her hands on her hips. "Remember that time you were convinced your eighty-year-old neighbor was a spy for the Venezuelan government? Or what about when you almost electrocuted yourself trying to find the hidden listening devices the NSA had installed in the walls of your house?"

Penelope pursed her lips. "Still no proof I was wrong about either, thank you very much."

"Hey!" a familiar voice called out through the postclass crush of bodies. Josie spun around and caught her breath as she spied the tall, black-haired figure of her boyfriend, Nick Fiorino, threading his way through the crowd.

"Hey, gorgeous," Nick said, planting a kiss on Josie's cheek. "Miss me?"

Nick pulled her close and Josie let out an audible sigh. Out of the corner of her eye, she could have sworn she saw Penelope grimace.

"Can you believe they found another body?" Nick shook his head. "How many is that now? Like a dozen?"

"Sixteen," Penelope said quickly. "Although coverupcadet .com suggests the actual number may be more like two dozen, if you take into account the missing-persons reports of the last six months and cross-reference them against people known to be in the vicinity of a wooded area." She chuckled nervously. "This is why I don't leave the house."

"Wow, Pen," Nick said. "That's, um . . ." He glanced sidelong at Josie, grasping for words.

"Insane?" Josie suggested.

"Fine, don't believe me." Penelope narrowed her eyes. "But we'll see who's insane when the feds catch the serial killer. Later." Then she turned on her heel and marched off down the hall.

"I don't think she likes me," Nick half joked.

Josie smiled at him. "You know how Pen is with . . . people."

Her friend Madison's meticulously groomed head of curls popped up beside Nick. "Can you believe it?" she said, slightly out of breath. "Another body!"

"I know, right?" Josie said.

A look of concern passed over her best friend's face. "Don't take that shortcut through the woods anymore, okay, Josie? If there's an animal out there stalking people, I don't want you to be the next victim."

Josie smiled. It was sweet that Madison was concerned about her. "Don't worry," she said lightly. "Penelope thinks it's actually a serial killer, so it's cool."

Madison's eyes grew wide. "A serial killer?"

"Let's not go there," Nick said.

"Anyway," Madison said, "Josie, what are you doing after school?"

Josie sighed. "I have to drive to Landover before my shift at the Coffee Crush."

"Landover?" Madison said.

"Yeah." Josie dropped her eyes. "I have to go pick something up from my dad's new place."

"Your dad's new place . . ." Madison's voice trailed off as she processed Josie's words.

Josie sucked in a breath as she felt Nick's hand grip her shoulder. Ugh. Better to just get it all out in the open. "My dad moved out last weekend." The words tumbled on top of one another as they raced out of her mouth. "Movers accidentally took the old mirror my mom used to keep up in her lab. She's dispatched me to retrieve it. That's it."

"Oh," Madison said. Then her eyes widened as reality dawned on her. "Oh!" She paused. "Okay, well, I'm taking my demon little sister to dance class, but I'll be home by the time you're off work. So call me, okay? If you need to talk?"

Josie smiled weakly. "Will do."

Madison nodded, then turned and headed down the hall. Josie's smile lingered as she watched Madison go. Her friend might be a bit of an airhead upon occasion, but she was also incredibly sweet and thoughtful. Two things Josie desperately needed in a best friend these days.

Nick leaned down and whispered in Josie's ear. "You okay?"

"Yeah." Josie took a deep breath, then let it out slowly. She *so* didn't want to drive all the way to her dad's new condo by herself. The thought was so depressing. "Any chance you can ditch track practice and come with me?"

"Sorry, gorgeous," Nick said with a shake of his head. "Regionals are in two weeks. Coach would kill me if I miss practice."

Josie tried to hide her disappointment. "Oh."

"Walk me to the gym, though?"

Josie nodded absently. "Yeah, okay."

They navigated the halls in silence, Josie wrapped up in her thoughts. Her parents' separation had hit hard. One day they seemed like their normal, happy selves, but practically overnight things had changed. Small fights at first, then before Josie knew it, her parents' nightly screaming matches were the new normal around the Byrne household. In less than six months, her dad had moved out. Now Josie's home life was a hot mess. Her dad was still in shock and, like a lovesick teen, spent most of his time trying to get Josie's mom to take him back. Her mom had thrown herself into her work, going so far as to have a home lab constructed in their basement to avoid charges of child abandonment while she worked twenty-four-seven on her new experiment. Meanwhile, Josie could count on one hand the number of conversations they'd had in the last week that weren't about work or—

"Did you hear me?"

Josie's head snapped up. She and Nick were standing in front of the entrance to the boys' locker room. His hands were folded across his chest, and his dark brows were pinched together.

"Huh?"

Nick sighed. "Josie, were you even listening to me?"

"I'm sorry," Josie said. "I was just . . . I don't know. Lost."

"You've been like that a lot lately," he said quietly. "Between your parents and your science project, it's like you don't have time for anything else." It wasn't an accusation so much as a statement of fact. "Do you even remember what today is?"

Josie caught her breath. Was it Nick's birthday? Had she forgotten Nick's birthday? No, that was in October. Josie relaxed. Forgetting her boyfriend's birthday would have been a disaster.

"Never mind." Nick shook his head and stepped toward her. "Look, there's something I need to talk to you about. Something important."

Josie looked up at him. There was an edge to his voice that made her heart beat faster. "Is everything okay?"

"Yeah, yeah," he said quickly. "I mean, there's just a lot going on and I needed to—"

Deep in Josie's purse, an alarm went off. Her cell-phone reminder that she needed to be in the car on the way to her dad's if she was going to make it back to work on time. She'd already received a written warning because of her tardiness—usually because she was lingering at the track, watching Nick practice—so she needed to motor. "Crap," she said. "I have to go."

"Oh." The muscles around Nick's mouth sagged, reflecting more dejection and pain than his clipped, monosyllabic response. What was going on with him?

"Call me," Josie said. "After practice, okay? We'll talk tonight."

"Okay." Nick flashed his crooked half smile, the sadness of a moment before evaporated. He was his old, carefree self again. "Don't let any monsters attack you on the way back from Landover, okay?"

Josie snuggled her face into his chest. "I'll try."

THREE

JOSIE'S ANCIENT HATCHBACK SHUDDERED IN protest as she stepped on the accelerator.

"Come on." She leaned forward in her seat, willing the old car to go faster. "If I'm late again, I'm going to get fired."

As if in answer, the Ford Focus lurched forward. A hand-me-down from her cousin, it was almost as old as she was, and the engine screeched in protest as she held the pedal to the floor. The speedometer flickered, desperately grasping for forty-five miles per hour, and for a fleeting moment Josie thought the Teal Monster, as Madison had dubbed the car, might actually have some kick left in her.

Or not. The engine sputtered, momentum slowed, and Josie had to downshift to third gear.

"I hate you," she said, slapping the steering wheel with the palm of her hand. "Just so you know."

Josie's phone rang. Keeping one hand on the wheel, she reached into the center console and hit speakerphone. "Hello?" she said loudly, over the roar of her car's engine.

"Did you get it?" Her mom's voice was crisp and businesslike.

Josie whizzed around a turn and hoped her mom couldn't hear the screech of tires on the other end of the line. She eyed the rearview mirror, sending a death stare bouncing to the back of her car, where the oversized rococo monstrosity sat covered in a fluffy blue blanket, wedged into the flattened backseat through a feat of advanced car yoga.

"Josie, are you there?"

"Yeah, sorry." Glancing right and left, Josie careened through a yellow light just as it turned red, praying there were no state troopers around as she barreled through the intersection. A speeding ticket was the last thing she needed. "I've got the mirror," she said, before her mom could ask again.

"Good." Her mom cleared her throat. "I just had a shipment delivered at the lab. So I'll—"

"Be home late," Josie said, finishing her thought. It was a conversation they had at least twice a week, whenever her mom got a shipment of materials delivered to her lab at Fort Meade. Top secret stuff, but Josie guessed it was the ultradense deuterium her mom used in most of her experiments. If so, it might be a few days before her mom surfaced from the lab.

"Right." Her mom paused. "Okay, well, drive safely. I'll call you later."

Josie clicked off her phone. Part of her was relieved when her mom worked late: the tension between them recently had been almost unbearable. But since her dad had moved out, the house was lonely, and the idea of spending another night there by herself was incredibly depressing.

Her mood sinking like lead in water, Josie flipped on the radio. It was programmed to the AM news station.

"From the evidence at the scene," a man said in a cool academic voice, "we have determined that the attacks were not caused by a bear. They appear to be the work of a predatory cat of some kind."

A reporter cut into the prerecorded statement. "When pressed for information, Captain Wherry stated that local investigators are targeting known collectors of exotic animals in hopes of finding the cause of the recent attacks. For WPTN, I'm Morgan Curón."

Josie rolled her eyes. A cat? Really? Sixteen dead bodies and all the authorities could come up with was an exotic cat?

Maybe Penelope was right: it *was* a cover-up.

"Time for weather on the nines," the news anchor said in his overly cheerful radio voice. "And we're looking at glorious weather for this April fifteenth."

Josie's stomach dropped. Today was April fifteenth?

Holy crap, no wonder Nick had looked so upset when she left. Today was their one-year anniversary.

And Josie had completely forgotten.

Shit, shit, shit. Major relationship screwup. How could she have forgotten? It was just a few weeks ago that she and Nick had been at the mall and he'd pointed out a necklace he thought she might like in the window of a chain jewelry store. Entwined hearts with little red stones at the apex of each. No wonder he'd been acting so weird that afternoon. He was waiting for her to wish him a happy anniversary so he could give her the necklace.

She reached for her phone; she needed to talk to him right that second. But he'd be in the middle of practice. Damn. She'd have to wait until after her shift and then maybe they could celebrate tomorrow?

She was the worst girlfriend ever.

Josie sped around a corner, tapping the brakes as lightly as possible so as not to lose momentum, and veered onto Leeland Road. Another glance at the time. 3:50 p.m. Ten minutes. She pushed Nick and their anniversary from her mind. There was nothing she could do about it, and right now she had to focus on getting to work. As long as she didn't get caught at the railroad crossing she was totally going to make it.

Wishful thinking. Josie heard the peal of bells before she even saw the flashing lights. Train coming.

Crap.

Option A: slam both feet onto the accelerator and pray her car had enough power to slip under the rapidly descending crossing arm. Option B: slow down and wait for the train. Option A: decent chance of a gruesome, fiery death. Option B: decent chance she'd get fired.

Kind of a close call, but after a moment's hesitation, Josie hit the brakes and screeched to a stop just as the railroad-crossing arm locked into place across the road.

It didn't take long for Josie to regret her sensible decision. Immediately, she realized it was a government transport train leaving Fort Meade. Probably the same one that had just delivered the shipment to her mom.

Oh, the irony.

Josie counted the cars as they ambled by. *Seventeen, eighteen, nineteen.* She checked the clock. 3:57 p.m. "Come on!" she said through clenched teeth.

Twenty-two, twenty-three, twenty-four. Josie leaned over the steering wheel and craned her neck, trying to get a view of the rails stretching south through the thick greenery of forest that hugged both sides of the road. She could barely see twenty feet down the tracks. Was there an end in sight? She couldn't tell.

Twenty-six, twenty-seven, twenty-eight. Josie reached for her cell. She'd call work and explain. See? It wasn't her fault. She would have been on time if it hadn't been for the stupid train. How could she control that?

3:59. With a heavy sigh, Josie scrolled through her contacts to the coffeehouse's number and hit the green button.

Josie wasn't quite sure what happened next. The Teal Monster idled at the crossing, the occasional shudder of the strained engine rumbling beneath her. Then, suddenly, the car lurched so violently that Josie's head smacked into the roof. She screamed—half from surprise, half from fear—and smashed her foot onto the brake pedal. Had someone hit her? She frantically looked into the rearview mirror but saw only the barren expanse of Leeland Road twisting into the woods. Confused, she turned all the way around to make sure a deer hadn't accidentally rammed her. That's when she noticed the mirror. It lay cockeyed in the back, and the blue blanket had slid to one side. The mirror must have shifted in the backseat while she was stopped at the crossing.

Huh?

She reached back to see if the mirror had been damaged, when a light flashed—fierce, white, and so intense that a searing pain shot through her eyeballs to the back of her skull and left her irises screaming for mercy. It was a clear, sunny afternoon in the middle of April, but the light that filled Josie's car blinded her as if she'd been sitting for hours in utter darkness and someone had suddenly shone a spotlight in her face. She slapped a hand over her eyes, desperate to block out the blinding flash. Blood thundered through her temples, and her eyes ached against the piercing light. Josie buried her face in her hands, and felt the car shudder . . .

Then everything went dark.

FOUR

A HORN BLARED. IT SOUNDED CLOSE, YET MUFFLED.

Then a voice. "Hello? Josie? Are you there?"

Josie blinked her eyes open, half expecting to still be blinded by the mysterious flash. Instead, Leeland Road stretched before her, open and empty. The train was gone. The crossing arm sat vertical and inert, the warning bells dead silent.

Her car was still running, her cell phone still gripped in one hand, and her manager's voice pierced the haze that had settled over her brain.

She absently lifted the phone to her ear. "H-hi," she said lamely.

"Josie, do you have any idea what time it is?"

Another horn blast. An irate driver in a pickup truck swerved around her through the oncoming traffic lane, flipping her the bird as he passed.

"I said," her manager repeated. His voice was steely. "Do you have any idea what time it is?"

Josie shook her head, trying to jar her brain back into working order. Time? What time was it? Her eyes drifted to the dashboard clock.

"Four oh-nine?" She couldn't keep the question out of her voice. Ten minutes? She'd been at the train crossing for ten minutes? That was impossible.

"Exactly," he said. "You're fired."

She heard the phone go dead, yet Josie didn't move. She stared at the digital clock display wondering what the hell had just happened.

4:21 P.M.

Josie eased the Teal Monster onto the soft shoulder of Leeland Road and cut the engine. She felt disoriented and confused, and her head still ached from the blinding flash of light that seemed to come from nowhere. She sat in the car, her heart pounding, and tried to figure out what she was going to do next.

She could have gone home, but to what? An empty house and no one to talk to. Not what she needed.

Other options: Penelope would be home, posting on one of her favorite online forums, but she'd immediately theorize that Josie's experience at the train tracks was part of a government mind-control experiment gone haywire or something equally off the rails, and Josie wasn't quite in the mood for that. Nick would still be at track practice. She hated bothering him while he was training for regionals, but maybe if she texted to explain what had just happened . . .

Josie paused. What *had* just happened to her? She had

absolutely no clue. One minute she was counting train cars, then the Teal Monster jumped off its tires and something blinded her. A flash. From the train, maybe? She thought it had come from that direction, but what on the train could have produced a flash that painfully bright? She remembered squeezing her eyes shut against the blue-white light. And then . . .

Nothing.

She needed to talk this through with someone right away. Someone who would listen and wouldn't judge. Like Madison.

Josie drove crosstown, the stupid mirror sliding back and forth in her trunk at every stop sign. All this drama for a mirror. She wanted to stop the car, haul the thing out, and smash it into a million pieces.

At the sight of Madison's car in the driveway, Josie breathed a sigh of relief. She ran up the driveway, taking the wooden steps to the enclosed patio two at a time, and rang the doorbell.

Josie crossed her right foot behind her and tapped the toe of her pink tweed Converse impatiently while she waited. *Come on, Madison! Answer the damn door.* After what seemed like forever, Josie rang the bell again, leaning on it so the old-fashioned chime tolled half dozen times.

Still nothing. Maybe Madison had the music cranked up in her room and couldn't hear?

Josie retreated down the steps and snaked around to the backyard. Madison's house was in one of the newer developments, with lots of land in between the homes and absolutely no fences, unlike the craftsman Josie's parents owned in the old part of town, where the lots were practically on top of one another. Josie half expected to hear Madison's favorite Pandora station blaring from the open window of her second-floor bedroom, but the whole house was oddly quiet.

Where the hell are you, Mads?

She pulled out her phone and checked the time. Four forty-five. Nick might be done with practice. It was worth a shot. She hit the call button and held her breath.

As the phone rang in Josie's ear, another sound drifted down from above. A tinny rendition of Josie and Nick's song. Which was also his custom ringtone for her calls.

Josie froze. Her phone continued to ring before it went to voice mail. "Hey, this is Nick. You know what to do."

Josie hit redial before the beep. She didn't even hold the phone to her ear, her arm lank by her side as she gazed up at the house. Once again, the opening chords of their song drifted down from the second floor. Through the open window in Madison's bedroom.

With a shaky hand, Josie ended the call and immediately dialed Madison's cell.

Another cell-phone ringtone pierced the stillness of the afternoon—"Weird Science" by an old eighties band called Oingo Boingo—which Madison had programmed for Josie.

From the room above, someone silenced the phone after just a few seconds of ringing.

"Shit," said a male voice.

Nick's voice.

Josie caught a flicker of movement at the curtain in Madison's window. A flutter as if someone had peeked out, then quickly let the fabric fall back into place.

"Shit." Madison's voice echoed.

Josie felt all the warmth drain out of her body. Her hands went numb, and the landscaped backyard blurred in and out of focus. The realization was slow and painful. Her best friend. Her boyfriend. The oldest cliché in the book.

"Seriously?" Josie said out loud. Her voice shook. "On our anniversary? *Seriously?*"

Nick's head of disheveled black hair filled the window. "Josie," he said. "I can explain."

"Explain? Explain *what*?" Josie tottered backward across the uneven lawn, then forced her legs to work. She needed to get to the car. She needed to get out of there.

Josie rounded the front of the house just as the patio door creaked open.

"Josie!" Madison screamed. She was still buttoning up the cashmere sweater she'd worn to school that day. "Wait."

Josie broke into a run, desperate to get to the Teal Monster.

Nick was faster. She could feel his runner's stride pounding up behind her as she yanked open her car door. "Josie, stop!"

"Screw you." Josie ducked inside and locked the door. Nick slammed his fist onto the driver's-side window, but Josie didn't even look at him. She couldn't. She fumbled with the keys; her hand shook violently as she turned over the ignition and she could already feel the hot tears pouring down her cheeks.

Josie took one look as she peeled out of the driveway. Madison stood on the lawn with her hands covering her face. Nick was in the middle of the street, arms outstretched toward her retreating car.

He hadn't even bothered to put on his shirt.

"IS THAT YOU, JOSEPHINE?"

Josie froze midtiptoe. Dammit. Her mom was supposed to be staying late at the lab like, you know, she mentioned on the phone not even two hours ago. And when her mom said she was staying late at work, she meant it like 99.99 percent of the time.

But no. Not today. Today of all days, her mom surprised her by coming home early.

Perfect.

Josie had driven around for almost an hour, trying to decide what to do. A variety of choices crossed her mind, everything from plunging her car into the Anacostia River, to driving back to Madison's house to tell them both exactly what she thought of them, to several other options that would have gotten her thirty to life in a state penitentiary.

For the first half hour or so her phone had rung off the hook. First Nick, then Madison, then Nick again. Rinse, repeat.

Then the texts. First Madison, in a rapid, manic stream.

Madison: **Josie, please just listen.**

Madison: **It's not what you think.**

Madison: **I mean, it is, but it's not like that.**

Madison: **Nick just needed someone to talk to.**

Madison: **And you've been so busy.**

Madison: **And things just happened. I didn't mean them to. I swear.**

Then Nick. His texts came more slowly, as if he labored over what to say.

Nick: **I'm sorry.**

Nick: **I didn't mean to hurt you. It just happened.**

Nick: **You've been so distant lately.**

Nick: **I know that's no excuse.**

Nick: **I don't know what else to say.**

Josie had ignored them all. She didn't want to talk to either of them. Especially not Nick. She didn't want to hear him beg for forgiveness. Or worse, maybe he wouldn't. Josie recalled the conversation they had after school. *There's something I need to talk to you about.* Maybe this had been his way of breaking up with her?

"Josephine?" her mom repeated. Her voice was louder, and Josie could clearly hear her footsteps ascending from the basement.

She should have stayed in the car.

"Josephine!" Her mom stood in the doorway that led to the basement lab, still in her white coat, with the top half of her dark brown hair twirled up on the top of her head and secured with two ballpoint pens.

"Is everything okay?"

Josie opened her mouth to say something, but the words froze on her tongue.

"What?" her mom said.

Josie flinched. She wanted to tell her mom the truth—about Nick and Madison, about her job, and about the train. She wanted a squishy hug, to feel her mom's long fingers comb through Josie's hair and for her mom to tell her that everything was going to be okay. But there had been such a strain between them the last few months, a divide that neither of them seemed able to cross, and the last thing Josie needed at that moment was to be rejected by her own mother.

"I'm fine."

"Are you sure?"

"Yeah."

26

Josie leaned against the wall and closed her eyes. She felt suddenly dizzy; the cramped quarters of the hallway spun around her. She just wanted to crawl into bed, pull the covers over her head, and pray that when she woke up, she'd discover that she'd gunned the engine on her car and outrun the oncoming train.

Maybe then, none of this would have happened.

"Where's the mirror?" her mom asked abruptly.

Right. The real reason her mom was even talking to her. "I left it in the garage."

"Fine, fine," she muttered more to herself than to Josie. "I'll move it downstairs to the lab." Then she cleared her throat and turned suddenly toward her bedroom door. "I have to go out tonight."

Josie shook herself. "Oh." Great. Was her mom dating now?

"Just back to the lab," she said, as if reading Josie's mind. "Running an experiment. Need to check in. You'll be okay here?"

Josie shrugged. "Sure."

"Good." Her mom paused as if she was going to add something, then shook her head again in that odd, distracted way. "Get some rest, Josephine. You look tired."

2:37 A.M.

Time abandoned her.

Josie had been lying on her bed in the dark, staring at the ceiling for what felt like days, yet the alarm clock on her nightstand mocked her. It had only been four hours.

Stupid clock.

Her mom said she looked tired, but that was an understatement. She was exhausted, plain and simple. Hours of crying would do that. Her temples throbbed from the headache that ravaged the very depths of her brain, and her raw, bloodshot eyes ached beneath swollen lids. Her limbs were heavy, a mix of fatigue and despair, and her entire existence felt futile.

Her body and mind were completely worn down, yet she couldn't sleep. Not for half a second had she slipped into blissful unconsciousness. She'd been aware of every moment that passed, even the sound of her mom quietly opening the front door when she got home, and dragging something heavy down the hall and into the basement. The stupid mirror, no doubt. Josie had been wide awake for all of it.

She'd tried to fall asleep, of course, for hours. All her usual tricks: counting sheep, pretending she was on a tropical island with Nick—she even looked for comfort in her favorite childhood stuffed animal, Mr. Fugly Bear. Whenever there was a thunder-and-lightning storm, her dad would bring her Mr. Fugly Bear (so named because he was missing an ear and the "thumb" off his right paw due to a washing-machine incident), who was the bravest, most rugged bear in town and would protect her from any and all danger. He'd prop Mr. Fugly Bear up against Josie's pillow, facing the window in case any monsters tried to crawl in that way.

Whether or not Mr. Fugly Bear could protect Josie from a trampled heart was never put to the test. He always sat on one of her bookshelves, but suddenly he was gone. There was another teddy bear on the shelf that looked vaguely familiar, but no Mr. Fugly. She must have moved him when cleaning up her room, accidentally shoved him to the back of a shelf or something.

Even he knew when to jump off a sinking ship, apparently.

And so she just lay there, staring at the ceiling. She couldn't erase the last view of Nick from her mind: shirtless, standing in the middle of the street in front of Madison's house.

Eyes open or closed, she couldn't get that image out of her mind. And it stayed with her, mocking her pain, it seemed, until sleep finally overtook her.

3:59 A.M.

The car shudders in protest as she steps on the accelerator.

But only for an instant. The BMW's precision engine kicks in immediately and she relaxes into the leather seat as the speedometer jumps five miles per hour.

She strokes the calfskin-wrapped steering wheel. "I love you," she says out loud. "Just so you know."

She glances at the digital clock on the dashboard. Two minutes to four. She should only be a few minutes late, as long as she doesn't get caught at the train tracks.

Of course it's her own fault she's running late, but whatever. Totally worth it to watch Nick at track practice after school.

She speeds around a corner, tapping the brakes as lightly as possible so as not to lose momentum, and veers onto Leeland Road. Up ahead, she can hear the peal of bells even before she sees the flashing lights at the bend in the road. Train coming.

There's only a split second to decide, but it's a no-brainer. She slams on the accelerator. The engine revs and the car careens forward as the arm of the railroad crossing descends. She holds her breath in anticipation and she grips the steering wheel so tightly her knuckles ache. She can feel the tension in her fingers, the strain of her muscles as she wills the car onward. Will I make it? Too close to call. *Her heart races and her breath comes in short gasps; the anticipation is palpable. Will she die in a glorious explosion as the train hits her car at full speed? She smiles. At least then all her problems would vanish.*

The car shoots under the descending arm with inches to spare. For an instant she's blinded by the lights of the speeding train, then her car flies down the far side of Leeland Road.

She's not sure if she's relieved or disappointed that she's still alive.

Josie sat bolt upright.

Her heart raced, and she was sweating so badly her light cotton pajamas clung to her damp flesh like plastic wrap.

Darkness surrounded her. She was in her bedroom. In bed. Safe. *It was just a dream.*

Was it? Josie held her hands up in front of her face. Her fingers curled inward, stiff and sore, as if they'd held something in a death grip.

Like a steering wheel.

SIX

1:15 P.M.

SHE NEVER FELL BACK TO SLEEP. AFTER THE nightmare, a mix of insomnia and despair weighed on her, and left her sobbing in her bed late into the morning. So it was some kind of miracle that she managed to get herself to AP Physics just as the late bell rang.

She'd wanted to stay in bed, lock her bedroom door, pull the covers over her head, and stay there until . . . forever. But missing physics would have put their project—and their grade—in jeopardy, and Josie couldn't do that to Penelope, especially since the Penrose experiment had been entirely her idea. Besides, she doubted the news of Madison and Nick's affair would have gotten around yet, so at least she'd be spared that indignity. Holding on to that one gleaming ray of good news in an otherwise wretched day, Josie had hauled her ass into the shower and made a half-hearted attempt to look as if her world hadn't collapsed around her.

A decision she now regretted.

Was it her imagination, or had the classroom fallen eerily silent? She couldn't look at anyone, didn't dare lest the precariously controlled sobbing that had overwhelmed her for most of the morning erupt again, but she had the acute sensation that every head in the classroom had turned to face her.

Josie slowly walked across the room to her lab table, eyes fixed on the tiled floor, painfully aware of how tragic she looked. Her unwashed hair had been yanked back into a ponytail and she clearly hadn't put much thought into the jeans, graphic tee, and stripy grandma sweater she'd pulled on. Her shoes completed the fashion disaster. She'd pulled her closet apart for her favorite pair of pink tweed Converse, but she couldn't find them, and in the end she just slipped on a pair of beat-up flip-flops that looked as if they'd taken one too many trips through the washing machine. Last, she'd attempted to disguise her dark under-eye circles with a clown-sized dollop of concealer, and to mask her red, bloodshot eyes with a dose of Visine that would have put Niagara to shame.

Yep, she was a disastrophe. Pathetic.

Penelope fidgeted on her stool as Josie sat down next to her. She was agitated, barely able to contain herself, and as Mr. Baines began to explain how he'd be evaluating their proposals, Penelope kept glancing at Josie, taking a breath as if she was going to say something, then looking away. In fact, everyone appeared to be stealing furtive glances at Josie whenever Mr. Baines turned his back. She was clearly the most interesting science experiment in the room.

Her illusion that word of Madison's and Nick's affair hadn't gotten out? Obliterated.

As soon as Mr. Baines started his rounds, Penelope broke her silence. "Oh my God," she said in a strained whisper. "You're here. I mean, you're okay. I mean, I was so worried because you weren't answering your phone and then everyone was talking about Nick and Madison, and then I saw the necklace at lunch and—"

Josie's head snapped up. "Necklace?"

Penelope cocked her head to the side. "Yeah. Nick gave Madison a necklace. Entwined hearts."

"Entwined hearts?" A lump rose in Josie's throat. "Gold with little red gemstones?"

"Yeah." Penelope cocked her head to the side. "How did you know?"

Josie groaned. "My anniversary gift." Nick had given it to Madison.

Penelope's eyes grew wide. "Wait, you *do* know that they've been getting it on behind your back, right?"

Josie winced. "Yes," she whispered.

"Oh, good." Penelope caught her breath. "I mean, no. I mean, I'm so sorry."

Josie stared at the table.

"So they decided to come clean?" Penelope continued in her high-pitched whisper.

Josie shook her head. "No. I caught them."

"Shit!"

Zeke and Zeb, the Kaufman twins, turned around at Penelope's exclamation. They were Nick's teammates on the varsity track team. Perfect. That was the last thing Josie needed: Nick's friends reporting back on the pathetic state of his ex-girlfriend.

"Shh!" she hissed at Penelope.

"Sorry."

She should have stayed home.

"I'm glad you're here," Penelope said, her voice low and steady. "I really was worried."

Josie nodded. She appreciated Penelope's concern, even if she couldn't quite process it.

"I wanted to punch Madison in the face when I heard," Penelope continued, talking nervously. "She was flaunting the necklace around in Humanities. Even Nick looked uncomfortable. Fidgety, and every time she touched him, he kind of stiffened up. It made my skin crawl the way she was acting, like they'd been dating forever and not just screwing behind your back for the last two months."

"Two months?" Josie's stomach dropped.

Penelope's hand flew to her mouth. "I didn't mean to tell you that."

"Who's saying it's been going on for two months?"

"Um . . ." Penelope lowered her voice. "Everyone?"

"Everyone?"

Penelope slapped her hand over her mouth again and let out a tiny squeak.

Josie lowered her forehead onto the smooth, cold metal of the lab table. Two months? Nick had been lying to her for two months?

How had she not seen this? Not known? How could she have been so stupid?

"Miss Wang. Miss Byrne." Mr. Baines strolled up to their lab table, clipboard in hand. His lips were pursed, and his wide-set eyes crinkled just at the corners as if he was secretly amused by their setup. "A standard beam-splitter experiment? I expected something less boilerplate from the daughter of Dr. Elizabeth Byrne."

Josie met Mr. Baines's gaze. She'd always suspected he rather passively disliked her, but as he stood there before her, the hint of a grin tugging at the corners of his thin lips, she realized it was a less passive and more active animosity bubbling under the surface.

"We're attempting to prove the Penrose Interpretation," Penelope said quickly, her voice rising an octave.

"Really?" Mr. Baines said. His eyes never left Josie's face.

"Y-yes," Penelope stuttered. "We just need to build the vacuum to replicate conditions outside the Earth's atmosphere and—"

Mr. Baines cocked an eyebrow. "A vacuum? That's it?"

"And mirrors," Penelope added, somewhat lamely.

"More like smoke and mirrors," Mr. Baines said with a throaty laugh. He scribbled in his notebook and turned to examine the next table. "Good luck with the unprovable theory."

"It's not unprovable," Josie mumbled.

Mr. Baines paused and turned back to her. "I'm sorry?"

"It's not unprovable," Josie repeated. This time, her voice sounded strong and forceful, no hint of tears. It was as if something snapped inside her at Mr. Baines's condescension, and suddenly all Josie wanted was a fight.

Mr. Baines walked back to their table. "I believe Penrose *himself* would disagree with you."

Penelope poked Josie violently in the back with her pen, practically begging her to shut the hell up. Too late.

"Well, then Penrose *himself* is an idiot." Josie said it louder than she'd intended. Penelope gasped, and all around her, Josie could hear the rustling of bodies as people focused on the escalating confrontation.

"Hm." Mr. Baines sniffed the air as if he detected a rotten odor in the air. He looked Josie directly in the eye and she met his gaze steadily. She wasn't about to back down. She'd learned more about parallel-universe theories by the time she was ten years old than Mr. Baines knew now. Her parents had spent their entire careers attempting to prove the many-worlds theory to explain quantum irregularities, and names like Niels Bohr and Hugh Everett III were more familiar to her than Harry Potter or Anne Shirley. If Mr. Baines wanted to go toe-to-toe with her on this subject, she was ready for him.

Instead, he looked away and flipped the page on his clipboard in a hurried fashion. "Well, I'm glad to see you haven't let certain *personal* events distract you from your work."

Josie's face burned. In an instant, the pain, horror, and indignity of her situation swamped her, made even more painful by the realization that not only did every student at school know what happened to her, but her snooty physics teacher did as well.

Josie desperately tried to fight back the tears that welled up in her eyes, but it was no use. Penelope, the lab table, the entire classroom blurred out of focus. As the first of the heavy droplets spilled down her cheeks, Josie spun around and ran out of the room.

SEVEN

3:35 P.M.

YOU SHOULDN'T BE HERE.

Josie ignored her inner voice of reason and continued to stare out the passenger window of her car. Parked on the hill above the athletic field, the Teal Monster half-hidden behind a Dumpster, she could just see the boys' track team running pyramid drills. She remembered those practices well. She'd sit in the bleachers, focused on homework, occasionally glancing up to find the tall, muscular form of her boyfriend sprinting around the all-weather track. Even now, stealing a moment with him from her hiding place in the car was oddly comforting.

That's so pathetic.

"Shut up," Josie said out loud.

Awesome, Josie. Talking to yourself while you stalk your ex-boyfriend. Quite a life you've carved out for yourself.

A pack of boys in mismatched red-and-white shorts and loose-fitting T-shirts rounded the upper turn. The middle-distance runners were pushing themselves through the last four hundred meters. They ran in a small pack, about eight guys in all, and at that distance they looked two inches tall. The Kaufman twins stuck out like identical sore thumbs, their long, bleached-blond hair flopping with each stride in almost disturbing symmetry. Then Josie's eyes drifted to the dark-haired runner behind them. Nick.

He ran with a telltale stance—straight up and down with a high kick to the knee. And as the pack cleared the corner, heading down the final straightaway, Nick slipped into an outside lane, whipped around the twins, and pulled ahead. Josie couldn't see his face but could picture it in her mind. Cool and calm, no display of fatigue or stress. It was his signature finish. While the other runners strained, red-faced, to keep up with him, Nick always had something left in the tank.

As usual, Nick crossed the imaginary finish line several feet ahead of his nearest rival. He threw his arms in the air and jumped around as if he'd just won a gold medal. The other runners dribbled across the line and bent forward, hands on knees, while Nick continued his mock celebration. Then one by one, they all meandered to the inner field for stretches.

Josie sighed and leaned her head back against the headrest. It was almost like old times, if "old times" was just twenty-four hours ago. Nick at practice, Josie watching. She could almost imagine . . .

Josie froze. Below, another figure stepped onto the field: slender, elegant, poised even when picking her way across the spongy surface of the track. Josie could tell right away it was Madison.

Her curls rippled in the spring breeze, and before she was halfway to the field, Nick caught sight of her. He stood up slowly, glancing to his right and left as if from embarrassment, and sauntered across the field to meet her.

Madison reached out and grabbed Nick by the waistband of his shorts, pulling her to him. Then right there on the track, she kissed him.

Nick broke off the face sucking after a few seconds, and Josie watched as Madison reached a hand to her neck and lifted something to her lips. She kissed the object before letting it fall back into place. The necklace.

"Fuck you!" Josie shouted. She pounded on the steering wheel with both fists. She hated them both so much. How dare they be so happy? How dare they have done this to her? "Fuck you! Fuck you! Fuck you!" Then she accidentally hit the car horn with her fist.

Madison and Nick instantly looked up toward the Teal Monster's hiding place. Josie scrunched down in her seat. This was a disaster. How could she have been so stupid? Spying on her ex-boyfriend and ex–best friend. Josie's blood ran cold. She was going to be the laughingstock of the entire school.

Without sitting up, she turned the ignition over, released the parking brake, and eased her car around the Dumpster. She waited until she was completely out of sight of the track before she sat up in her seat.

She could barely drive home amid the sobs.

EIGHT

3:59 P.M.

JOSIE WOULD HAVE GONE STRAIGHT TO BED THE second she got home, if it weren't for the explosion.

She was dragging her tired, worn body down the hallway when the foundation of the house rocked as if an earthquake had hit. Josie had to brace herself against the wall to remain upright. At the end of the hall, the basement door flew open, and a bright light flashed through the house, so intense it momentarily blinded her.

It took Josie a few seconds to process what had happened. The flash. The feeling that the house had jumped off of its foundation.

Josie swallowed, her throat suddenly parched, as a creepy-crawly feeling spread across her skin. This had all happened before. In her car, by the side of the train tracks just twenty-four hours ago. Could it be a coincidence? Or something even stranger?

You're being ridiculous. Josie shook her shoulders, tossing off the inexplicable fear that had overcome her. She didn't believe in coincidence, or déjà vu, or any of that crap. This was a pattern, and the one thing she'd had instilled in her since childhood by her two scientist parents is that patterns are not random. They always exist for a reason.

Josie set her jaw and marched down the hall.

Time to find the reason.

The basement lab was in a state of chaos. Books and equipment were scattered across the floor, dumped from a metal shelving unit that had tilted over onto the large stainless steel table in the middle of the room. The floor was strewn with broken glass, which crunched under the soles of Josie's flip-flops, but she hardly noticed. Her eyes were fixed on a piece of equipment in the corner. Mounted on an elaborately rigged series of sawhorses and tables that curved around one corner of the basement, down the full length of the house, and back around the next corner, was a laser.

Not just any laser. Josie recognized the double undulators, compact accelerator, and experimental bending magnets right away. It was a prototype of a compact X-ray free-electron laser—an X-FEL—the multimillion-dollar piece of equipment Penelope had suggested they "borrow" from Josie's mom for their science-fair entry. And it was sitting in Josie's basement.

Wouldn't someone at Fort Meade notice that an X-FEL the size of a minivan and worth more than the crown jewels had suddenly gone missing from a heavily secured government facility? How the hell had it gotten into Josie's house?

Josie eased her way around an overturned table for a closer look at the laser. She'd never seen this version of an X-FEL before but she'd heard her parents discussing it excitedly over dinner for years. It had been one of the priority projects up at Fort Meade: millions in funding, a team of A-list scientists and engineers, top secret specs no one had ever seen.

Josie bent down and examined one of the undulators. It was one of the most high-tech, cutting-edge pieces of equipment in the world and yet . . .

Something wasn't right. This rig wasn't shiny and new and gleaming with custom-made components. It was old, gritty, and looked as if it had been pieced together with odd parts and discarded materials from earlier prototypes. Josie peered at the accelerator tube, her nose so close her breath made foggy little clouds against its metal surface. She could clearly see the seaming where different pieces of the cylinder had been fused together. An X-FEL of that caliber should have had a custom-designed accelerator of all one piece, and this one looked almost home-made.

Josie snapped upright. Homemade? Had her mom built a duplicate version of a top secret laser *in their basement*?

"What the hell is going on?"

The words might have come from Josie's mouth, but they didn't. She spun around, stumbling over a heavy steel box, and saw her mother standing at the top of the stairs.

"Oh my God," her mom gasped, taking in the full extent of the damage.

"Yeah, I'm fine, thanks," Josie said under her breath.

Her mom inched down the stairs, as if testing her weight against each step. Her eyes were wide with shock as she scanned the basement from left to right. "What happened?" she said at last, her voice shaky. "Tell me what happened."

"There was an explosion."

Her mom whirled on her. "Did you turn it on?" she said breathlessly. "Did you turn on the laser and cause an explosion? Where is the deuterium?"

"Wait, there was deuterium in the house?"

"Tell me!" her mom snapped.

Josie shook her head. "I was upstairs. There was an explosion. It blew the door open."

Josie's mom glanced up at the basement door. "Blew the door open?" she said absently.

"Yeah," Josie continued, "and I found the lab like this."

"Found the lab like this . . ." Her mom's voice trailed off.

"Mom, what's going on? Why do you have the X-FEL in the basement? And why does it look like you made it yourself?"

Her mom turned back to her and opened her mouth to say something, then clapped it shut. She stared over Josie's head at something against the far wall of the basement. Josie turned, following her gaze to the mirror propped up in the corner.

"Get it out of here," her mom said without looking at Josie.

"Huh?"

"The mirror. Get it out of the lab. Now."

"Why?" Josie stared at her mom. The mirror? Really? There

was a bootleg weapons-grade laser in the house and her mom was concerned about the mirror?

"I . . . ," her mom started, her eyes faltering. "I don't want it damaged. It was my grandmother's."

Josie sighed. *Fine, whatever.* She crunched her way to the back of the basement, lifted the mirror, then shimmied through the mess and up the stairs.

As she reached the hallway, she looked down at her mom to ask what she was supposed to do with the mirror. But the words froze on her lips. Her mom sat on a stool, head in her hands.

Josie had no idea what was going on, no hint of what her mom was involved in. Locked doors, homemade lasers, explosions, secrets.

Maybe this had all contributed to her parents' separation? Maybe there was something going on—something major—that had shut her mom off from her family? Josie made a mental note to ask her mom about it. But not now. With her mom still sobbing in the basement, Josie quietly closed the door.

4:20 P.M.

Josie rested the mirror against the wall outside her bedroom and stared at it. So many odd things had happened since she picked up the stupid thing from her dad's apartment. Could they all be connected or was it just a weird coincidence?

There's no such thing as coincidence. That was practically a mantra around the Byrne household. So if it wasn't a coincidence, there was something about the mirror that connected the disparate events of the last twenty-four hours. Something concrete and logical. There had to be.

She'd seen the mirror once before, at her mom's lab on a "bring your kid to work" day back in elementary school. Her mom said the mirror helped inspire her when she was trying to solve a problem in the lab, though why she decided to bring it home a few months ago, Josie had no idea.

It stood about five feet high, with short legs on either side and a rounded top. Garish and ostentatious, the frame was heavily embellished with opulent wood carvings—jagged leaf flourishes that jutted out onto the surface of the mirror, connected by swirling vines that got denser and more entangled as they extended upward. At the top of the mirror, the heavy carved foliage entwined to form a kind of woodland crown, right in the middle of which was an angelic face. Josie's arms got goose pimply as the delicate face stared at her with dark, unseeing eyes in the muted light of the hallway.

Part of her wanted to beat the mirror to a pulp: smash the glass, dismember the frame, and stomp up and down on its remnants until there was nothing left but dust and slivers. Instead, she found herself dragging the ugly thing into her room, where she shoved aside a beanbag chair and leaned it against the wall.

If the mirror was somehow connected to the flash of light and the explosion in her basement, she was going to figure it out. Maybe it would fix whatever her mom was dealing with. Then maybe, just maybe, Josie could fix her family too.

NINE

3:59 A.M.

SHE GLANCES UP AT THE SUN AS SHE WALKS ACROSS the track. *Almost three full hours before sunset—plenty of time to get home before dark.*

A pack of boys in mismatched red-and-white shorts and loose-fitting T-shirts rounds the upper turn. She steps onto the inner field and pauses next to a pile of gym bags.

The boys blow past her at a full sprint. Except one. From the back of the pack, he slows his pace, running straight up and down with a high kick to the knee. Cool and calm, with no display of fatigue or strain, Nick stops inches from her.

"Hey, Jo."

She smiles. "Nick."

"What are you doing here?"

She takes a step toward him. "You said you had something for me. Remember?"

"Oh. Right," he says between deep breaths. "I just didn't think you'd want it right now."

"I do," Jo says. "Is that okay?"

"Of course."

She follows Nick across the field to a pile of backpacks and jackets. He bends down, unzips the front pouch of his bag, and removes something wrapped in blue tissue paper. "I think this belongs to you." He puts the packet in her hand.

She trembles as she slowly peels away the layers of tissue. "Oh, Nick!" She gasps.

It's a necklace on a gold chain. Two entwined hearts.

"Yeah," he says, a black curl flopping over his eye. "I thought you'd want it."

She reaches up and brushes the hair from his face, letting her hand linger against his cheek. He doesn't move. She trails her hand down his chest and she can feel his heart pounding. She doesn't care that he's sweaty. She doesn't care that he smells like the inside of the boys' locker room. She presses her body into his and tilts her head up toward him. He looks down at her with those piercing brown eyes as she stands on tiptoe, aching for his lips. . . .

Josie let out a moan as her eyes fluttered open. Instead of Nick's face just inches from her own, all she saw was darkness. The bluish light of the moon streamed in through her window, illuminating a patch of floor and bureau, including a loose photo of her and Nick. It was taken just a few weeks ago.

When Nick was already cheating on her.

The image of Madison kissing Nick on the track flooded Josie's mind. Between the explosion in her mom's lab and the mystery of the mirror, Josie had almost managed to forget her most recent humiliation.

Almost.

Ugh. Tomorrow was going to be a disaster at school. The embarrassment of getting caught spying on them was salt in the wound of their betrayal. Everyone at school would be talking about it. How was she going to face the shame?

Josie fought the panic welling up inside her. She just needed to get some sleep. Things would seem better in the morning. She rolled on her side, determined to put all thoughts of Nick and Madison out of her mind, and looked at the clock just before she shut her eyes.

4:00 a.m.

TEN

"JOSEPHINE, ARE YOU GETTING UP TODAY?"

Josie stared at her bedroom ceiling. Getting up for what? What was the point?

So much for feeling better in the morning.

"Did you hear me?" Her mom cracked the bedroom door. There was a pause where her mom must have registered that Josie was still, in fact, in bed, then Josie felt a whoosh of air as her mom threw the door open. "You're not even awake yet?"

Silence. Was she going to ask what was wrong? Josie wasn't sure if she was hoping for it or dreading it.

"Are you feeling okay?"

"No," Josie croaked.

There was the sound of footsteps across the hardwood floor, stopping short of Josie's bed. "I'm sorry." Her mom paused. "You should stay home."

"Okay." Maybe she could just stay in bed forever and never go back to Bowie Prep? That seemed like the best-case scenario.

"I'll call and check in on you from the lab. Try to get some rest."

Yeah. Rest.

She can't sleep.

She sits up in bed, pushes her sleep mask to her forehead, and squints against the light. She never has insomnia. Always sleeps like the dead. But she's been tossing and turning for hours. Time to give up.

She throws the blue floral comforter back and swings her legs over the bed. The carpet is soft and lush as she walks across the room to the bookcase. She wiggles her toes in it as she tries to decide on a book.

She chooses a volume of Keats. A gift from her mom. She's never read it but it seems like it would fit her romantic mood. She reaches for the necklace that hangs just beneath her throat and fingers the delicately woven gold hearts. Nick and Jo. Intertwined forev—

The word forever *freezes on her tongue. She stares at the antique mirror in the corner of her room. It perfectly reflects her bed.*

But instead of an empty bed and rumpled comforter, sound asleep in her bed is a girl.

She glances back at her bed. It's empty. But when she returns to the mirror, she can clearly see the image of someone asleep in the bed. Her *bed. She takes a step closer to the mirror just as the girl rolls over. She can see the face clearly now. It's not just a girl.*

It's her. Identical.

But that's impossible.

She's across the room in a second, her face inches from the mirror. That room, that girl. They look so real. Like the glass from the mirror has evaporated away to nothing. She reaches out her hand expecting to feel the cold, smooth surface of the mirror, but instead the space feels dense, thick, and spongy like gelatin. Her fingertips permeate the gooey nothingness beyond the frame of the mirror, warping the reflection of the girl asleep.

Is it really a reflection? What's happening?

The sleeping girl sits up.

Josie's eyes flew open. She sat straight up in bed and stared at the mirror. For a split second, so fast she wasn't sure it was real or just a lingering image from her dream, Josie thought she saw someone in the mirror.

A girl. *Her.*

Before Josie's brain could even register what she saw, the image was gone and the mirror was just a mirror, reflecting the chaotic mess of Josie's room.

Josie squeezed her eyes shut, trying to recall what she'd just seen. A girl who looked so much like her, standing in the mirror with her hand outstretched as if she were going to reach through the mirror into Josie's room.

Just like in her dream. *Holy shit.* Josie jumped out of bed. Late afternoon light streamed through the slats in her closed blinds. Her heart thundered in her chest and she was breathing heavily. Fear-induced adrenaline raced through her veins, leaving her dizzy and disoriented.

She'd been having another dream. A dream about her, but not her. Just like all her dreams recently.

Except this time when she opened her eyes, she knew she was awake. Wide awake. She knew she saw someone in that mirror. Someone who looked exactly like her. A twin. A doppelgänger.

Josie looked at her alarm and caught her breath.

4:00.

That time was familiar. What time was it when she dreamed that Nick had given her the necklace? She vividly remembered the red digital readout on her alarm clock: four in the morning. Which meant she'd had the dream at exactly 3:59.

She tried to think back to the first dream she'd had, the one where she'd been driving a Beemer and had outrun the train at the crossing. It had been the middle of the night and she didn't think much about what time she'd woken up, but could it have been the same? Could it have happened at 3:59?

Josie's heart fluttered in her chest. She was having weird dreams, always at the same time. Was she going crazy? Was it just a coincidence?

There is no such thing as coincidence, she said to herself. *There must be a logical explanation. This is a pattern, so it must have a reason.*

"Calm down," she said out loud. "Just calm down and you'll figure it out."

The words had the desired effect. Josie's breathing began to normalize. Her pulse slowed; panic and fear ebbed from her mind.

3:59. One minute to four. What was the connection? She just had to think. What was she usually doing at that time? Homework in the library. Hanging out with Madison. Driving to work . . .

Josie groaned. On Monday, she'd gotten stuck behind that train. At 3:59. It was the exact moment her life started to spin out of control. Her brain must have locked on to that time, like it was the last moment of happiness she was ever going to have.

Josie flopped back down onto her pillow and yanked the comforter up over her head. Even her subconscious was sabotaging her. Still, the fantasies of a Nick who still loved her and who gave a necklace to *her* instead of to Madison were alluring. Josie snuggled into the covers. Maybe she'd just live in those dreams and forget real life altogether.

It couldn't be worse.

3:59 A.M.

She can feel the dry grass beneath the blanket, practically each individual strand as the weight of her body presses them flat against the ground. Some are thicker than others. Weeds, most likely. Maybe a dandelion or two. But cushy nonetheless, like a pillow from Mother Nature.

She stretches her arms over her head and arches her back. She loves the warmth of the late afternoon sun, and the tickling breeze from the east. She feels so content, so alive, so blissfully happy.

She hears a crunching of grass, and rolls onto her side, propping her head up with her hand. Silhouetted against the afternoon sun,

Nick strides across the field.

"Thanks for coming," she says.

"Of course," he says with a tight smile. He sits down on the blanket and eyes the picnic basket and thermos of lemonade. "You didn't have to do all this, Jo."

"I know." She sits up and opens the picnic basket, removing sandwiches and potato salad. "But I wanted to."

She pours lemonade and hands Nick a glass. He doesn't drink it. "Is everything okay?" she asks.

He nods slowly but doesn't look at her. "How's your mom?"

"Fine," she says after a suitable pause.

"Do you . . ." His voice trails off. "Do you ever wonder what happened?"

"I don't want to talk about it." It's true and yet it's not.

He still doesn't look at her, but his voice is soft. "I'm sorry."

"I know."

He puts the untouched lemonade down on the blanket, leaning it against the basket. "Look, there's something I need to say to you."

She catches her breath. "Yes?"

"Jo." He pauses and swallows hard. "I—"

Josie never heard what Dream Nick was going to say. She bolted upright in bed, wide-awake, as a blood-chilling scream echoed through her house.

ELEVEN

4:00 A.M.

"*NOOOOOOOO!*"

Josie's heart thundered in her chest. "Mom?"

"Get off me!" her mom shrieked from her bedroom.

"Mom, are you okay?"

"Get off!" Her mom's voice cracked. "I don't know what you're talking ab—"

She screamed again, a piercing cry of pain and fear, followed by the sounds of a struggle and something smashing against the floor.

"Mom!" Josie leaped out of bed, and sprinted across her room and down the hall. A high-pitched shriek froze Josie in her tracks. Muffled and distant, it sounded like an animal, definitely not Josie's mom. The unexplained attacks flashed into her mind. Could the police have been right? Some kind of exotic cat killing people in the night? If so, how the hell did it get into the house? And how was she going to save her mom?

Josie grabbed a vase off the table in the hallway. Maybe she could distract the animal long enough to get her mom out of the house? It was the best plan she could think of as she barreled into her mom's bedroom and flipped on the light switch.

A single bulb illuminated the room, instead of the usual two; one lampshade had been knocked askew, exposing the bare bulb. The matching lamp, which had stood on the nightstand closest to Josie's mom, lay broken on the floor. Josie blinked, her eyes adjusting to the bright ball of light before her, and through the fluttering of her eyelids, saw her mom alone in bed. Her eyes were clenched shut, her arms flailing around her as if trying to fend off an unseen assailant.

"I don't know!" her mom repeated, her voice a mix of panic and pleading. She paused, then spoke again more frantically as if in answer to an unspoken question. "I don't know what you're talking about!" She gasped, her arms frozen above her; then she rolled up into the fetal position, covering her head with her arms. "No! No, please!" she sobbed.

"Mom?" Josie dropped the vase on the bureau and dashed to her mom's side. "Mom, are you okay?"

Her mom continued to roll from side to side, pawing at the air. "Get it off! Get it off me!"

"Mom, it's a dream. It's just a dream." Josie reached out her hand and laid it on her mom's leg.

Instantly, her mom sat up, gasping for breath like a woman drowning. Her eyes flew open and looked frantically around the room, wild and unseeing, finally settling on Josie.

"Josephine," she said breathlessly.

"Mom, are you okay?"

"Yes." Her mom ran a hand through her dark, wavy hair, which hung lank and damp in her face. Josie noticed for the first time that her mom was drenched in sweat. "Yes, I'm fine."

"You were screaming," Josie said.

Her mom looked up. "Was I?"

Josie nodded. "Screaming and crying, and you were fighting with something that wasn't there."

"I see." Her mom sat for a moment, staring into the dark hallway silent and lost, as if she'd forgotten Josie was in the room. "Did I say anything?" she said at last.

"You said 'Get it off me' and 'I don't know' like a bazillion times."

Her mom slowly turned and looked at Josie. Her cool, collected demeanor was back. "Don't exaggerate, Josephine," she said calmly.

But Josie wasn't going to be sidetracked. "Mom, what the hell is going on?"

Her mom sighed. She swung her legs over the bed and slipped her feet into a pair of slippers. "It was just a dream."

"A nightmare."

"Yes, I suppose." Her mom cast a cursory glance at the smashed lamp, then dismissed it and walked down the hall.

Josie trailed after her. "You suppose? Mom, you're drenched in sweat. And did you see what you did to the lamp?"

Her mom didn't even glance over her shoulder. "I saw."

"Well?" Josie pressed. "What were you dreaming about?"

Her mom walked into the kitchen and flipped the switch, flooding the room with stark, fluorescent light. She took a deep breath, letting it out slow and steady. Then she smiled, her face and body completely relaxed, and sat down at the table. "I don't remember." Josie's mom pressed the palms of her hands to her eyes. "I think perhaps I'm tired. Could you make me a cup of tea?"

"Tea?" Her mom hated tea. She was a gourmet, organic coffee drinker all the way. "Mom, you never drink tea."

Her mom jolted. "Yes, well . . ." Her voice trailed off and she averted her eyes. "I'm trying to be healthier. I think the coffee has been affecting my sleep."

It was true; her mom looked exhausted. Her face was sagging, her eyes sallow and ringed with purple, and she'd completely lost that girlish lightness she'd always possessed.

Josie set the kettle on a burner and went to the pantry. Did they even have tea in the house? She'd never seen any. She instinctively grabbed for the black canister that held her mom's favorite French roast. It felt lighter, less dense, and when she popped it open she found that the custom ground coffee had been replaced by bags of Earl Grey.

"Mom," Josie began tentatively, as she draped a tea bag over the side of a mug and poured the scalding water into it. "Maybe you should take some time off work? You've been going at it pretty hard."

"I'm fine!" her mother snapped.

Josie flinched. "Okay."

Her mom immediately shook her head. "I'm sorry. Perhaps you're right."

Josie sat down across from her. Her eye drifted up to the sunflower clock above the kitchen window. It was just a few minutes after four o'clock.

Her body went rigid. Was it possible? Josie was having another dream about Nick at the same time her mom was having a nightmare, once again at 3:59? That couldn't be a coincidence.

"I've been having strange dreams too," Josie said tentatively. "Every night at the same time."

"What time?"

"3:59."

Her mom's chair scooted back across the linoleum floor with a screech. "I'm tired," she said, pushing the untouched tea away from her. "I'm going to try and get some sleep."

"Mom?"

"I'm going to bed." Her mom swept out of the kitchen, switching off the light as she disappeared through the doorway. "And I suggest you do the same."

Josie sat at the table in the dark as she listened to her mom stomp down the hall. Her bedroom door slammed, then the house fell oddly silent.

What the hell was going on? Even based on her mom's behavior lately, this was totally outside the norm. Josie had never seen her mom so tense and on edge, snapping at every little thing. Work and her failing marriage were taking a toll. Josie slumped forward at the table, resting her chin in her hand. What could she do to help?

Out of the corner of her eye, Josie thought she saw an object pass by in the darkness outside the kitchen window.

It was just a split-second image, as if something had been illuminated by a camera flash before fading back into the darkness of the night, but Josie could have sworn she saw what looked like a large wing soar past the window. Then in the distance, another animalistic scream.

An eagle? Josie thought. A wing and a shriek; it made sense. Or maybe an owl. Weird that it would be so close to the house; it must have been hunting something. Josie was oddly relieved. At least it wasn't the exotic man-eating cat supposedly responsible for all the unexplained deaths recently. That was something.

Josie yawned. If nocturnal birds were out hunting, it meant she needed to be in bed, sound asleep. Back to school in the morning, back to face the hell that was her social life. She was going to need all the sleep she could get.

12:45 P.M.

"ARE YOU OKAY?" PENELOPE BLURTED OUT WHEN Josie took the seat across from her in the cafeteria.

"You mean more or less okay than I've been for the last few days?"

Penelope cocked her head to the side. "Either?"

Josie shrugged. Between the dreams, her mom, and the nightmare that had become her existence at school as teen-gossip topic du jour, *okay* wasn't really a word that applied to her life anymore.

"That good, huh?" Penelope said, reading between the lines.

"That good." Josie unwrapped her bean-and-cheese burrito and cracked open a soda while Penelope munched on a bag of Fritos. They ate for several moments in silence, until Josie heard a laugh from the corner of the cafeteria. A light, glittery giggle, and one she knew only too well. Before she could stop herself, she turned around and saw Madison sitting next to Nick at the varsity track team's table, her head buried in his arm.

Nick turned and at that moment caught Josie watching him.

His eyes flicked down to Madison, still snuggled next to him, then back up to Josie, a look of apology in his eyes.

Yeah, like that was good enough.

"You've got to ignore it," Penelope said in her matter-of-fact way.

Josie turned back to her. "Ignore it? How the hell am I supposed to ignore it?"

"I don't know," Penelope said. "But you've got to figure it out. Stat."

"Why bother?" Josie threw her arms wide. "Everyone already knows. It's only matter of time before I'm the butt of every joke at the school."

"Oh, you already are."

"What?"

Penelope nodded. "Yeah, apparently the new word for when your boyfriend cheats on you with one of your friends is *Byrned*. It's trending on Twitter. Even more popular than the unexplained animal attacks."

Josie groaned and sank her forehead onto the table. She appreciated that Penelope always called it like she saw it, but every once in a while a little tact might have been helpful.

"My point is that you've got to start acting like it doesn't bother you. Or at least don't stalk him at track practice, okay?"

"Is there anything I do that's private anymore?"

Penelope shook her head. "Zeke and Zeb told everyone about it in homeroom yesterday. By lunch, it was all over the school that you were stalking Nick and Madison."

"Shit."

"And it's not going to help you, okay? You don't want him back." It wasn't a question. It wasn't a suggestion. Penelope was laying down the law. "So do what you have to do to move on. Because Nick and Madison already have."

3:30 P.M.

As soon as she got home, Josie made a beeline for her bedroom.

Time to purge.

Penelope was right. She'd been pining away for Nick, waiting for him to realize how miserable he was without her and to ask if she'd take him back. But no more.

She plugged her iPod into portable speakers and scrolled through her song list until she found suitably angry music. P!nk. Perfect breakup music. She pumped up the volume and hit play.

Josie grabbed her plastic garbage can and planted it in the middle of her room. Everywhere she looked, something reminded her of Nick. A memento, a tchotchke, a gag gift. Little things, sentimental only because she'd given them that power.

The movie ticket from their first date was pinned on her corkboard. She ripped it down, sending the pushpin spiraling off to the other side of the room, and dropped the ticket in the trash.

She caught sight of the three-inch-tall lime-green bunny that sat on her dresser. Nick had won it at the county fair in one of those rigged ringtoss games and given it to her. Josie snatched it up and launched it into the garbage.

"Two points!"

This was turning out to be more fun than she'd thought.

Photos, gone. Concert-ticket stubs from his favorite band, gone. On the dresser, Josie grabbed an old vase with a red silk rose sticking out of it. They'd gone to Ocean Beach for the day and he'd bought the fake rose from a boardwalk peddler while they were chowing down on hot dogs and French fries beachside. Josie had put it in her favorite vase—an old fifth-grade art project that converted a wine bottle into a mosaic piece of "art"—and given it a spot of honor on her dresser. Now she wanted nothing more than for both flower and vase to be out of her sight. She was about to dump both in the trash when she paused.

The vase was different.

Crazy, Josie realized. A standard wine bottle, probably one of her mom's favorite chardonnays that seemed to fill up the recycling bin with alarming frequency these days. It had been covered with small squares of chopped-up glossy magazine pages—bits of color and texture, movement, and shadow all layered upon one another to form a pop-culture mosaic. The bottles had then been covered in two thick layers of glue, left to dry for what seemed like months, and finally sent home on the last day of school as the prized fifth-grade "art" project.

But Josie had loved that stupid thing. She remembered how her parents had donated magazines to the cause. Her dad's *Newsweek* stack and her mom's bedside collection of *InStyle*—both had been ravaged for just the right colors and patterns. And the fruit of her labor had sat on her dresser for years.

Only this wasn't it.

Sure, it looked similar, but right away, Josie could tell it wasn't hers. The color scheme was off—all pastels and muted colors, while Josie's bottle had been covered with vibrant hues. And it was clean. Every other item on Josie's dresser was blanketed in a light coating of dust, but this vase and the silk flower it held had been recently dusted.

Josie was still pondering the weirdness of the vase that was hers and yet wasn't, when her cell phone rang. She didn't even look to see who it was before she answered.

"Hey, Josie."

Blood thundered in Josie's ears, blocking out P!nk, and all of the bravado and girl-power strength she'd managed to conjure up during her purge drained from her body in an instant at the sound of Nick's voice.

THIRTEEN

3:51 P.M.

"ARE YOU THERE?" NICK ASKED.

Josie's mouth was dry. "Yeah."

"Oh. Good." Nick paused. After a few seconds, Josie heard him clear his throat. "I'm glad you finally took my call." He paused again as if waiting for Josie to respond, but she couldn't have if she wanted to. Her brain had seized up, and all ability for rational thought had abandoned her.

"I wanted to talk to you before you saw me at school. I mean saw *us* at school. Madison and me, but . . ." His voice trailed off. "But yeah, I understand why you didn't want to talk."

Yeah, sure he did.

"I feel . . ." Josie heard him swallow. "Bad."

Bad? *He* felt bad?

Nick didn't wait for a response. "I guess I just want you to know that I didn't mean for this to happen."

"Oh. Okay." How exactly was Josie supposed to respond to that?

"I know I should have told you that Madison and I had been spending time together after you started working at the Coffee Crush. I mean, it wasn't anything at first—I just really needed someone to talk to. And then . . . well . . ."

And then you slept with her. Yeah, Josie had that part pretty clear in her mind.

"Not that I'm making excuses," Nick continued. "I know I hurt you. But . . . I don't know. Maybe you'll be better off without me."

Josie laughed out loud. She couldn't help it.

"What's so funny?" Nick sounded hurt.

"Are you actually trying to tell me that I'm better off because you cheated on me?" Josie said through bursts of laughter.

"I don't know. Maybe?" She could picture his nonchalant shrug, which only pissed her off.

"Maybe? Like maybe you did me a favor by cheating on me? Toughened me up by breaking my heart? Saved me from pain by giving *my* necklace to *her*?"

"I didn't give it to her," Nick snapped.

"Oh yeah? Then why is the necklace you bought for me hanging around your new girlfriend's neck, huh?"

Nick was silent for a moment. "I was going to return it." His voice was strained. "But she found it in my room and wanted it."

"Oh."

"I didn't know she was going to tell everyone I'd given it to her. That wasn't my fault."

"Right," Josie said, her temper flaring once more. "Because

none of this is your fault, right? You're Boyfriend of the Year."

"Look," Nick said. He sounded angry. "How would you even know I bought the necklace for you? It's not like you remembered our anniversary."

Josie's face burned. He was right. She'd totally forgotten their anniversary in the middle of everything else in her world falling apart. She was about to apologize when she remembered that whatever gift Nick had bought to celebrate their year together, he'd still been sleeping with Madison for almost two months. Suddenly, the gesture seemed hollow.

"So now you're trying to blame this on me?"

"No," Nick said quickly. "But you did forget our anniversary."

Josie set her jaw. "You're trying to make yourself feel better. I get it. But understand this—there is no scenario in this universe or any other that makes what you and Madison did acceptable, okay? There's a special place in hell for backstabbing friends and cheating boyfriends, and the two of you have reservations."

"You want this to all be my fault," Nick said. "Fine."

"It *is* all your fault," Josie interrupted.

"Maybe you should take a look in the mirror, Josie. There were two of us in that relationship. Ever think that maybe this is partially *your* fault?"

"Are you kidding me?"

"You haven't exactly been available lately, you know," Nick said bitterly.

"Well, gee, Nick. My parents are going through a divorce." Josie let the sarcasm drip from every syllable. "What did you expect?"

"You think you're the only one with problems?" Now Nick was getting pissed off. "We've all got shit going on. Did you even know my brother has cancer?"

Josie caught her breath. Tony had cancer? How did she not know that?

"We found out two months ago. I wanted to tell you, but you never had time. I felt like you had too much going on, so when Madison and I were hanging out one night, I told her. The rest just . . . happened."

So it was her fault, in a way. Nick cheated on her because he felt like she wasn't there for him. Ugh, why hadn't he told her? Or had he tried and she just didn't notice? She'd been so wrapped up in her own drama, it was a real possibility.

Nick took a deep breath and let it out slowly. "Look, I don't want to fight. I just needed you to know that I didn't mean to hurt you. And I'm sorry."

"Okay." Josie felt deflated. Her quick burst of anger had evaporated as soon as she heard about Tony's cancer. "Thank you," she said somewhat lamely.

"Good-bye, Josie."

"Bye."

3:57 P.M.

Josie's hands were shaking as she tossed her cell phone onto the bed.

She wasn't the only one going through life drama, but in her own pain and grief she'd managed to box out the one person in her life she cared about most. She pictured Nick's face Monday during their last conversation. There had been something wrong, something he desperately wanted to talk to his girlfriend about, and Josie didn't have time.

Josie leaned against the windowsill and stared out into the backyard. The yew bushes that lined the fence on all three sides were ridiculously overgrown. The lawn was mostly weeds, dotted with barren patches of dirt and a minefield of gopher holes. It seemed like everything was falling apart: yard, house, life . . .

Josie's heart ached for Nick. He and his older brother were very close, and though Nick wasn't always the best at expressing his feelings, Josie knew he must be devastated at the thought of losing Tony.

Maybe Nick was right. Maybe Josie was partially to blame. Maybe she did need to take a look at herself. Josie turned away from the window toward the old mirror.

Only Josie didn't see her own reflection.

From where she stood at the window, the antique mirror reflected her bed. And there, snuggled under the same blue-and-white floral comforter cover, was a girl. She wore a sleep mask, but even with it obscuring part of her face, in the bright lights of the room, Josie realized she was staring at someone who looked exactly like her. A doppelgänger asleep in her bed.

Josie glanced at her bed. Nope, it was empty, the covers and pillows a disheveled mess, just the way she'd left them that morning. But there, in the mirror, she could clearly see the image of herself sound asleep in her room.

Wait, was it her room? The girl, the bedclothes, even the night-stand were the same. But the room in the reflection clearly wasn't Josie's. The floor was different—lush, cream-colored carpet where the hardwood floors in Josie's room were covered in worn, striped throw rugs. The giant print of Seurat's *A Sunday Afternoon on the Island of La Grande Jatte* that hung above Josie's bed wasn't in the reflection, replaced by a black-and-white panoramic photo of Paris. And the alarm clock on the nightstand wasn't Josie's old hand-me-down from her mom, but a sleek, modern clock with solid blue numbers that cut through the brightly lit room.

Numbers? Josie took a step closer to the mirror and squinted at the clock. It took her brain a moment to register the time it showed and the realization dawned on her slowly. 3:59.

Wait, didn't she just have this exact same dream? But in reverse? Josie whipped her head around to look at her own alarm clock and caught the readout just as it clicked over to 4:00. 3:59? Again?

Josie turned back to the mirror.

The girl in the bed was gone.

FOURTEEN

4:15 P.M.

JOSIE SAT ON THE EDGE OF HER BED AND STARED at the mirror for what felt like an eternity. The dreams she could explain away: stress, exhaustion, fantasy fulfillment. But this? She was wide awake, sober, functional. And she'd seen the reflection of herself, sleeping on her bed, in her room.

Only it wasn't her room or her bed. Similar, but not the same. Not at all. And obviously it wasn't her reflection.

Was she losing her mind? Josie needed to talk to someone about it, someone who would listen and wouldn't judge and might just be able to offer some insight. There was only one person who fit that bill.

Josie's dad picked up on the first ring. "Hey, Jo Jo," he said. She could almost picture the crooked, boyish smile spreading across his face. "How's my favorite daughter?"

"Your only daughter," Josie said.

"Semantics."

Josie laughed. They'd played out that same interchange a bazillion times.

"So what's going on, sweetie?" he said. "Aren't you supposed to be at work?"

"Um . . . I have today off." That was a conversation for another time. "Can I ask you something?"

"Of course, Jo Jo. Shoot."

Josie took a deep breath. "Is there any history of mental illness in our family?"

Her dad snorted. "Well, I'm completely nuts. Clearly."

"That's not what I mean."

"Oh." Her dad was instantly serious. "Okay. Well, I think one of my grandfather's brothers ended up in a sanitarium. Is that what you mean?"

"Maybe." He could have been a schizophrenic, which would explain Josie's dreams and visions. "What about on Mom's side?"

"Is there something wrong with your mother?" he said quickly.

Josie hesitated. She shouldn't have. She should have just said, "No, of course not, Dad. She's totally fine." But she didn't. Just a half second while the memory of the previous night's incident raced through her brain, but that was all her dad needed.

"I knew it. Josie, look, I didn't want to say anything before, but I think there's something seriously wrong with your mom. Has been for some time. I read an article about how brain cancer can radically alter a person's personality: their likes and dislikes, even their voice and mannerisms."

Josie gripped the phone. "You think Mom has brain cancer?"

"Maybe."

All the blood drained out of Josie's face. "What?" Her voice faltered.

"Er . . ." Her dad caught himself. "I mean, of course not." He paused, and Josie could hear him drinking something on the other end of the line. "But since I brought it up, has she been complaining of headaches recently? Had any dizzy spells or blackouts?"

"No." Josie said. *Brain cancer? Really?*

"Okay. Well, that's good." He almost sounded disappointed. "Does she ever ask about me? You know, like after you came and picked up the mirror?"

"Sure," she lied. She couldn't bring herself to tell him that not only did his estranged wife never ask about him, but whenever Josie brought him up, her mom immediately changed the subject.

"Good. Next time she brings me up, tell her that I'm seeing someone, will you?"

Josie's jaw dropped. "You've got a girlfriend?"

"Met her at the gym. She's a yoga instructor. Tall, blond. Kimber's the real deal."

"Kimber?" Josie asked. "Kimber Janikowski?"

Her dad paused. "How did you know that?"

Josie pounded the palm of her hand against her forehead. "Kimber went to my high school, Dad. She was a senior when I was a freshman." Could her week get any worse?

She heard her dad suck in a breath. "Really?"

"She was prom queen, Dad."

He fumbled with his phone. "Hey, Jo Jo, I've got a meeting. Real quick, was there something you wanted to talk about?"

Real quick. Ugh. "It can wait."

"You sure?"

"Yep." *Never more so.*

"Okay, I'll call you later. Love you, Jo Jo."

"Love you too, Dad."

4:30 P.M.

Josie sighed. So much for that.

Fine. She could deal with this problem by herself. She was an only child, after all. She'd just attack it scientifically, like her parents had taught her. Josie grabbed a notebook and pen from her backpack, and settled into the pillows on her bed.

    Step one: formulate a question.

Easy. What the hell is going on?

    Step two: research.

Er, not as easy. Though she did have a few pieces of information at her disposal. The train, for starters. She could assume it was coming from Fort Meade, and therefore had dropped off a shipment of deuterium for her mom. Ultradense deuterium was central to her mom's research into creating micro black holes. It wasn't inherently radioactive or particularly dangerous, but Josie would have to research its properties to find out if it could have accounted for the flash.

Then there was the mirror. First the incident at the train, then the explosion in her mom's lab—the mirror was present both times. And Josie had clearly seen the reflection of the girl—Jo, if her dreams were correct—in the mirror, and in one of those dreams, Jo had seen *her* in the same mirror. Not that it made any sense, but at least there was a connection.

Lastly, the time. 3:59. The flash, the explosion, the dreams. They always happened at the exact same time.

Step three: hypothesis.

Josie absolutely rejected any kind of paranormal explanation. Nope, not possible. Everything that happened had a sound, scientific explanation. So assuming she wasn't losing her mind, she was left with a scientific possibility. The same girl, the same room, same time. Parallel universe? There she was, back at her parents' favorite subject. The thesis they'd both spent their careers pursuing: the many-worlds theory. Even Josie's own attempt to prove the Penrose Interpretation was rooted in the idea that a single particle can exist in two different places at the same time. Penrose theorized that with anything bigger than a dust particle, its multiple states would collapse, so that you only ever saw the particle in one fixed position. Josie loved the simplicity of the Penrose Interpretation—none of the crazy multiple-worlds theories like what her mom had been working on for years. But if Jo was real, and her world was real—two identical particles bigger than a speck of dust existing in different places at the same time—Josie's science-fair entry was total bunk.

Oops.

Step four: test your hypothesis with an experiment.

That was the step that made Josie's stomach drop. She looked up at the mirror. There was only one way to find out if that mirror was a portal to a parallel universe.

She'd have to confront the mirror. At exactly 3:59.

3:55 A.M.

Josie sat the floor of her bedroom with her blue-and-white comforter pulled over her shoulders. She'd set her alarm clock for 3:30 a.m. just in case, but it was a needless precaution. There was no way in hell she was getting any sleep that night.

Josie looked at the clock. 3:57. *Come on.* Why was it that whenever you were waiting for something, time seemed to slow down? It was mocking her and her ridiculous theory.

Was it so ridiculous? If the many-worlds theory was correct, if an infinite number of parallel universes existed, was it such a stretch to assume that at some point in the space-time continuum, two of them would intersect? Josie wasn't ready to explain exactly *how* that might happen, but she was certainly prepared to consider it a possibility.

3:58. Josie stood up and let the comforter fall to the floor. If she was right, there was actually another world on the other side of this mirror. A world that she'd been seeing in her dreams each night. A world where a girl who was her but not her lived a life that was hers but not hers.

And if it was true, the theoretical concepts of parallel universes were about to be blown wide open.

Josie could see the reflection of her alarm clock. Any moment now. She held her breath, unable to peel her eyes away from the mirror, as the time hit 3:59.

The image blurred. Josie's reflection distorted as if she were staring at it through a pool of water. Ripples cascaded across the surface of the mirror, obscuring her reflection entirely, then dissipated. The image resharpened and Josie found that she was staring at her own face, her own eyes once more. Only the girl in the reflection had blond highlights, bright and shiny where Josie's hair was a duller blond, and the girl in the reflection wore a denim pencil skirt and a red gingham tank top, while Josie was in her shortie pajamas.

Not a reflection.

Josie stared at the girl. The girl stared back.

This was Jo. The girl from Josie's dreams.

Neither said a word but Josie could tell by the look on Jo's face that she was excited too. They'd seen the same thing, come to the same conclusion, on opposite sides of the mirror. The girl held up her hand, reaching out to touch the mirror, and Josie did the same. The surface rippled like a pebble dropping into a pond, and instead of a hard surface, the glass was soft and liquid. It was denser than water, though, and as Josie pushed her hand into the substance beyond the edge of the mirror frame, it felt like she was pressing her hand into a tub of pudding. Josie wiggled her fingers in the substance and the image distorted. It wasn't warm or cold, just spongy and thick. Jo did the same, reaching her hand into the expanse of the mirror.

Then Josie felt it. She was touching Jo's flesh. Palm to palm.

Josie stared at her hand. She could feel the warmth of Jo's

palm. She was awake, no bones about it. This was real. This was really happening.

She looked up and met the other girl's eyes. "Jo?"

Jo cocked her head to the side, as if she couldn't quite understand what Josie said, then her eyes widened. She nodded. Then her lips moved, slowly. Josie couldn't hear her words; her voice was just a muffled sound through the mirror. Jo repeated it, speaking even slower. Josie could just read her lips.

"Who are you?"

Josie opened her mouth to respond, but the image blurred again. Jo pulled her hand away. Josie did the same, just in time. The image in the mirror rippled, distorting Jo's face in a squiggly mass of waves, then resolidified until all Josie could see was the pale, panting image of her own face in the mirror.

FIFTEEN

3:58 P.M.

ONLY AN ACT OF GOD WOULD HAVE KEPT JOSIE away from the mirror at 3:59 the next afternoon. She'd been restless all day at school, barely able to focus on her classes and, for the first time that week, blissfully unaware of the whispers that erupted every time she walked into a room. She didn't care, not about Madison or Nick or her physics project or her parents' divorce. She only cared about Jo.

A girl who lived a life that was sort of like hers, but different. Better. A girl who was still Nick Fiorino's girlfriend.

An idea had taken hold in Josie's mind. Ever since she'd learned about Nick's brother, she'd been eaten up with remorse over the way she'd treated Nick the last few months. What if she could go back and change things? What if she could go back and be there for Nick, listen to him when he needed her?

Maybe time travel was out of the realm of possibility, but now there was another Nick. A Nick who still loved her. Maybe she could still be there for him. Fix her mistakes with Nick, even if it was just for one day.

Josie shook her head. She was being totally ridiculous. To do that, she and Jo would have to switch places. Was that even possible?

Josie glanced at the clock. *Hurry up!* In her hand she held a letter, the contents of which she knew by heart. Since they couldn't talk through the portal, Josie thought she'd write Jo a note outlining what she knew about the mirror, the flash, and the connection between their worlds. She'd spent her entire lunch hour slaving over it, rewriting it at least three times, to make sure she didn't sound totally and utterly insane.

> *Dear Jo,*
>
> *Since we can't really talk, or in case you aren't in the mirror today, I thought I'd write to you and let you know that I'm real, that this—whatever this is—is real.*
>
> *I'm not sure where to start but here are the basics. I'm Josephine Byrne but everyone calls me Josie. I live in Bowie, Maryland, I'm a junior at Bowie Prep, and it's 2013.*
>
> *I'm not really sure what's happening to us, but I know it started last week. I was in my car waiting for a train to pass. There was a flash and I think I blacked out or something. Next thing I knew I started seeing you in the mirror and . . . yeah.*

Then yesterday.

Josie had originally written *I started having dreams like I was seeing life through your eyes* but she'd deleted that part. She didn't know if Jo was experiencing the same phenomenon or not, and thought it might be better to leave out the creepy details for now.

Something is connecting us, every twelve hours at 3:59.

It's a portal between our universes, maybe caused by the flash

at the train tracks? That's the only theory I have right now. I

don't know how it happened, but I know that this is real.

I'll be in the mirror tonight.

Sincerely,

Josie Byrne

Josie didn't even need to look at the clock to know it was 3:59. As if on cue, the surface of the mirror rippled and rolled across the pane like the tide washing up onto the shore, then retreating into the sea. When the image came back into focus, Jo stood facing Josie.

She wore powder-blue silk pajamas and embroidered blue slippers. Her hair was brushed up into a high ponytail, and clasped in her hands was a small, white envelope.

A letter.

They'd had the same idea.

Josie smiled. She and her doppelgänger were thinking the

same thing at the same time. Jo gazed at the envelope Josie held in her hand, then her eyes met Josie's and she smiled as well.

Okay, Josie said to herself. Time to see if her theory was sound. She plunged her arm into the gelatinous substance of the portal. She reached all the way through, up to her shoulder, and felt her hand break through to the clean, light air of Jo's room.

Jo gingerly lifted the letter from Josie's hand, allowing her fingers to graze Josie's wrist. She'd done it intentionally, somehow Josie just knew, to make sure the hand was real: flesh and bone. Josie would have done the same. There was a piece of her that still thought maybe this was all a dream. Or a hallucination.

But the sensation of Jo's fingers touching her skin dispelled any doubts. Josie might not have been able to explain why it was happening, but Jo was real and the portal was real, and the letter that Jo gently placed in Josie's outstretched hand was certainly, most definitely real.

Josie drew her hand back through the portal into her own world, clasping Jo's letter so tightly her knuckles ached.

It was a white, rectangular envelope almost exactly like the one Josie had used. Her hands shook as she turned the envelope over and read the clear, steady handwriting on the front:

To the Girl in the Mirror

Josie looked up in time to see Jo's image begin to blur. She was waving and she mouthed *bye* as her face faded away and was gone.

Immediately, Josie flopped down on her bed, tore open the envelope, and pulled a handwritten letter from inside.

Hi.

That's such a ridiculous way to start, isn't it? I mean, it's like I'm writing a letter to myself. Only I'm not, am I? Because that would be crazy.

Like this isn't crazy.

I'm hoping you'll be there in the mirror again tonight. If for no other reason than to prove to me that I'm not crazy. But just in case you're not, I'm writing this letter.

I'll start with the obvious, I guess: Who are you? Where are you? And why is it that I can see you in my bedroom mirror every twelve hours at the exact same time?

I'm Josephine Byrne but most people call me Jo. I live in Bowie, Maryland, I'm a junior at Bowie Prep, and it's 2013.

If you get this, please write back. That way, I'll know. Know I'm not crazy, that is.

Though I suppose if you do write back, that's almost as bad.

Sincerely,

Josephine Byrne

4:10 P.M.

Josie must have reread the note a dozen times. *Josephine Byrne.*

Same name. Same high school. Same year. Same girl.

The same girl but different. Of that Josie was convinced. Jo still had Nick, while Josie had lost him. She wondered what else Jo had: Were her parents happily married? Was she popular at school? Were they rich? Was she interested in science and math like Josie?

So many questions Josie was desperate to learn the answers to, the most important of which was why this was happening to them in the first place. Maybe together, she and Jo could make sense of what was going on? There was only one way to find out.

It was time she and Jo had a talk. Face-to-face.

SIXTEEN

3:59 A.M.

JOSIE WAS WIDE AWAKE, STANDING IN FRONT OF the mirror at the exact moment its surface undulated like the ebbing tide, opening the door between her world and Jo's. There wasn't any note gripped in her hand. This time, she planned to answer Jo's letter in person.

She hadn't slept at all that night. Not that she really needed to on a Friday night, but she'd tried nonetheless, setting her alarm for 3:30 again, just in case she drifted off, but the adrenaline that coursed through her body made her antsy and impatient, and as the minutes slowly crept toward the awaited hour, Josie actually got less tired, more alert, more eager to see what would happen.

But as the rippling waters of the mirror gave way to the room on the other side, Josie's heart sank. Empty. No Jo.

Two things were immediately apparent, though. First, even though all the overhead lights were on, the late afternoon sun streamed through the open windows on the west side of Jo's room. 3:59, but the wrong 3:59. Where Josie's timeline put her in the wee hours of the morning, eastern Maryland still swathed in a heavy blanket of darkness, in Jo's world, it was the afternoon. Their universes were twelve hours apart.

No wonder Josie's dreams had always taken place at the end of Jo's school day. No wonder Jo had been wearing her pajamas earlier that afternoon. And when she saw Jo sleeping with all the lights on, wearing a sleep mask, it must have been the middle of the night. Kind of weird that she slept with the lights on, but whatever.

Josie continued to stare into Jo's room, Jo's world. The space was the same: the room, the dimensions, the window and closet and bed all in the same exact place. But Jo's room was clearly that of a wealthier girl. Instead of Josie's mismatched bedroom furniture of hand-me-downs, roadside pickups, and craigslist purchases, Jo's room had been decorated. The bed frame was brushed chrome, low to the ground, and piled with a giant pillow-top mattress, a far cry from Josie's rickety wooden four-poster—missing a post and propped up at one corner by an old footstool. Jo's dresser and bookcases were arranged with an almost meticulous precision. Where Josie's bookcases looked as if someone had dumped their contents on the floor, then quickly shoved them back on the shelves, the books on Jo's were neatly lined up, spines out, grouped by size. Perfume bottles stood sharply at attention, again in height order, and an array of silver jewelry stands flanked the dresser, each holding a specific bounty: earrings, bracelets, necklaces.

The entire room sparkled and gleamed under the harsh

recessed lighting, like an ultrasleek hotel room that had just been visited by the housekeeping crew. Josie found it hard to believe that anyone lived in such a clean, controlled environment, let alone a sixteen-year-old high-school student. They looked so much alike, but clearly, she and Jo were very, very different.

Josie leaned closer to the mirror, trying to get a glimpse of the door to Jo's room and perhaps down the hallway of her house. Forgetting that the glass pane of the mirror had dematerialized, Josie's head went right through into the thick goo of the portal.

"Shit," Josie said out loud, but her voice was muffled and distorted. She lost her balance, stumbled forward trying to right herself, and tripped on the bottom edge of the mirror's frame, which sent her flailing through the mirror into Jo's room.

She fell in slow motion through the portal, right up until the moment she broke the plane into Jo's room. Then her momentum sped up and her shoulder slammed into plush carpet, momentarily sucking the breath out of her lungs. She squinted her eyes closed against the full force of the electric lighting as she sat up, rubbing the arm that had broken her fall. Through the mirror she could see her room: dimly lit by her bedside lamp, her cluttered belongings looked so little-girlish in comparison to Jo's sophisticated décor. It was a whole different world.

Universe, more exactly. She was in a parallel universe, the existence of which science had been trying to prove for decades.

And which Josie had proven in one clumsy moment. Awesome.

Josie's eyes rested on Jo's desk, where a pen and paper stood neatly lined up beside a framed, smiley photo of Jo and her parents. Perfect. Jo might not have been there, but Josie could prove that she had been.

She dashed across the room and wrote a quick note.

I'm real. And I walked through the mirror. Meet me

tonight?

—Josie

Josie smiled, hoping the note wouldn't freak Jo out too much. That's when she saw it. Out of the corner of her eye, she saw the image in the mirror distort as the surface began to ripple. The image of her own bedroom came in and out of focus. The portal was starting to close.

Josie threw herself toward the mirror. As she passed through, she could almost feel the mirror beginning to solidify. The gooey interior felt more like hardening concrete. Her bedroom was pulling away from her, racing down a long hallway. Josie pumped her legs, desperately trying to step into her own world before the portal closed for good. Instead of the split second it had taken her to fall through into Jo's room, Josie felt as if she'd been in the portal forever. What happened if it closed before she reached her room? Where would she be?

The weight of the portal grew heavier and denser, and for one sick moment Josie felt as if the space around her was going to crush the life from her body. Her lungs burned, and Josie gasped for air. She could still see her room, distant, dark. She had to get there. Had to. With all the strength left in her, Josie leaped forward, arms outstretched, desperate to catch hold of the mirror's frame. It seemed too far away. Too far to reach. Her eyes closed; her mind went blank.

Then her hand felt the edge of the frame. She clawed at it and pulled her body through. As soon as she rolled onto the hardwood floor of her bedroom, her lungs worked and Josie gulped in huge mouthfuls of air.

She glanced back and saw her own reflection in the mirror. She'd just made it.

4:00 A.M.

Josie stood up, her back creaking in protest. She'd fallen through the mirror. She'd been to the other side, and she'd almost gotten trapped there. Passing back through the mirror, just at the moment the portal started to close, reminded her of the theoretical descriptions of passing the event horizon into a black hole. Time elongated. Physical matter stretched. And your body felt like it was being pulled apart.

Note to self: don't get caught in the portal.

Still, she'd done it. She'd been to the other side.

Jo's room had been so clean, so rich. The photo on Jo's bureau showed a happy family, not one ripped apart by divorce. Then Josie thought of Nick, Jo's Nick. Nick, who met Jo for picnics in the park. Nick, who gave Jo a necklace of two entwined hearts. In Jo's world, Nick still loved her. In Jo's world, Josie could make up for what happened between herself and Nick. . . .

Josie stared at the mirror, which currently reflected just the cluttered, spastic mess that was her room. But there, just on the other side, was a place where all of Josie's woes didn't exist.

All she had to do was walk through the mirror.

SEVENTEEN

3:59 P.M.

JO WAS IN THE MIRROR AS THE IMAGE DISSOLVED from Josie's jean shorts and tank top to Jo's satin pajamas. This time, Josie didn't waste a second. She took a deep breath and plunged into the portal.

"Oh my God," Jo said as Josie's feet landed on the soft carpet of her room. "You came through."

"I know," Josie said, somewhat breathlessly. "Cool, huh?"

"Um, yeah." Jo sounded like *cool* wasn't quite the adjective she'd use.

They stared blankly for a moment, each examining the other. Josie knew what Jo saw. Her dirty blond hair was a tangled mess and her face was devoid of makeup, typical Saturday fashion for someone with no place to go. Meanwhile Jo's bright blond tresses fell on either side of her face in perfect spirals that cascaded over her shoulders, even though it was the middle of the night.

"So we're the same person or something," Jo blurted out. "Is that it?"

"Kind of," Josie said. She wasn't sure she wanted to get into a long discussion of theoretical quantum theory if she only had a minute until the portal closed.

"I don't know why, but it scares me," Jo said.

"Maybe because it makes absolutely no sense?"

"Yeah, I mean, look at us." Jo spoke quickly. "Except for the hair, we could be—"

"Twins," Josie said, finishing the thought. "Right?"

Jo didn't answer. Instead, her eyes were fixed on the other side of the mirror. Josie turned around and followed Jo's line of sight to a photo on her dresser. A photo of Josie and her mom.

"Is . . . is that your mom?" Jo asked.

"Yeah." Jo seemed transfixed by the photo. "It was from a banquet at the lab where she works. Some kind of awards thing."

Jo continued to stare. "When was it taken?"

"Last month."

"Are you guys close?" Jo asked. "You and your mom?"

Josie shrugged. She wasn't sure how much she wanted to reveal. "We used to be. But for the last six months or so, things have been a little . . . strained."

Jo turned her head sharply. "Six months? That's . . . a long time."

"Yeah, I guess." Jo reached her hand out toward the photo, pausing at the cusp of the mirror's frame. She hesitated, then let her hand fall to her side.

Josie smiled. "It's okay, you know. You can go through. Kinda feels like you're swimming through a pool of Jell-O, but it only lasts a second."

Josie's heart raced as she watched Jo stare at the photo of her and her mom. She was secretly hoping that Jo would go through into her room and see that it wasn't such a big deal. Maybe she'd kind of like it over there. Maybe she'd consider switching places with Josie, you know, just for a day. Maybe . . .

Her eyes involuntarily darted to Jo's necklace. Two entwined hearts. Jo and Nick. *Josie* and Nick.

"That necklace," Josie said. "Is it from your boyfriend?" Josie couldn't help herself. She had to know if what she'd seen in the dreams was real.

Jo's gaze slowly turned to Josie. "My boyfriend?"

"Yeah." Josie pointed to the necklace. "Was that a gift from him?"

"Yes," Jo said at last. "It's from my boyfriend."

Josie smiled. "It's beautiful."

Jo turned back to the mirror. "Do you want to switch places?" she blurted out.

Josie face lit up. "I was thinking the same thing."

"Twinsies." Jo laughed. "Tomorrow. Let's do it tomorrow night." She looked back into the mirror. "Well, night for me."

"Sounds perfect." Josie was having a hard time keeping the excitement out of her voice. "For twenty-four hours?"

Jo smiled. "Yeah, that'll be enough."

Yes, it would. Enough time to see Jo's parents happy and

together. And enough time to set things right with Nick.

"Deal."

The image in the mirror began to ripple. "Shit!" Josie bolted for the portal. "Gotta go."

"Wait." Jo grabbed Josie's arm as she started to duck through the mirror. "Your hair. Do you think you can dye it to match?"

Josie had never dyed her hair before, but this was one hell of a perfect opportunity to try. "Will do."

Jo smiled. "See you tomorrow."

EIGHTEEN

11:30 A.M.

JOSIE GRABBED A HAND TOWEL OFF THE RACK and wiped a hole in the steamed-up bathroom mirror just big enough to see her reflection. Her hair was turbaned up in a blue bath towel, still hidden from view. A discarded bottle of hair dye and plastic gloves were shoved in the garbage can, next to a cardboard box that showcased flowing golden tresses that looked as much like Jo's as Josie could remember.

Picking a color out of the bazillions of choices at CVS had been a challenge. Candle Glow or Desert Flower? Medium Ash Blond, Medium Champagne Blond, Medium Golden Blond. They all just looked blond to Josie, and in the end, she tried to pick the one that looked the most like Jo's professionally colored and highlighted hair. Golden Sunset may have sounded like a bad chick flick, but as a hair dye, Josie hoped it would give her dirty blond hair the bright, shimmery look she was after.

It had to be right. Had to. In just a few hours she'd be going through the mirror.

Josie took a deep breath. Moment of truth.

She bent over and untwisted the towel, then whipped her head back and checked out her new look in the mirror.

Even though her hair was still wet, Josie could see the change immediately. The golden color shimmered in the harsh bathroom light. Her face seemed brighter and more alive. She ran her fingers through her hair, all soft and satiny. No mistaking it now; she was definitely a blonde.

Picking out hair dye might have been complicated, but mimicking Jo's bouncy 'do was going to be a whole other shit show. Josie's styling routine consisted of brushing out her wet hair before bed, then hoping that when she woke up it hadn't dried with some bizarre cowlicks that made her look like Alfalfa's big sister. Which it usually did—thus Josie's wide array of headbands and ponytail holders.

Jo, on the other hand, must have spent an hour every morning doing her hair so it fell in those buoyant, lively spirals around her face. Just like Madison. Ugh. Maybe that's what boys liked? Josie clearly hadn't a clue.

She pulled a plastic shopping bag out of the bathroom cupboard and dumped her haul on the counter. Velcro rollers, round brush, some sort of spray gel. Did girls really do this *every* morning?

Twenty minutes later, Josie had managed to get most of her hair dried and twirled up in rollers. She looked a little bit like a blond geisha with huge mounds of hair piled up on her head. She did one last pass with the hair dryer, then carefully pulled the fat rollers out of her hair and ran her fingers through to loosen the curls.

Then she stood in front of the mirror and stared.

She looked exactly like Jo.

Someone gasped, and Josie turned to find her mom standing in the doorway. Her eyes were wide and she looked terrified. Like she'd seen a ghost.

"I dyed my hair," Josie said lamely.

Her mom continued to stare.

"Um, do you like it?"

Without saying a word, Josie's mom reached out her hand and caressed Josie's cheek with her fingertips. Her mom had been so distant lately, since before Josie's parents had separated, cold and closed and work obsessed. It was the first time in months Josie felt an actual sense of connection to her mom. It reminded Josie of a better time, before things had gotten so strained within their family.

Fighting back a lump in her throat, Josie reached out and hugged her mom.

Her mom sank into the embrace, and they held each other for a moment, then without warning, her mom pushed away.

"Mom? Are you okay?"

"I'm fine." Her face looked pinched as if she was in pain.

"I'm sorry, I—"

"I'm fine," her mom repeated. Then she spun around and disappeared into her room.

Ugh.

* * *

Josie held her breath as the mirror began to ripple.

Finally.

It was finally happening.

She'd get twenty-four hours as Jo—an entire day to put things right with Nick. All she had to do was make the time to let him know that she was there for him, whatever he needed to talk about. If she'd only done that before, maybe Nick wouldn't have turned to Madison.

Josie squeezed her eyes shut, pushing the image of Nick and Madison from her mind. Instead, she imagined the weight of Nick's arms around her waist, the pressure of his lips on her own. And what else? Josie's eyes flew open. She'd never thought to ask Jo how far she and Nick had gone. Whatever. She didn't care. If she was only going to get one day, she wanted it to be memorable.

As before, as soon as the rippling dissipated, Josie grabbed her backpack and launched herself through the mirror.

"Your hair looks good," Jo said as soon as Josie landed.

Josie smiled. "Thanks."

"Daddy's asleep." Jo didn't make any move toward the mirror but stood resolutely in front of it. Like Josie, she carried a bag on her shoulder, though hers was a designer tote bag, not a beat-up school backpack. "And Teresa will be up in a few hours to begin breakfast. I'm usually downstairs at six thirty sharp, so try not to be late."

"And your mom?" Josie was looking forward to a normal family meal, just like it used to be back home.

Jo tilted her head. "Sleeping," she said after a pause.

"Okay." Josie waited for Jo to step through the mirror but still, she hesitated.

"I left you a cheat sheet on my desk. Where to go, who people are. All the details."

"Me too," Josie said. "Anything else?"

Jo opened her mouth to say something, then pressed her lips together and shook her head curtly.

Josie's turn. "Mom'll be at the lab until late, but she usually texts to say when she'll be home. I left my phone on the dresser."

Jo nodded. "Me too."

"So I guess . . ." Josie's voice trailed off.

"Yeah." Jo took a deep breath. "Okay. Here I go."

She stepped gingerly, like a skater testing the ice on a frozen lake, unsure whether the next step might send her crashing through into the frigid depths below. She stuck her arm into the mirror first, clenching and unclenching her fist as if she was testing the air, then sort of jumped into Josie's room.

Jo turned and smiled. Which is when Josie remembered the necklace that still hung around Jo's neck.

Without thinking, Josie shoved her head through the mirror. "The necklace!" Josie said as soon as she emerged into the clear air of her room. She reached out her hand.

"Oh, right." With painful slowness, Jo removed the necklace and dropped it into Josie's palm.

Josie pulled back through into Jo's room and clasped the necklace on right away, then gave Jo the thumbs-up.

Suddenly a look of concern passed over Jo's face. She grabbed a pen and paper off of Josie's desk and scribbled something quickly, holding the note up just as the image began to blur.

"Don't go out—" Josie read out loud, trying to decipher the letters through the rippling mirror.

But that was all she saw. The portal was closed.

NINETEEN

4:02 A.M.

"DON'T GO OUT?" JOSIE REPEATED. CRAP, WHAT had the rest of the note said? *Don't go out . . .* Alone? After curfew?

Whatever. It didn't matter. Josie spun around and assessed Jo's room. She squinted against the light reflecting off the crisp, white walls. Yikes, why was it always so bright in there? She scanned the room, searching for the light switch, but didn't find anything.

No light switch? That was weird. There had to be a dozen recessed lights in the ceiling, illuminating every inch of the bedroom. How could there not be a switch to turn them off?

Maybe it was one of those electronic remote-control systems. Fancy. She wished Jo had mentioned it, but whatever. It wasn't like she was going to get much sleep in the next twenty-four hours anyway.

Twenty-four hours. For an entire day this was all hers. The room, the life, the boyfriend. Josie's eyes drifted to Jo's closet. And the clothes!

Josie knew it was shallow, but it was like living a Cinderella makeover scene in a movie when Josie threw open Jo's closet, exposing the largest wardrobe she'd ever seen. Meticulously organized: shirts, blouses, jackets, skirts, pants, dresses—each arranged by color from left to right.

The shelves above had been custom built as shallow cubbyholes, each holding a single pair of shoes. Heels, sandals, flats, boots—they were all separated by type and color. Well, that was certainly something she and Jo did *not* have in common: no one would ever accuse Josie of being OCD. Hell, maybe Jo would organize her room while she was there? Bonus!

Josie started to flip through hangers. She had to find the perfect outfit for today. Something that would be very "Jo."

One hour and a dozen outfit changes later, Josie settled on the perfect look. A wispy baby-doll dress in a lemon-yellow floral print. It was romantic, whimsical, and brought out the light gold of Josie's hair in a way none of her dark T-shirts ever had. She added textured ecru tights and tan ankle booties with a bow on the back, and spun around in the mirror.

Perfect.

It was almost five o'clock by the time Josie carefully laid the yellow dress on the back of Jo's boudoir chair and finished hanging up the rest of the discarded outfits. She hadn't slept in almost two days and the intensity of the overhead lighting was starting to give her a dull headache. A fruitless search for some kind of media remote only uncovered a half dozen sleep masks in Jo's nightstand. Crap. She didn't want to sleep, per se, but she at least wanted to close her eyes for half an hour before she had to head downstairs and start her masquerade.

Oh well; at least she had a sleep mask. That would black out the incessant lights. Josie sat down on the edge of Jo's bed and pulled the largest mask out of the nightstand drawer.

That's when she saw it.

Movement in the window.

Josie stared into the darkness of what would have been the backyard at Josie's house. Inky, impenetrable darkness. The lights from the room made no inroad into the blackness of the night. It was as if the dark swallowed up the light. A black hole from which nothing escaped.

Yet as Josie stared out into the void, she saw it again: an image flashed in the window.

It was just a split second, like a snippet of a film strip that appeared from nowhere and disappeared into the darkness, but Josie was staring right at it this time. She could see the color—brown with traces of black and gray—and the outline of a head with a long beak framed in the window.

Then a shriek tore through the silence. A cross between a bird and grinding metal, the scream was like nails on a chalkboard and it set all the hairs on the back of Josie's neck standing straight up. Though unnerving, it was not unfamiliar. She'd heard that sound before, in the dead of night back home.

The shrill cry faded as whatever made it disappeared into the night. A bird, most likely. Like the owl Josie thought she saw in the kitchen window the night her mom had the horrible nightmare. Harmless and normal, Josie told herself.

Weird that she didn't see it clearly as it sailed past her window. Just that single flash of a beak, so instantaneous if she hadn't been looking right at it, she would have thought it was a trick of the light. Surely the glow from her window would have illuminated the entire bird?

Why are you stressing about this? Josie had enough to worry about that day. It was just a bird. Nothing out of the ordinary. *Get some sleep.*

But she still pulled the blinds closed before she crawled into bed.

TWENTY

6:01 A.M.

A MELODY INVADED JOSIE'S SLEEP. IT WASN'T familiar, just a soft fragment of song that was getting louder and louder by the second. Ugh. Where was she?

Josie opened her eyes, and found nothing but darkness. Panic gripped her. Was she blind? She reached her hands up to her face and felt the silken mask over her eyes.

Right. Jo's sleep mask. Jo's alarm. Jo's life.

She pushed the mask up to her forehead and was instantly blinded by the harsh overhead lights. With her eyes pinched closed, she reached out a hand and flailed around for the alarm until she inadvertently slapped the right button to silence its annoying tune.

Well, that's one way to wake up in the morning.

It took several minutes for Josie's eyes to adjust to the brightness, but eventually she was able to pry her lids open and roll out of bed. Dawn was just breaking; early rays of light peeked into the room through the slats in the blinds, duller than the artificial illumination overhead, but comforting somehow. Josie tiptoed over and pulled the blinds open.

The first blush of sunrise tinged the sky, promising a bright, cheerful spring morning. Unlike in her house, Jo's bedroom was on the second floor. Josie gazed down onto manicured hedges and painstakingly maintained rosebushes, a far cry from the overgrown, gopher-infested mess that Josie's bedroom looked out upon.

Josie yawned. She was tired, excited, and nervous for how the day would unfold. Could this charade actually work, or was she going to get called out as an impostor exactly thirty seconds into breakfast?

Calm down. She could do this. As long as she *looked* like Jo, no one was going to question if she didn't exactly *act* like Jo.

After shower, hair, and makeup, Josie donned the outfit she'd chosen and looked at herself in the old mirror. She'd tried to do her hair as much like Jo's as she could—parted on the left and tucked behind one ear—and she hoped the effect was close enough. Same with the makeup. Jo's medicine cabinet looked like a Sephora display case. Josie tried to remember Jo's face and applied foundation, blush, eye shadow, liner, mascara, and gloss accordingly.

It was more effort than Josie had put into her appearance in weeks, but as she admired the effect in the mirror, she smiled. She looked like Jo.

Josie studied Jo's cheat sheet, then turned back to the mirror. She looked like Jo; she could act like Jo. No one would know the difference, especially not Nick.

Time to find out.

"Good morning, Miss Josephine."

A short, wiry woman with jet-black hair and thick, old-fashioned glasses was placing a thermos carafe on the table as Josie entered the dining room. According to her cheat sheet this was Teresa, the Byrnes' housekeeper. Teresa saw Jo every single day and didn't hesitate in greeting Josie as "Miss Josephine." This was going to be easier than she thought.

"Good morning," Josie said, hoping the fluttering in her stomach didn't make its way into her voice.

Teresa didn't look up but continued setting the table for breakfast. Two place settings. Only two.

"Why are there only two plates?" Josie asked. Did Jo not eat with her parents? That wasn't in the cheat sheet.

Teresa tilted her head to the side. "I'm sorry, Miss Josephine?"

Crap. From Teresa's reaction, Josie was clearly supposed to know why there were only two places set for breakfast. One of Jo's parents must be away from home, or maybe went to work earlier. Or maybe just didn't eat breakfast? Ugh, she had no idea.

Josie forced a laugh. "Sorry," she said lightly. "I . . . I forgot."

Teresa lifted an eyebrow—an almost imperceptible millimeter—then turned and walked out of the room without another word.

Josie sat down at the table and bit her lip. Hopefully she hadn't just blown everything with her misstep. Her hand shook as she reached for the carafe and poured herself a cup of coffee. She needed to get a grip. She was fine. No one was going to assume she was an impostor, especially not based on one—

"What are you doing?"

Josie looked up from the table and saw a man standing in the doorway, one hand braced against the frame. She knew the face: the pale blue eyes, tanned skin, and streaked blond hair so like her own. It was her dad.

Only not quite. They had the same boyishness about them—a crinkle at the corner of each eye from excessive smiling, a softness about the mouth—but Jo's dad was a slightly more put-together version of her own. Slicked-back hair, designer suit, and carrying a tablet in one hand, this Mr. Byrne looked significantly more professional.

He stared at her for a moment; those piercing blue eyes examined every inch of her, face, dress, finally the hair. All the warmth drained out of Josie as Mr. Byrne's eyes lingered on her newly dyed locks. Dammit, she was going to get caught. He knew she wasn't Jo. How stupid had they been, thinking they could fool their respective parents? Panic swept over her. How was she going to explain this?

Josie was debating whether or not to make a run for it, when a smile spread across Mr. Byrne's face. "I'm just teasing you, princess. Don't look so serious."

Josie let out a breath. So Jo's dad was a trickster. Ha. Ha-ha. *So funny.* "Sorry," she said. "I guess I'm just tired."

"I'd say." He strode across the room and sat down at one of the place settings. "You looked as if you'd seen a ghost or something."

Teresa reappeared as if by magic and scurried to Mr. Byrne's side. She loaded his plate with scrambled egg whites and toast, then poured him a cup of coffee and whooshed out again without a word.

Josie smiled, but her eyes drifted toward the door, hoping someone else was going to make an entrance. Where was Jo's mom?

"Is everything okay?" Mr. Byrne asked.

She hesitated. "I was just . . ." Crap, what should she say? Jo must have left something out. Maybe her mom was traveling for work? She was supposed to know that.

"I know," he said softly. "I miss her too."

Right. Jo's mom wasn't there. Phew. *Would it have been so hard to mention that, Jo?*

With renewed confidence, Josie helped herself to a piece of toast. Her stomach was in knots and she prayed the sustenance would calm her nerves.

Mr. Byrne ate in silence, fingering his tablet on the table next to his plate. Josie didn't say a word. This seemed to be their normal morning routine, and she didn't want to do anything out of the ordinary.

"Are you going to see Nick after school today?"

"I think so," Josie said.

"Good. I like that boy, despite what happened."

What happened?

"And it was nice of him to return the necklace to you."

Return the necklace?

Mr. Byrne shoved the last morsel of toast into his mouth and drained his coffee. "Remind him about my offer, will you? Could really use a boy like that around the office. A government job right out of high school is an excellent opportunity, even if he has to work a few years at the Grid before he could transition into my department."

Josie's head was spinning as Mr. Byrne stood up and walked around to her side of the table. Something happened? What was the Grid? And Nick *returned* the necklace? Josie thought it had been a gift from boyfriend to girlfriend, just like the one Nick had given Madison. What was Jo's dad talking about?

"Have a fantastic day, princess." Mr. Byrne planted a kiss on the top of her head. "I'll be home late, so don't wait up."

TWENTY-ONE

7:15 A.M.

JOSIE'S MIND WAS A BLUR BY THE TIME SHE CLUM-sily grouped together what she assumed were her school things and closed the door to Jo's room behind her. She was missing a piece of the puzzle. Had Jo not told her something? Or was she blowing Mr. Byrne's comments completely out of proportion?

Stop trying to figure it out, Josie told herself. She was just a visitor and would be back in her own miserable life before she knew it. So what if Jo's mom was away on business? At least Josie got to spend some family time with Mr. Byrne, who was sweet and attentive and not a heartbroken mess dating a former prom queen half his age. Besides, the most important part of her day was still ahead: Nick.

Josie slipped Jo's cheat sheet out of her satchel as she headed downstairs. "Car's in the garage off the laundry room behind the kitchen." Got it. She took a right into the kitchen and tried to look easy and casual as she passed Teresa. The housekeeper stood at the sink meticulously washing the breakfast dishes. She didn't look up as Josie walked by.

As in every other part of the house, bright lights flooded the Byrnes' garage, glistening off the chrome fixtures. But Josie barely noticed the flood of lights. Her eyes were locked on the sleek black car before her.

The two-door BMW coupe looked as if it had just come off the showroom floor. Gleaming black with enormous performance wheels and a smoky glass moonroof, it looked like something James Bond would drive. She climbed into the leather driver's seat and sat there, afraid to touch anything. While her old Focus had exactly two buttons on the dashboard—air-conditioning and hazard lights—Jo's car was like the command center on a nuclear submarine. With a tentative finger, she engaged the push-button ignition. Instantly, the car came to life as the mirrors, steering wheel, and seat all moved into the perfect position for Josie's frame. The in-dash navigation screen welcomed "Josephine" with a personal greeting, and a series of flashing lights and beeps told her that everything had been checked and rechecked, and they were ready for launch. Er, for her drive to school. Same thing.

Josie almost felt sorry for Jo, who'd have to limp through suburban Bowie in the shuddering, temperamental disaster that was the Teal Monster. She probably should have warned Jo about that tricky ignition.

Oops.

It took her a few tries to find the visor button that opened the garage door; then with a deep breath and the school's address programmed into her GPS, Josie eased the car down the driveway.

"Turn left ahead," the car's mellifluous computer voice told her at the end of the driveway. Just like home, Josie turned left on Round Tree Lane. The houses looked similar on the treelined street. But also different, like everything else about Jo's world. There were a lot of brand-spanking-new McMansions, as well as totally remodeled older houses like the one Jo lived in. Originally a small craftsman like Josie's house, one here had been transformed into a modern two-story home complete with attached three-car garage.

Then there were the massive streetlights in front of every house in the neighborhood. Every single house. In addition, most had floodlights mounted on their exteriors—above the front door and the garage. Apparently, everyone was paranoid about not having enough light.

Despite the fact that this neighborhood was significantly more upscale than the one in which Josie lived, there were several houses that looked completely abandoned. Windows boarded up, lawns overgrown and gone to seed. A few even had collapsed roofs. And each abandoned house had a large sign staked into the lawn: NO GRID ACCESS.

Josie wondered what that was all about.

While Jo's neighborhood may have seemed strange, Bowie Prep, on the other hand, was relatively familiar. Same imposing brick façade, same smattering of kids scurrying to and fro. The parking lot was packed by the time she got there, except for one spot right near the front. It didn't seem to be handicapped or reserved. Someone must have just left. Finally, something was going Josie's way.

For the first time since she walked through the mirror, Josie felt at home. Bowie Prep in Jo's world looked a whole hell of a lot like Bowie Prep in Josie's, except cleaner and brighter. Still, things were in the same places—the entry hall, school office, courtyard all right where Josie would have expected them. Even her locker, number 441, was in the same place as Josie's number 441. Everything was the same.

Except one thing. Here, people noticed her.

"Hi, Jo!" a couple of girls said in unison as they passed her in the hallway. They looked vaguely familiar, though certainly no one Josie was friendly with back home, but she smiled in return like they were best friends. A group of guys greeted her around the next corner, then a trio of nervous underclassmen smiled at her tentatively as she stopped at her locker. It was like she was school royalty or something. Everyone knew Jo Byrne, and apparently for all the right reasons, whereas back home, Josie was just known as the sap who got "Byrned" while her boyfriend and best friend got it on behind her back.

Josie checked her cheat sheet for Jo's locker combination. 35-12-8. Exactly the same as her own. It was amazing the things that were the same.

And the things that weren't.

Jo had English for first period and as the warning bell rang, Josie made her way upstairs for class. Though she'd been combing the halls for Nick since she arrived, she still wasn't prepared to find him standing at his locker near the top of the stairs.

She froze, staring at him. He looked exactly as Josie had seen him in her dreams. The two Nick Fiorinos could have been carbon copies of each other. Black, wavy hair left slightly long so the thick strands were able to curl up in heavy coils behind his ears. Dark brown eyes, almost black, and heavy eyelashes longer than any boy had a right to. Strong nose and chin, right out of a Roman sculpture.

Josie felt her hands trembling and prayed she hadn't broken out in a sweat. The last time Josie had spoken to her ex-boyfriend face-to-face, he'd been shirtless in front of Madison's house, pounding on her car window, an image Josie wanted to douse with mind bleach.

But this Nick wasn't her ex-boyfriend. He was her boyfriend. She'd been in love with Nick for as long as she could remember and here, for twenty-four hours, she could fix what was left broken between them.

Nick closed his locker, and turned to find Josie staring at him. His eyebrows pinched together, obviously confused. "Jo?"

Josie's heart pounded. It was as if he'd never cheated on her, never broken her heart. A lump rose in Josie's throat and without thinking, she launched herself at him, wrapping both arms tightly around his neck.

"Whoa," he said, immediately trying to pry her arms away. "Jo, are you okay?"

Josie suppressed a sob and clung to Nick more fiercely.

"Hey!" Nick whispered harshly in her ear. "What the hell are you doing?"

Josie jerked her head up as Nick wedged his hands between them, pushing her roughly away by the shoulders. His face was hard-set as he stared at her, his eyes narrow and wary. He was clearly confused and disturbed.

No more confused and disturbed than Josie. There was something in Nick's face and demeanor that wasn't right. He wasn't the loving, gentle boyfriend Josie expected. *Oh no.* Josie's stomach dropped. Had Jo and Nick broken up in the twenty-four hours since she and Josie had made the plan to switch places? That would have been Josie's luck, wouldn't it? To have gone through all this just to be in the exact same space with her ex-boyfriend.

Josie took a breath and calmed herself. Maybe Nick had the same problem with Jo that he'd had with Josie? Maybe he needed to talk about something and Jo hadn't been available?

"If you need to talk," she offered, "about anything, I'm here anytime you—"

In line with Josie's luck, the bell rang for class. Nick took the opportunity to bail. "I gotta go. We'll, um, talk later?"

"Yeah," Josie called after him as he disappeared into the throng. *You bet your ass we will.*

This day was *not* going according to plan.

TWENTY-TWO

11:15 A.M.

JOSIE DASHED INTO THE SECOND-PERIOD PHYSICS classroom as the final bell rang. Barely on time, as usual. She smiled to herself. You can take the girl out of the universe but you can't take the universe out of the girl.

She had no real excuse for almost being late. Even though she was dazed from her interaction with Nick, physics was in the exact same room as in her own version of Bowie Prep, but it had taken her freaking forever to get there. Every hall she walked down, it was like everyone made a point to say hello to her. No one approached her, no one walked with her to class, but people were falling over themselves to smile and be polite. Still, Josie noticed a distinct lack of genuine warmth in their salutations. In fact, Josie thought she detected a trace of fear from most of the students as they fired off a quick "Hi, Jo!" then scurried back into the anonymity of the crowd.

It was kind of like being the world's most popular leper—the focus of everyone's attention and no one's affection—and it made her incredibly uncomfortable. Was that what it was like to be popular? A kind of cold, fearful isolation?

But the moment she entered the physics classroom, all of her discomfort faded away. The room was an exact replica of her own beloved Bowie Prep science lab. The same metal tables and ancient stools. The same equipment lining the walls in floor-to-ceiling bookcases. Even the same students at the same tables, including the Kaufman twins in the front of the room, and the Swedish exchange student sitting prim and proper near the door. And at the same table—without a lab partner—was Penelope.

"Hi, Pen," she said, taking the empty seat next to her old friend. "How's it going?"

Penelope started and cast a furtive glance at Josie from behind the thick, black hair that hung half in her face. Josie saw in Penelope's eyes the same look she'd seen from some of the students who greeted her in the hallway: fear.

"Look, I already told you," Penelope said, her voice guarded and low, her eyes fixed on the lab table. "I'll make sure you pass, okay?"

"Um, okay."

"Just do what you promised."

Josie was utterly confused. "What I promised?"

Penelope's head snapped up. "The Grid. You promised to make sure we don't get cut off."

"Oh!" Josie smiled and tried to act like she had any idea what Penelope was talking about. "Of course. Already taken care of."

Penelope's body relaxed somewhat.

Mr. Baines clapped his hands and the class came to attention. Josie pulled a notebook and pen from her bag, and caught the look of confusion on Penelope's face as she stared at both.

The lecture was pretty standard, a lesson on fields: electromagnetism, strong nuclear force, weak nuclear force, and gravity. Practically remedial as far as Josie was concerned, so she didn't even bother to take notes. Hell, she could have taught that class. Penelope appeared to be of the same mind-set: Josie saw her occasionally scribble down a name or an equation, but for the most part she doodled on her page. At one point she caught Josie watching her draw a diagram of relativity, showing the grid lines of space warping around the mass of a giant object. Penelope quickly flipped to a new page in her notebook, and carefully shielded her page from Josie's view for the rest of class.

Bored and disturbed by the fact that Penelope was not only *not* Jo's friend but appeared to be terrified of her, Josie zoned out for most of the lecture, until one of Mr. Baines's questions grabbed her attention.

"Which brings us to the last question before the bell," he said, with a dramatic flourish at the equations he'd spent most of the period diagramming on the whiteboard. "And your homework assignment for tonight. Despite being the weakest of the four fundamental fields, gravity is also the most important. Tell me why. At least five hundred words."

A groan rippled through the class, and Josie was surprised. Really? That was hard? She couldn't help herself; she laughed out loud.

"Miss Byrne," Mr. Baines said, his voice full of concern. "Is everything okay?"

"Yes, sorry," she said, composing herself.

Mr. Baines's glance shifted to Penelope, then back to Josie. "Is everything okay with tonight's assignment?"

Really? The teacher was asking *her* if the assignment was okay? Josie looked nervously around the classroom. "No, it's fine. It's just kind of easy."

She had no idea why she said it. Perhaps her combative nature with her own version of Mr. Baines was bubbling to the surface. But as soon as the words flew out of her mouth, she regretted them. The color drained from Mr. Baines's face, and a chorus of whispers raced through the room. What had she said? What mistake had she made now?

"I just meant," she said nervously, trying to make it better, "the idea that gravity is the only field that works on all particles regardless of mass is pretty basic, right? And the only field that can unite quantum mechanics and general relativity in one . . ."

Josie's voice trailed off. Every single person in the room was staring at her, eyes wide, in several cases mouths agape. No one said a word; no one moved. They just stared at her like she was sitting there in class completely naked.

She turned to Penelope, who stared at her too, but with something more than the shock reflected in every other face. Penelope's narrow eyes were closed to thin slits, wary and alert, and her brows were scrunched low.

Josie swallowed hard. Did Penelope suspect that Josie was an impostor?

The bell rang, saving Josie from any further muck-ups. Mr. Baines repeated the assignment and scurried from the room without even a look in Josie's direction, and the rest of the students followed suit. It was as if the room were on fire, people were so anxious to get out of there.

Josie packed up her things slowly. Holy crap, she'd better keep her mouth closed for the rest of the day before she ruined the whole masquerade. She stood up and saw Penelope standing silently by the door of the empty classroom.

Her chin was jutted out and her arms folded across her chest. "What was all that about?"

Damn. Josie must have made quite a faux pas. "Sorry," Josie said. "I didn't realize I was being rude."

"Rude?" Penelope laughed drily. "You're Jo Byrne. You own this school. Hell, you have your own parking spot reserved every day. No one would ever think you were rude."

"Oh." Josie was confused. "I just thought . . . I mean, everyone got quiet."

Penelope tilted her head to the side, scrutinizing Josie. "You know why."

Josie's mind raced. "Um . . ."

"You've never answered a question in class."

So science wasn't Jo's strong suit. Of all the things they had in common, Josie found it ironic that an aptitude for science wasn't one of them. "Oh, well, you know I'm not good at science."

Penelope pulled her chin back. "You've never answered a question in any class. Ever." Then she caught her breath. A look of fear washed over her face and before Josie could say anything else, Penelope spun around and dashed out the door.

TWENTY-THREE

6:15 P.M.

JOSIE SAT IN THE BLEACHERS, WATCHING NICK at track practice. She'd been there for almost three and a half hours, waiting.

He'd avoided her at lunch; that was clear. Josie knew from Jo's cheat sheet that they had third lunch together, but Nick had never appeared in the cafeteria. It had been the weirdest lunch period of her life. Just like in the hallways between classes, people were constantly stopping by her table to say hi and ask if she needed anything, but no one sat down near her. In fact, no one sat down at the table. She had the whole, long cafeteria table to herself.

If this was popularity, Jo could keep it.

By the beginning of fourth period, she would have talked to the school janitor, given the opportunity. She was desperate for conversation.

She and Nick were supposed to have fourth-period European History together. Finally, she figured he'd be forced to at least sit in the same room with her. Apparently, not so much. Same as lunch, Nick never showed.

But if this Nick was anything like her Nick, track practice was the one place he would absolutely, positively be. Josie was right. Twenty minutes after the final bell, Josie saw him trot out onto the all-weather track in his usual red-and-white track shorts. He'd glanced in her direction and paused. Josie had waved at him, but instead of waving back, he'd turned and sprinted to the far side of the field for his stretches.

Ugh. It was like she was reliving her own crappy life. What was going on?

She had less than twelve hours to spend with Nick. She was determined to make every second count.

Even if that meant camping out on a hot, metal bleacher for three hours while Nick went through the longest workout in the history of track workouts.

It was déjà vu all over again. Sitting in the bleachers watching Nick at track practice, while Nick basically ignored her very existence.

This had to be a parallel universe. Nothing was more parallel than what Josie felt.

It was the slowest three hours of her life, for sure. With the exception of the bodies moving around the track, there wasn't much to look at. Although every once in a while, Josie caught a movement out of the corner of her eye, a figure in the trees on the south side of the track. But when she'd look in that direction, there was never anyone there. Josie shook her head. She was just being paranoid, like Penelope and her talk of serial killers and dismembered bodies in the woods. Ridiculous. Those deaths took place in a different world, far from where Josie was now.

Nick was the last to leave the track. The coaches and managers were already packing up when he finished his last sprint. Again, he glanced at the bleachers. He must have seen her. But instead of coming over to talk to her, he turned on his heel and headed straight to the boys' locker room.

What the hell? He was avoiding her, of that Josie was sure. Was it about Tony? Josie was determined to find out.

She just had to find him. And there was one place Nick would have to show up.

Josie shouldered her bag and marched into the school parking lot. There were only two cars left: Jo's black BMW and a beat-up old SUV.

Bingo.

Fifteen minutes later, her patience paid off. Nick exited the side door of the gym and made a beeline for his car.

"You want to tell me why you've been avoiding me all day?" Josie asked, stepping out from behind his car. Her mock-up of Jo's confidence was finally starting to feel more "make it" and less "fake it."

Nick flinched and dropped his keys on the ground. "Shit, Jo. You scared me. What are you doing here?"

"I want to know why you're avoiding me."

He bent down to pick up his keys and slowly straightened up. "Avoiding you?" he said. "I don't know what you're talking about."

"Really? Where were you at lunch? And fourth period?"

Nick looked her dead in the eye. "I was excused for both."

"Is this about Tony?" Josie blurted out. "If you want to talk about it, I'm here for you."

Nick flinched. "What are you, my mother?"

"I'm your girlfriend," Josie erupted. She wasn't sure which Nick the anger was directed at. Maybe both.

"I'm sorry, what?"

"You heard me." She totally failed at keeping the exasperation out of her voice. She pulled the necklace out from under her sweater. "Remember this?"

"Your mom's necklace? What does that have to do with it?"

Josie's mouth went dry. "My *mom's* necklace?"

"I told you the other day when I gave it back to you."

Returned. That's what Mr. Byrne meant. Josie felt as if she'd been punched in the stomach. It wasn't a gift; Nick had just been returning something to her.

"It got mixed up with my brother's things after the accident," Nick continued, emphasizing every word, like he was talking to a small child who might not understand.

"The accident . . ." Josie shook her head. Was that why Jo's mom wasn't around? Had there been some sort of car wreck or something? Something to do with Tony?

Nick let out an exasperated sigh. "Look, I've told you at least twice so let's make this the last time. You and I are just friends. That's all we are and that's all we'll ever be. So no more picnic invitations; no more hugging episodes like in the hall this morning, okay?"

Nick's face hardened as he spoke. Josie knew that look. She'd seen it before on her ex-boyfriend's face. Just once: the last conversation they had before she caught him cheating with Madison. Nick had wanted to talk to her, but she didn't have time, and the same fleeting look passed over his face.

That's what she saw in this Nick. Disgust.

The realization came crashing upon her, like a spring thunderstorm barreling down the Potomac Valley. Nick hated her.

Josie felt her body sway. It was happening again, same as before. Her skin had gone clammy. Her brow beaded up with sweat, but she felt cold and shivery as if she was running a high fever. She pressed her hand to her temple and noticed that the parking lot of Bowie Prep was tilting ever so slightly to the left. As she started to lose her balance, she could have sworn she saw a figure duck behind her car.

"Jo? Are you okay?" Nick moved toward her, placing a hand on her shoulder, but Josie shook free. It was even worse here than it was back home. Not only was this Nick not in love with her, he absolutely hated her.

Josie's face burned. She was so humiliated, like she was reliving Madison and Nick's betrayal. She hadn't thought anything could be as bad as that moment, but the hatred she saw in Nick's eyes was definitely worse. She wanted to get out of there, to run as far away from Nick Fiorino as she possibly could, in this universe or any other.

Nick glanced up at the horizon. "Sun's going down. You'd better get in my car. I'll drive you home."

"Get in your car?" Was he crazy? Josie backed away. "I'm not going anywhere with you." She wasn't going to be the victim anymore. She wouldn't put herself in the position to be hurt by this Nick in the same way she'd been hurt by her own. It was the only thing she could control.

"Jo, wait!"

Too late. Josie didn't care if Jo's BMW sat in the school parking lot all night. She needed to get out of there. Now. She swung around and stumbled around the corner of the gym, out of Nick's sight.

TWENTY-FOUR

6:45 P.M.

HOW COULD SHE HAVE BEEN SO STUPID? HOW could she have thought things would be any different here? Whatever she'd seen in her dreams, whatever Jo had led her to believe, was all a fantasy.

Shadows started to creep across the landscape as Josie wandered aimlessly beyond the front lawn of Bowie Prep. She glanced at her watch. A few more hours until she could cross back through the mirror to her own wreck of a life. A life that suddenly didn't seem so bad.

Josie paused when she reached the sidewalk. Nick was right: the sun was going down and it would be dark soon, and her feet hurt in the high-heeled booties. She should walk back to the parking lot and drive Jo's swanky car home. But she couldn't. Nick might see her, and that . . . well, she'd had enough humiliation for a lifetime at the hands of Nick Fiorino. It was only four miles or so back to Jo's house. She'd just suck up the pain and walk.

The streets were mostly deserted. No one sat on their porches enjoying the warm spring evening. No one was out walking their dog. No one pushing kids in strollers. A few cars whizzed past her, and several of them honked at her. Well, at least someone somewhere in some universe still found her attractive.

As dusk stole across the town, an unnatural chill descended. Josie looked up, expecting to see towering thunderheads piling up into the heavens, but the sky was clear, though perhaps darker than Josie would have thought for that time of evening.

The bright streetlamps bathed the neighborhood with light, but without warmth or cheerfulness. Unlike the ones on Josie's block back home, these were starkly blue, sterile, and extremely intense. In house after house, blinds were being drawn, shutters latched, like every household was hunkering down for the night. As Josie tramped along, she got a creeping feeling up the back of her spine. The entire town had an air of hostility.

Maybe it was the strangeness of the neighborhood, or maybe it was her confrontation with Nick, but in addition to seeing figures in the shadows, Josie now thought she could hear someone walking behind her. Footsteps, heavy and sharp, matching her beat for beat. But every time she turned her head, there was no one behind her.

Without thinking, Josie quickened her pace.

Up ahead, a trail cut through the thin woods that surrounded the neighborhood. Just like her favorite shortcut back home, it would eliminate a half mile off her walk. The sun's rays had completely disappeared, leaving the light purply glow of twilight as night rapidly approached. But she knew this trail like the back of her hand, and the sooner she got back to Jo's bedroom, the better. It was a no-brainer. She rounded the corner and ducked into the trees.

As soon as she was off the street, the atmosphere changed. It was silent. A complete and total lack of sound. The wind didn't blow; there was no backdrop of chirping birds or the occasional car zipping by on the street that was just a few yards away. It was as if she were in a vacuum, utterly devoid of life.

Something wasn't right about this place: the woods, the night, the whole damn world. She expected her eyes to adjust to the encroaching darkness after she got out from under the intensity of the streetlamps, but the woods stretching before her looked darker than they should have. Sure, it was night, but the last beams of sunlight should still have lingered on the horizon. She wasn't sure why, but she began to jog down the path. She could see the light at the end of the trail, signaling the street on which Jo lived, but it seemed forever away. Again, she could have sworn she heard something behind her, rustling the low foliage that lined the trail. This time she didn't look back, but broke into a dead run. She glanced up at the sky. It was inky black and dotted with stars.

There was movement above her. A dark form blocked the stars from her view. Just as before, it was only a flash, a momentary glimpse of something that looked like wings flapping in the darkness. Deep brown, threaded with black and gray. Gone in an instant.

That's when she heard it.

It sounded far away at first, a dim rustling noise, but in the complete absence of sound, it was jarring. The noise grew louder, rushing toward her from above. Faster and faster, like an enormous flock of birds swooping down on her. She knew that sound. She'd heard it before. A grating, shrieking flapping of wings in the darkness.

The sound outside the window.

In the darkness.

The bright lights, rooms without switches, houses shuttered up against the coming of night. Suddenly it all made sense. There was something in the dark, something that came with the onset of night. Something dangerous. Something to be feared.

And Josie was in the middle of the woods without any light at all.

The noise grew exponentially louder with every passing second. She pressed her hands against her ears to block out the painful, deafening sound, but it did no good. The noise of the darkness swamped her, dulling her senses and slowing her down.

Josie had a sensation of wind rushing by, air beating with the onslaught of dozens of wings. She caught glimpses of movement, of flesh and talons and beaks, but nothing concrete. It was as if they were moving in and out of a spotlight, and she could only catch a fleeting glance as they passed above her, swooping through the dark woods amidst their deafening shrieks.

The speed of the flying creatures increased, and suddenly Josie felt like she was surrounded by them, an impenetrable wall of these monsters of the dark.

Panic blinded her. "Help!" Josie cried out. "Someone help me!"

She felt one of the creatures swoop around her, circling directly above. Then something swept across her head, brushing her hair. It felt like a wing, only harder. Less like feathers and more like leather. A second wing glided across her back. This time she felt the fabric of her sweater tear as something sharp ripped through it.

Suddenly, there was a shift in the air rushing around her. A pause in the movement and the sound, the eye of the storm. A single shriek tore through the silence, then another echoing ahead. Another and another, as if the creatures were communicating to the rest of the flock. She heard a rumbling in the distance, crescendoing with each passing second. They were coming back. The swarm had been called back.

A talon slashed across her arm. Josie cried out as a searing pain shot from her wrist to her elbow, and she could feel the hot trail of blood trickling from the wound.

In an instant, the air swirled above her; the beating of wings pressed against her from every side. They were swarming, circling, preparing to attack. The light at the end of the trail faded, blocked by the swarm. She waved her arms in front of her face, attempting to cut her way through whatever blocked her path. The creatures of the darkness sliced at her hands, at her arms, at whatever open flesh they could find.

Whatever lived in the night was trying to hurt her.

To kill her.

Josie forced her legs to move as she blindly stumbled forward, but they were on her now. Pecking and cutting, forcing her down.

Josie sank to her knees and covered her head with her arms, trying to protect herself. This was it. This was how she would die.

Without warning, they stopped. She could still hear their screeching, but it was muffled. She felt a weight on top of her, like a body shielding her from attack.

"Hello?" Josie said.

"Quiet!" a voice barked. Harsh and raspy, barely discernible above the chaos surrounding her. "They'll follow your sound." She felt an arm around her, then a hand on her wrist.

Suddenly she was being pulled to her feet and practically carried down the trail. She stumbled and tripped, but the strong arm around her waist kept her moving.

Light flooded her eyes and Josie felt the hard concrete of Round Tree Lane. She half expected to be bombarded again, but the screeching and fluttering was gone. Whatever attacked her in the darkness had vanished.

She turned, looking for the person who had saved her life, but all she saw was a pair of car headlights bearing down on her.

"Jo!" a voice yelled. A voice she knew. "Jo, what the hell are you doing? Get in the goddamn car!"

Nick.

Josie shielded her eyes as another set of lights illuminated the street. Floodlights mounted on the roof of Nick's SUV. They cut a swath through the dark expanse to where Josie stood under the streetlamp. She stumbled forward, feeling like all the strength had been drained out of her.

Blood poured down her arms and she could feel a sharp pain

at the back of her neck. She reached the SUV, steadying herself against the hood as the engine idled.

"Hurry up," Nick barked. "We've got to get you out of here."

Right. Out of here. Yes, back to the mirror. She had to get back through the mirror.

Nick reached over and opened the passenger door, and Josie whipped around it, careful to keep her body in the safety of the light as she climbed into Nick's car.

She slumped in the worn leather seat, panting. Interior lights of the car illuminated every inch of the cabin. And for the first time, Josie was thankful for them.

"What the hell were you thinking?" Nick asked. His voice was gruff but laced with concern and panic.

"Th-thank you," Josie stuttered. Her teeth were chattering, her body wracked with shivering. "You . . . you saved my life."

"You're lucky I followed you." Nick pulled his sweatshirt over his head and draped it over her shoulders. "What you were thinking walking home at dusk? And the path through the woods? You were practically asking for the Nox to attack."

Nox. Is that what they were? It seemed like such an innocuous word for what lurked in the dark.

Nick ran a hand through his thick, dark hair. "You're lucky you made it through the woods to the street. Most people don't make it five feet once the Nox catch them."

"Someone," Josie panted. "Someone carried me out."

"Carried you out of the dark woods?" Nick shook his head. "No one's alive in there, Jo. Not once the sun goes down."

No one was alive in the woods. That was impossible. She'd felt an arm. She'd heard a voice.

"What is with you today?" Nick continued. "It's like you're a totally different person."

"You have no idea."

"Huh?"

Josie kept quiet. It was no good trying to explain anything to Nick, since she'd be gone in a few hours and then the old Jo would bring things back to normal. Nick would just write it off as "lady problems" or temporary insanity, and Josie would pretend this sojourn into Jo's world never happened.

After a moment, Nick sighed. "Fine. Don't talk to me. I'll take you back to my house and get you cleaned up."

"No," Josie said. Her teeth were still chattering. "Take me home."

"Jo, you're covered in blood."

"Take me home," she repeated. She couldn't risk not being there for the next window. She had to get home.

"Suit yourself. But if your dad gets pissed off, it's your problem."

3:55 A.M.

Despite a half dozen Advil in the last few hours, Josie's head still pounded. Her body felt like it had been poisoned—sluggish, heavy, and aching all over.

Her ripped-up forearms didn't help matters. While the Nox, as Nick had called them, had only inflicted a few wounds on the back of her neck before she made it out of the woods, her arms looked as if she'd gone three rounds with a Weedwacker. Most of the cuts were shallow, with a few exceptions, and after a painful hour in the bathroom cleansing the deeper gashes and taping them up with gauze and butterfly bandages, she figured they'd heal okay.

But what the hell were those things? She knew now what Jo had been trying to tell her when they switched places: *Don't go out after dark.*

Yeah, thanks for the heads-up.

At five minutes to the appointed time, Josie was ready to go. She'd changed back into her own clothes, shoving the blood-covered yellow dress and Nick's sweatshirt deep into the bottom of the hamper, and left Jo's room exactly as she'd found it. Everything would look better now: her parents' divorce, her mom's weirdness, even Nick and her social standing at school. All of it seemed bearable when weighed against the homicidal monsters that lived in the darkness just outside the bright lights of Jo's room.

She thought she'd be sad to have to go back to her own life, but as the surface of the mirror rippled, Josie smiled. She was ready to go home.

She wanted to feel her own bedsheets; smell the musty air of her dilapidated, water-damaged house. Before the image on the other side was even fully in view Josie reached her hand into the undulating surface of the mirror.

Josie felt the thick, spongy interior of the portal as she pushed her arm through. She was about to duck into the portal and go through to her own bedroom, when her fingertips grazed something solid and rough.

Huh?

She leaned into the gooey substance of the portal until her shoulders rested against a hard surface. It was solid and heavy, and it wouldn't budge. She pulled away, and slowly, the image on the other side of the mirror came into focus. A gray concrete wall.

The wall of the basement in Josie's house.

In an instant, Josie realized what had happened. Jo had conned her. She'd conveniently left out several details about her life—a life that kind of sucked, apparently—and now that she was in Josie's life, she had no intention of coming back.

Panic. Josie reached up as far as she could, trying to find an edge, something she could wedge her fingers between and maybe force the mirror off the wall. She submerged herself in the portal, and tried to push the back side of the frame away. But it wouldn't budge. Jo must have secured the mirror with something, sandwiching it tight against the concrete.

The mirror began to ripple again and Josie pulled her body out of the portal. As her own reflection rematerialized, cold reality slapped her in the face.

Josie was trapped.

TWENTY-FIVE

6:55 A.M.

JOSIE DIDN'T REALIZE SHE'D FALLEN ASLEEP until a knock at the door woke her up.

"Are you awake?"

Josie rolled over in bed. Her eyes were closed, but it was still dark in her room.

She stretched her arms over her head. It had all been a dream— a horrible, wretched nightmare. She was at home in her bed and her mom was waking her up so she wouldn't be late for school. Another normal day.

Thank God.

"Miss Josephine, you're going to be late."

Miss Josephine? Josie's eyes flew open and she realized she was wearing a sleep mask. Jo's sleep mask.

She was still in the nightmare.

"Miss Josephine?" Teresa cracked the bedroom door. There was a pause, then she heard Teresa take a sharp breath. "Miss Josephine, your arms. Are you okay? What happened? If your father finds—" Panic rose in her voice as each thought crossed her mind.

Josie wiggled her arms beneath the covers so Teresa couldn't see the full extent of her wounds. "I'm not feeling well, so I'm not going to school."

"But what shall I tell your father?"

Josie rolled over, turning her back on Teresa. "Just tell him I'm sick." She didn't care what Teresa thought; there was no way in hell she was going to school today. She needed to figure out a way home.

"Oh." Teresa lingered at the door for a moment, then Josie heard her slowly close it. "Of course, Miss Josephine."

Josie rolled onto her back and stared around Jo's room.

Your room.

Josie shook her head, forcing the thought from her mind. She was not going to be stuck here. She'd figure out a way home. Somehow.

What if she couldn't? She hadn't told anyone back home about Jo and the mirror. So far, she'd been able to snowjob everyone in Jo's world into believing that she was their daughter, classmate, whatever. Wouldn't Jo be able to do the same thing in Josie's world? Her mom had been so weird lately, so distant and distracted by work; would she even notice there was something different about her daughter? Would anyone?

Maybe her dad. Then again, he'd been so wrapped up in the divorce, he might attribute his daughter's weirdness to that.

There was no one else. No one who'd notice. And no one

who'd miss her even if they did.

Hell, maybe people would like Jo better.

Josie swung her legs over the side of the bed and stood up. She paced the room aimlessly, her mind racing. Nick had made it clear that Jo had been after him for quite some time, to no effect. But there was another Nick. Maybe Jo would want to try with him?

And if she succeeded, she'd never want to go home.

What if Josie was stuck here? Other than Jo's father, who seemed to care for her in a kind of jovial, fatherly way, what was here for her? Josie slumped down in Jo's leather desk chair. For the first time, she prayed Madison and Nick's romance was solid and long-lasting. The only way Josie was getting home was if Jo wanted to switch back.

She sat there for what felt like hours, gently swinging back and forth in Jo's swivel chair. What was she going to do?

After a while, Josie realized her eyes had rested on an object on Jo's bookshelf. She wasn't sure how long she'd been staring at it, but suddenly, recognition dawned.

She was staring at her vase. The wine-bottle vase covered in magazine squares that she'd made in fifth-grade art class.

Josie sprang to her feet and snatched the vase off the shelf. She knew instantly that it was hers. *So that's what happened to it.* Her vase and Jo's vase had switched.

But how?

Josie let the vase fall back onto the shelf with a clunk. It hadn't come through the mirror with her—of that she was pretty sure. She'd have noticed a flying inanimate object. And yet here it was, as real and solid as anything else around her, which meant the connection between their worlds extended beyond the physical confines of the mirror.

And if the vases could move back and forth between the worlds without the portal, maybe she could too?

A list of things that had randomly gone missing flooded Josie's brain. Her pink tweed Converse, Mr. Fugly Bear. Things she'd looked for and couldn't find over the last week, since the mirror landed in her bedroom.

Were they here? In this house?

Josie took a deep breath. There was only one way to find out.

2:15 P.M.

Josie waited impatiently all day, but at two o'clock Teresa went out to run errands. Finally. Josie needed to spend some time perving around the house, and she much preferred to do it unobserved.

She'd spent most of the day making a list of things to look for, things that had gone missing or at least seemed odd or out of place in her house since the day at the railroad crossing. The vase, her shoes, and Mr. Fugly Bear were obvious—they were objects Josie had actively missed—but as she thought back on the last week, she realized that the leapfrogging of items between the two worlds went deeper. Incidents that seemed a mere annoyance at the time suddenly had more meaning.

Like the Tinkerbell magnet on the fridge. Josie had come home from school last week and found several pizza-delivery coupons scattered on the kitchen floor. They'd been pinned to the refrigerator door by a large Tinkerbell magnet Josie had bought on a family vacation to Disney World. She'd gathered up the coupons and found another magnet to hold them in place without really thinking about what had happened to poor Tink.

Now she knew.

And those were just the things she'd noticed. Maybe there were more objects zapped into Jo's world and vice versa? And if they could be, why couldn't Josie?

She'd already done a full sweep of Jo's room and bathroom, but other than the vase, she hadn't found any of the missing objects. She decided to start downstairs in the kitchen, the most logical place to find a refrigerator magnet.

The sleek stainless steel refrigerator was devoid of decoration: no magnets or family photos or pizza-delivery coupons in sight. Similarly, the kitchen counters were empty, just squeaky-clean granite countertops polished to within an inch of their lives. Teresa took her job very seriously.

Josie checked the pantry as a matter of course. Its contents were similar to the one in her own kitchen—it even had the same black canister set, all uniform and lined up in rows three deep on a shelf—but no kitchen magnets or anything else that reminded her specifically of home.

Josie was starting to despair when the living room, laundry room, and formal dining room all turned up empty. Was she wrong? Was the vase just a fluke?

There were three bedrooms upstairs. Jo's room she'd already gone over with a fine-tooth comb, so she tackled Jo's parents' room next. Large and luxuriously decorated, it looked more like a hotel suite than a master bedroom. The enormous king-size bed sat on a raised step on the far side of the room, flanked on either side by floor-to-ceiling windows. There was not one but two walk-in closets—his and hers—which were each about as large as Josie's bedroom back home. Not to mention the bathroom complete with sauna, whirlpool bathtub, and a glass-enclosed shower that could accommodate an entire basketball team. If Josie had a bathroom like that, she might never leave.

Searching a room that size was no easy task. But surely one of the objects on Josie's list must be there. In one of the closets, in a drawer, in the ridiculously large bathroom? Yeah, no. After an hour, Josie gave up in defeat.

One more place to check. The guest room.

Situated on the same side of the house as Jo's room, the guest bedroom was oddly sparse. Bed, nightstand. That was it. Not even a dresser, just a small closet on the far wall. Oh well, at least it would be easy to search.

The nightstand was empty, as was the space under the bed. But when Josie yanked open the closet door, she gasped.

On the floor in the middle of the closet was a box filled with a variety of miscellaneous objects. Sitting right on top was Mr. Fugly Bear.

Josie crouched down and lifted Mr. Fugly out of the box. Yep, definitely him. Missing an ear and a thumb. Her favorite childhood toy, here in a closet in Jo's house.

Creak.

Josie froze. *What was that?* She waited, crouched in the closet, and held her breath. After what felt like forever, Josie slowly exhaled. Just the house settling. If Teresa or Mr. Byrne were home, she'd have heard them come in. She was being paranoid.

Shaking off her fears, Josie hauled the box out of the closet. In the bright lights of the unused room, she could see another familiar object: a pair of pink tweed Converse. Then another and another. A bottle of her mom's favorite perfume. A Christmas card from Josie's cousins in Ireland. A book of tapas recipes from her mom's international-cooking phase. And a magnet shaped like the pixie from *Peter Pan*.

All of them here. All of them gathered and put in a box and shoved in this closet out of sight. They'd been put here deliberately. Josie shook her head. It must have been Jo. The vase might have gone unnoticed since it was so similar to the one that appeared in Josie's room, but a pair of pink Converse sneakers would have been a shock for Jo to find in her closet. Had Jo realized what they were and what they meant? Had she hidden them?

And more important, how did they get here in the first place?

Josie had no idea, but the key to getting home seemed to lie in figuring out the Mystery of the Missing Converse. She laughed lightly to herself. Best Nancy Drew title ever.

Okay, think. She leaned back against the bed. Regardless, these items had switched places with a counterpart on the other side, like Jo and Josie, only the objects were zapped at random. Josie hadn't seen these items moving through the mirror when it was open, so how did they get there?

Josie caught her breath. Maybe there was another portal?

Josie leaped to her feet. That had to be it! Another portal. Another rift between the two worlds.

Josie picked up the box and headed back to Jo's room. It didn't matter how or why, only that another portal existed. She just had to find it. Or create another one. Whatever it took to get home.

"I will," she said out loud as she gripped the handle to Jo's bedroom door. She felt hopeful again. Buoyant. "I'll get home if it kills me."

But as she threw open the bedroom door, Josie's stomach dropped. Her skin went cold, and her newfound sense of hope drained away.

Standing in the middle of the room, with a gun leveled at her, was Nick.

"We need to talk."

TWENTY-SIX

3:45 P.M.

TWO HOURS AGO JOSIE HAD BEEN DESPERATE TO get time alone in the house. Now she would have sold her first-born to have someone else around.

Nick's face was very calm. His voice didn't shake. His arm held the gun steady. There was something unnerving in the casual way he stared at her, as if holding her at gunpoint was a perfectly natural activity for a Tuesday afternoon.

"Who are you?" he asked.

A hundred thoughts raced through Josie's mind. How did he know? And what should she tell him? Lie? Tell him the truth? Would the truth sound more like a lie than an actual lie? Better not risk it.

"What the hell are you doing?" Josie said, doing her best impression of Jo. "Is this some kind of joke?" She shuffled her feet toward the door in what she hoped was a casual manner.

"Don't move," Nick said. Still calm. Still devoid of emotion.

Josie wasn't willing to give in. "Don't tell me what to do."

Nick shrugged. "I'm the one holding the gun."

Josie forced a laugh, desperately hoping she sounded light and airy. "Please. I can tell that thing is plastic from here."

Nick paused, then in answer he cocked the metal barrel. Definitely not a toy. "Right," he said. "Plastic."

Josie swallowed hard. Apparently there was a whole hell of a lot more going on than she could even imagine. She was running out of options.

Nick motioned toward the bed. "Sit."

"What do you want, Nick?"

"Sit down."

She could have made a break for it. But Nick was stronger and faster, not to mention the fact that he had a gun pointed at her chest. She probably wouldn't have made it downstairs, let alone outside, without taking a bullet in the back. And then where would she have gone? The neighbors? Could she trust anyone? Nope. Besides, who would believe her? Josie was out of moves. She dropped the box on the floor and sat down gingerly on the edge of her mattress.

"Good." Without taking his eyes off her, Nick dragged the desk chair over to the door and sat down, blocking the only exit. "Why don't you start by answering my question: Who are you?"

Josie laughed again. She couldn't help it. Nick sounded like he was doing an impression of a Nazi interrogator in every old movie she'd ever seen. "Really?"

"Cut the crap," Nick said. His voice had an edge to it now. Patience was wearing thin. "Who are you?"

"Josephine Byrne," she said with a cheeky grin. At least she wasn't lying.

"Bullshit."

"Look," Josie said with a broad smile. "Don't you recognize me?"

Nick shot to his feet. "I've known Jo since we were twelve, and I can say this with one hundred percent confidence: you are not Jo Byrne."

How did he know?

"I know her." Nick shifted his feet uneasily. "I know her personality, the way she talks and holds herself. The way she treats people. Ever since yesterday morning at school I've had this weird feeling that something just wasn't right. *You* weren't right. Zeke and Zeb told me what happened in physics. Then last night confirmed it. Either you've had major head trauma and don't actually remember who you are, or you're one of them." He paused and pointed the gun directly at her again. "And it's significantly more likely you're one of them."

"Who?"

"Do I look like an idiot?"

"Um . . ."

"I wouldn't put it past them to have you made up to look like Jo. Were you afraid of us? Of what we might discover? Could your secret research really be threatened by a couple of high-school students? That's pathetic. You hear me?"

Josie was starting to worry for his sanity. "Nick, what are you talking about?"

Nick ignored her question. He stormed up to her and grabbed her roughly by the shoulder. "Where are they? What happened to them?"

"I don't know who you're—"

Nick's fingers dug into the fleshy part of her neck. "WHAT THE FUCK HAPPENED TO MY BROTHER?"

Josie jerked away, trying to free herself. There was something in Nick's eyes that scared her. Desperation. Fearlessness. Whatever it was, he clearly wouldn't have thought twice about snapping her neck if push came to shove.

"Tony?" she said.

"Is that why you brought him up at school yesterday, huh? Were you trying to see how I'd react?"

Josie tried to wriggle free. "I don't know what you're talking about."

"Sure you don't. Not about Dr. Byrne either."

Josie stopped struggling. "What about Dr. Byrne?"

"Dr. Byrne? *Dr. Byrne?*" Nick pushed her down on the bed and climbed on top of her. He squeezed her throat, constricting airflow. "Jo would never call her mom that."

Josie pawed at Nick, desperately gasping for air. She didn't even care about the gun anymore, only prying Nick's hand off her throat. She kicked, trying to free herself, but he straddled her legs, rendering her almost completely helpless. She could feel her face burning, all the blood trapped as Nick methodically increased the pressure around her neck. Josie couldn't breathe, couldn't move. Her lungs burned, her eyes watered, and slowly, her vision began to go dark . . .

Just then, Nick released her. Josie's head lolled to the side as she gulped in huge mouthfuls of air. Her body felt limp and tired.

"One more time," Nick said. He'd regained his composure. She felt cold metal pressed against her cheek. The muzzle of the gun. "Who are you?"

Josie was screwed. She was Josephine Byrne—only not Nick's Josephine Byrne. How could she explain it to him without getting her head blown off?

"I'm not going to ask again."

"Okay!" Josie said, panting. "You win."

The gun didn't move. "Go ahead."

"Just hear me out," Josie said. Nick's face was impassive, his eyes quick and alert, like a tiger hunting its prey. But the knuckles on the hand that gripped the gun were white and tense. He was scared too.

"Quickly."

"My name is Josie Byrne."

Nick pressed the gun into her cheek. "I said—"

"Listen to me!" Whether it was the tone in her voice or the look on her face, it made Nick pull back as a wave of hestitation passed over him.

"Josie Byrne," she repeated. "Not Jo, *Josie*."

"What are you talking about?"

"I haven't had plastic surgery to look like Jo, okay? I *am* her." As soon as Josie said the words, she felt her face flush bright red. It was true, sort of, and even with Nick sitting on top of her holding a gun to her head, she felt a rush of excitement at saying those words.

Wow. That was completely fucked up.

"You're not Jo," Nick said, turning ever so slightly pink.

Josie ignored him. "We're the same person. Sort of."

Nick barked a disbelieving laugh. "Are you trying to tell me you're long-lost twins or something?"

"No."

"Then?"

Crap, what *was* she trying to tell him? "We're like the same person. The exact same person. Only not."

"A clone?" Nick sat back on the bed.

"No, not a clone." Josie pushed herself up to a sitting position. Nick still held the gun pointed in her general direction, but he seemed to have forgotten it was even in his hand.

"Because I wouldn't put it past the Grid to start cloning us." Nick looked out the window, clearly lost in his own thoughts.

Again, the idea of making a break for it crossed Josie's mind, but something held her there. Maybe ... maybe he could help her? She was going to need an ally if she was ever going to get home.

"I don't know anything about clones," Josie said truthfully. "But what I'm about to tell you is going to sound strange."

"Stranger than clones?"

"Actually? Yeah."

Nick half smiled. He was still tense, but there was an instant lightness to his face. "This had better be an awesome story."

Josie glanced at the clock. Five minutes to four. Well, that was the first thing that had gone right for her in the last twenty-four hours. At least she would have concrete, irrefutable proof of the completely insane story she was about to tell her gun-toting not-boyfriend.

"Well?" Nick asked.

It was now or never. Josie pointed to the mirror. "I came through there."

TWENTY-SEVEN

3:56 P.M.

NICK ARCHED AN EYEBROW. "YOU CAME THROUGH the mirror?" he asked skeptically.

"I know, it's crazy. But something happened last week and suddenly there was this connection between my world and yours and then—"

Nick snapped to attention. "Hold up. *Your* world?"

"Yeah. I—I don't come from here. I'm Josephine Byrne, but in another world."

"You mean in another dimension." Nick didn't sound incredulous. In fact, he said the words like they were common knowledge.

"Exactly."

"How?"

"Um . . ." Yeah, wasn't that the million-dollar question. Would he have any idea what she was talking about if she mentioned her theory about the ultradense deuterium? Doubtful. "I'm not really sure," she said instead. "Something happened and then I started having these dreams, like I was me but not me. Every night at the same time. Then I started seeing things in the mirror. Jo. This room. Every twelve hours at the exact same time. I realized I was seeing Jo's life, like through her eyes. Just for a minute. Every twelve hours."

"At what time?"

"Three fifty-nine."

Nick's eyes grew wide. "Three fifty-nine? You're sure?"

Josie nodded. "Positive."

Nick fell silent. He stared at the bed and bobbed his head up and down slightly. Was he trying to remember a month's worth of 3:59s? Josie looked away. Hopefully he wouldn't remember exactly what he'd been doing at those times. What snippets of his life Josie had been eavesdropping on.

"So if you're not bullshitting me . . . ," Nick started.

"I'm not. I swear."

"Yeah, yeah." Nick nodded. He was staring at the clock on the nightstand. "If you're not bullshitting me then in about thirty seconds there's going to be an image in that mirror that is not a reflection of this room, right?"

"Right."

"It'll be your room in another dimension."

Ugh. Josie shook her head. "Not exactly." Nick arched an eyebrow.

Josie was about to explain, when she caught sight of the mirror. It was starting.

"See for yourself," she said, nodding at the mirror.

Nick turned his head and, Josie saw with some satisfaction, his jaw dropped. He stared for a few seconds as the glass undulated, distorting the reflection of Jo's room. Nick slowly rose to his feet, the arm with the gun hanging limply at his side.

The concrete wall was still there, stark, gray, impenetrable. Nick reached his hand out to touch it, pausing just before his palm grazed the surface as if he wasn't quite sure what he was seeing and feeling was real. He gingerly brushed his fingertips against the mirror, breaking the surface of what, just seconds ago, had been solid glass. Josie watched as he swished his fingers around in the murky middle of the portal. He pulled his hand away and held it up before his face as he wiggled his fingers. Then he thrust his hand forward into the portal and pressed it flat against the wall.

Nick paused, then he leaned his body into the portal, testing his weight against the wall. He stood up straight, and with his fingers, traced the inside of the mirror frame looking for a break or a gap, just as Josie had done in the early hours of the morning, then he pushed his face into the wall, peering closely at the corner of the mirror, and poked at it with his finger.

Even though his body was blocking the mirror, Josie caught sight of the surface as it started to morph back into shape.

"Nick," she said. "Back up."

His head was completely submerged. Duh, he couldn't hear her.

The mirror began to resolidify. It washed over Nick's face and hands, still pressed into the concrete wall, viscous and shimmery, like liquid metal. Josie leaped forward and grabbed Nick by the back of his sweatshirt, then heaved with all her strength. He was choking now, suffocating on whatever made up the portal. It was like trying to pull someone out of quicksand. Nick felt stuck to the mirror. Horrific gurgling noises poured out of his mouth. Josie wrapped both of her arms around his waist, braced her foot against the frame, and pulled with all her strength.

With a sharp sucking sound, Nick's body was released from the mirror, and he and Josie tumbled backward onto the bed.

They lay there for a second, his body on top of hers. He was panting heavily, just as Josie had been a few moments before when he was choking her.

That's right. Nick had just tried to kill her.

She pushed his body to the side and shimmied out from under him. "See?" she said. "I told you it was crazy."

Nick passed a hand over his face. "Yeah."

"Yeah." Josie sat down in the chair and folded her arms across her chest. She didn't know what else to say. At last someone other than Jo knew her secret. At least it was out, the burden of secrecy removed. Whether or not Nick could help her was another matter entirely.

Nick slowly pushed himself into a sitting position, then stood up and walked over to the window. He left the gun on the bed, discarded, unheeded. As he stared outside in the late afternoon sunshine, Josie made a mental note that she was about three feet closer to the gun than he was.

"So you and Jo switched places."

"Yep."

"Her idea?"

"Actually, yeah." Josie conveniently left out the part about how she'd desperately hoped Jo would want to switch places. That wasn't a conversation she wanted to have with Nick.

"Okay." He still didn't look at her. "And then when you went to switch back out, you found the wall."

"Exactly."

"That's so like her," Nick said, more to himself than to Josie.

"Is it?"

Nick turned around. "Yeah. Selfish. Jo's used to getting what she wants. Mr. Byrne's a nice guy, but he's the government liaison with the Grid. Pretty powerful. Has his office up at Fort Meade on the Grid campus and everything. Jo likes to talk it up like she can decide who gets power from the Grid, and who doesn't. She uses it as a threat."

"Right." Josie remembered Penelope's comment in the lab, and the way people went out of their way to be friendly without actually wanting to be Jo's friend. She was a bully.

"It's weird, though," Nick said after a pause. "Why she'd want to stay there."

Once again, Josie couldn't prevent her natural reaction. She laughed out loud.

"What?" Nick asked, half turning toward her.

"Why wouldn't she want to stay there? This place is awful. She's in love with you, while you clearly can't stand her, and—"

"Whoa," Nick said, holding up his hand. "How did you know she's in love with me?"

Crap. Loaded question which Josie had no intention of answering. She cleared her throat and barreled on. "Everyone avoids her at school. She has no friends. Oh, and when the sun goes down the darkness tries to eat you alive."

Nick cocked his head. "No Nox in your world?"

"Hell, no. What are those things anyway?"

"Hmm," Nick said, ignoring her question. "Still, not enough to make her stay there. Not with her mom and everything. Unless . . ."

Josie started. "Wait, what about her mom?"

"She didn't tell you?"

Josie narrowed her eyes. "There's a lot Jo didn't tell me."

Nick laughed softly. "Yeah, that sounds like her too." Nick paced back and forth, ignoring her question about Jo's mom. Suddenly, he swung around. "Your mom, on the other side. She's okay?"

"Yeah, I guess. I mean, she's been kinda weird lately, but she's not sick or anything."

"And Jo knew this?"

Josie nodded. "Yeah."

He tilted his head to the side. "What does your mom do? Like for a living?"

"She's a theoretical physicist."

"Specializing in quantum gravity?"

"Yes!"

"Experimenting with ultradense deuterium?"

"How did you know?"

"I wonder . . ." Nick bounded across the room and grabbed Josie by the hand, yanking her out of the chair. "Come on."

Josie jerked her hand away. "Whoa, crazy. I'm not going anywhere with you."

Nick's eyebrows pinched together over his nose in a look of utter confusion. Then his eyes drifted to the gun on the bed. "Oh. Right. Look, I'm sorry about that, but you don't understand. I thought you were one of them."

"One of who?"

"I'll explain on the way. But we need to get out of here."

Josie folded her arms across her chest. "I said, I'm not going—"

Nick rolled his eyes, then snatched up the gun. Josie backed away, cursing herself for being so stupid. He was going to kidnap her.

Instead, Nick flipped the gun around so the barrel faced him, and handed it to her. "You can carry this if it'll make you feel better. But I need you to come with me right now. Please."

Josie tentatively reached out and took the gun out of Nick's hand. She'd never held a weapon before. It was heavier than she'd thought. "Why should I trust you?"

Nick smiled at her. A real, sincere smile. The first she'd seen from him. "Because I might be the only person who can get you home."

TWENTY-EIGHT

THE SUN CREPT TOWARD THE HORIZON AS NICK continued to drive. Josie fidgeted in her seat, craning her head to get a look at how dark it was getting, as her fingers lightly traced the bandages on her arms. The last thing she wanted to do was get stuck outside after the sun went down.

"We'll be fine," Nick said, reading her mind. He tapped the roof of his SUV. "This baby's got a full set of interior lights, plus the high-intensity floodlights I had installed on the roof. I go out at night all the time, no trouble. Trust me."

Josie glanced at the handgun in her lap. "Right."

"Besides," Nick said with a shrug. "There's plenty of light where we're going."

"And where's that exactly?"

Nick smiled, but didn't answer.

What was with all the mystery? She couldn't figure it out. Nick seemed to be taking a random route: first they were on Annapolis Road, then the old Crain Highway, before doubling back on

Route 32 to Route 50, almost exactly back where they started.

It wasn't until the second loop that Josie realized what he was doing.

"You think someone's following us."

Nick shrugged. "Maybe."

"Why?"

"You'll see when we get there."

"Oh."

They fell back into silence, but only for a moment. There was one question Josie was dying to ask.

"What are the Nox?"

"Good question." Nick made a right-hand turn onto the highway for the third time. "You really don't have anything like them where you come from?"

"Nope."

"You sure?"

"Pretty sure I'd know if there were man-eating monsters living in the darkness."

"Okay, okay. Don't get touchy." Nick glanced at her. "It's just hard to imagine life without them. A life where you can actually go outside at night or sleep in the dark."

"Was it always like that?"

Nick shook his head. "Not always." He sped up, keeping one eye on the rearview mirror. They were passing an off-ramp and at the last minute, he veered over two lanes and took the exit.

Josie grabbed the "oh shit" handle as the SUV screeched around the bend. Another quick turn and Nick slammed on the brakes and veered the car off the road behind a thick growth of scrub brush. Lo and behold, about sixty seconds later, a black sedan car sped down the same road they'd just been on.

Josie gasped. "You were right."

Nick held up his hand, and continued to watch the road. A few minutes later, the same car slowly drove by in the opposite direction, backtracking, looking for them.

Nick stayed put. After ten minutes, another car passed by—a black SUV this time. As before, it drove slowly, and circled back after a few minutes.

As the SUV disappeared back onto the highway, Nick exhaled deeply. "Okay, I think we're good."

Josie tightened her seat belt. "Wow."

Nick started the engine and shifted into neutral, then let his car slowly coast down onto the road. They had a clear view in either direction. No black cars in sight. Without waiting, Nick turned right and resumed normal driving speed and tactics as he crossed the train tracks.

"Who's following you?"

Nick shrugged. "The first was a government tail, most likely. The second was definitely from the Grid. That's who's usually following me, just in case I know something." He looked at Josie sidelong. "We're all being followed. Anyone who had a connection to Project Raze."

"Project Raze?"

"I'll explain it all when we get there, I promise," Nick said, cutting off the question on the tip of her tongue. "But yeah, the Nox. I'll give you the history-book version since apparently you're clueless."

"What gave me away?"

Nick laughed. "Besides walking down an unlit trail through the woods after dark?"

"Exactly."

"We're taught in kindergarten," Nick said, in a sugary-sweet tone, "that the Nox are like the boogeyman—they come to get children who are bad, in the night while they're sleeping."

"That's awful."

"Isn't it? You should see the picture books about it. Scare tactics to get kids to behave and follow the rules. Twenty years ago, parents would use them as punishment. If you were bad, you'd get stuck out on the back porch all night with just a single light above you to keep the Nox at bay."

Josie shivered. The idea of standing on a cold concrete porch, back plastered against the wall of the house while those things flapped and shrieked around her all night, was enough incentive to make even a hardened juvenile delinquent turn angelic.

"The truth," Nick continued emphatically, "is even more disturbing. The Nox didn't exist until about sixty years ago. At least not in our world. The government doesn't like to advertise this fact, but the truth is that the Nox were the by-product of Cold War government experiments attempting travel through space-time."

"Wait a minute," Josie said, straightening up in her seat.

"Someone *made* those things?"

Nick eased off the main highway onto a bumpy, uneven road. "More like accidentally found. Awesome, right? Man-eating monsters that live in the dark and that no one can see."

Josie cocked her head to the side. "No one can see them?"

Nick shook his head. "Nope. They're completely invisible. Can't catch them either. It's like they can disappear at will. One minute they're there, the next, gone."

"Oh." Josie thought about the gray wings sweeping past her in the darkness. Had she imagined she saw them?

They drove through an old warehouse district, completely abandoned from what Josie could tell. The broken pavement made her teeth clatter as the SUV slowly traversed what once had been a wide, asphalt surface. The buildings were in varying states of disrepair, from basic wear and tear like broken windows and missing roof tiles, to out-and-out vandalism where entire walls had been removed.

Nick pulled up in front of one of the more intact warehouses and stopped the car. It was a single-story edifice of corrugated metal, smaller than most of the others, with a storage shed built off one side, and tucked between two enormous, hulking structures that looked as if they were about to collapse in on themselves. Not that this one was much better. Every single window had been broken, leaving gaping, jagged holes in their panes, and the walls looked as if they were about to be utterly consumed by a heavy layer of rust. Beyond the broken windows, Josie saw nothing but the blackness of the unlit interior, which at least indicated that the roof was still intact since it kept the sunlight out. The walls seemed whole and unmarred as well—strong, and without the cutaway sections that were missing from most of the other structures in the area—and the large roll-up door that would have accommodated a big rig truck in its glory days looked structurally sound. It appeared to be padlocked to the ground with new, unrusted chains, as if to make sure no unwanted visitors prowled around. A lack of power wires in the warehouse district seemed to imply that human presence was uncommon, and Josie wondered why the shiny new padlock would be necessary. Once the sun went down, that area would be a bloodbath for anyone left lurking about.

Josie glanced at the sun, now much lower on the horizon than she was entirely comfortable with. "Where are we?"

Nick looked at her sidelong as he opened the door and slid out of the car, leaving the engine at an idle. "Nowhere. Literally."

Josie watched as Nick stepped up to the padlocked door. He seemed calm, almost buoyant, and displayed no signs of apprehension or concern for their current location. He pulled something from his pocket, then crouched to the ground. Josie could hear the jangling of metal, and in a few seconds, Nick had unchained and rolled up the old access door.

Silently.

The door had been oiled, so the runners made barely any noise as it opened. She'd expected the heavy screeching of rusted metal as the old door protested against use, but nope. Someone kept the inner workings of this warehouse in decent shape.

Nick was smiling as he climbed back into the car. He released the brake and rolled through the open door.

"Where are we?" Josie asked again.

There were three other cars in a little parking area. Nick pulled alongside and cut the engine. "The Fortress of Solitude."

"Huh?"

"Superman's lair," he said.

"Oh."

"Kinda the same thing, actually," Nick said in all seriousness. "We're off the Grid. Completely self-contained. They have no idea we're here." Nick opened his car door. "Speaking of, switch your cell phone off. No cells in here. Ever."

"Um, okay." She switched off Jo's cell, and following Nick's lead, climbed out of the car.

Josie gazed wide-eyed at the interior of the warehouse. From the outside, it had looked like another abandoned, dilapidated building, but inside was quite different. First off, it was well lit. The exterior had presented a mess of broken windows and absolutely no sign of life, but a warm orange glow permeated the interior space, strong and safe and inviting.

Huh. That was weird. She should have been able to see the light from outside. Josie craned her head to peer up at the windows that lined the top of the warehouse. Blackout curtains were duct-taped over each window so none of the interior light bled into the abandoned area. Wow.

Nick closed the gate, then motioned for Josie to stay put. "Wait here."

He didn't need to tell her twice.

Nick jogged to the far end of the warehouse, where a lounge area had been set up. Sofas, easy chairs, even a coffee table. A large dry-erase board on a wheeled stand took up the space near the sofas, and behind it, there was a makeshift kitchen with a fridge, a watercooler, and a long table that was covered in books, maps, and scattered papers. A large guy bent over the open fridge, peering into its interior. Two more guys lounged on the sofas—identical shocks of bleached blond hair on identical tall, lean bodies—while at the large table, a girl sat hunched over the books and papers, studying.

"What's up, Nick?" said a familiar voice.

"Where you been?" said another. The identical bleached blond heads sat up on the sofas and Josie immediately recognized Zeke and Zeb, the Kaufman twins.

The other guy slammed the fridge door. "Dammit," he said, turning around. "Who keeps drinking my Muscle Milk?" Josie knew that face. Jackson Wells, captain of the Bowie Prep football team.

"Dude," Nick said. "No one but you drinks that crap."

"Well, someone's taking it," Jackson said. He wandered to the edge of the table and leaned against it. "I just put two in yesterday."

"Guys," Nick said. "Listen up. Something's happened." Nick turned to Josie and waved, beckoning her over. "You aren't going to believe this."

Oh boy. That was an understatement.

Josie slid out from behind the car and walked toward the group. They all stared at her and as she got closer, Josie could see the faces even more clearly. Her eyes lingered on the girl sitting at the table, a brunette with a scowl on her face that could only be described as hatred.

Madison.

TWENTY-NINE

5:12 P.M.

"WHAT THE HELL, NICK?" MADISON SAID. "ARE you out of your mind?"

Jackson reached into the back of his pants, and when his hand reappeared at his side, Josie realized he was holding a gun. She suddenly regretted her boneheaded decision to leave Nick's gun in the car.

"Dude," Jackson said. "You shouldn't have brought her here. I thought we'd agreed on that."

"I know what she looks like," Nick said. "But she's not Jo."

"I'm not Jo," Josie echoed. Her voice sounded small and weak.

"Bullshit," Zeke said. At least she thought it was Zeke. Didn't matter which universe, she couldn't tell them apart.

"You can't trust her," said his brother.

Madison looked like she was ready to pounce on Josie and gouge her eyes out. "Her dad practically works for the Grid, Nick. He's one of them."

Nick shook his head. "He's just a liaison for the government,

Mads. You know that. Mr. Byrne's pretty harmless, despite what Jo leads people to believe."

"Don't care." Jackson's knuckles flexed over the gun handle. "You shouldn't have brought her here without giving us a heads-up."

Nick put his hand on Jackson's arm. "Chill. You're going to have to trust me on this one. She's not Jo Byrne."

Jackson's eyes never left Josie's face. "You, I trust. Her? Not so much."

"Just listen," Nick said. He nodded at Josie and smiled, all sign of strain or tension gone from his face. "Go ahead. Tell them exactly what you told me."

Josie felt the weight of four people staring daggers at her. Meanwhile Nick was still all smiles. Sure, he'd believed her story because he was there to see the mirror do its thing. But these people? She glanced at Madison, whose body was so rigid and tense she looked like a cheetah about to take down a gazelle. Jackson's eyebrows brooded low on his dark face, angry, intense. The twins stood behind her, shoulder-to-shoulder like an impenetrable wall.

They hated her, all of them. Well, hated Jo. And she doubted whether any of them would buy what she was selling. Still, at this point, she didn't have much of a choice. Nothing left to do but tell the truth.

It came out with surprising ease. Nick's beaming smile helped. She kept her eyes focused on his and he gave her the occasional nod and wink as she got to the really crazy parts. The train, the dreams, the mirror—it all flowed out of her like a faucet turned

172

on full blast. And when it was done, she realized that the mood in the warehouse had changed.

"Tell them what time it was," Nick said coolly when she was done.

"Three fifty-nine."

Zeb and Zeke exchanged a glance, and Jackson's jaw dropped. "Really?" he said.

Madison threw up her hands. "I can't believe you guys are taking her seriously."

"It happened a week ago yesterday. On the fifteenth. Six months to the day. Hell, to the second!" Nick strolled over to the large dry-erase board and flipped it over to the opposite side. It was a time line of some sort, with arrows and circles connecting a series of photos that had been stuck around it. He jabbed his finger at a point on the timeline and smiled. "And there was a huge shipment that day. On the afternoon train from Andrews. Now, it could be a coincidence, but I can't help but think the two things are related."

Josie was confused. "A huge shipment of what?"

"Ultradense deuterium," Nick said.

Josie caught her breath. "Oh my God. My mom got a shipment of ultradense deuterium on the fifteenth. On the same train that stopped me at the tracks. It can't be a coincidence." Josie's mind raced. "Same shipment, same train, same time. If there was an anomaly of some kind, that could have been enough to create the portal between our dimensions."

Nick turned sharply. "What kind of anomaly?"

"Not sure." Josie shrugged. "A previous weakness in the curvature of space? Or something violent enough to create one, like a massive, subatomic explosion."

"Goddammit!" Madison whirled on Nick. "I can't believe you fell for her bullshit. Nick, she's conning you. 'A massive, subatomic explosion,'" Madison mocked. "She's been after you for years and she'll do anything to get your attention."

"Mads, she took the trail through the woods. After sunset. She barely survived a Nox attack. No one who knows what they are would risk it."

"I wouldn't put it past her," Madison said coldly.

"She could have known you were following her," Zeb said.

"Did it for attention," Zeke added.

The idea that someone would willingly subject themselves to a Nox attack just to get the attention of a boy—even if that boy was Nick Fiorino—was so ludicrous, Josie laughed out loud.

Madison whirled on her. "You think this is funny?"

Josie pushed up the sleeves of her sweater, exposing her heavily bandaged arms. "Yeah, these are so funny."

"Too bad they didn't attack your face." Madison turned around and walked toward a sofa.

Josie wasn't sure if it was her entrenched hatred for the Madison who had betrayed her, or whether *this* Madison was just grating on her nerves, but something snapped.

"Hey," she said, spinning Madison around by the arm. "I don't know how to explain what happened to me or how I got here, but it happened. I don't particularly like being stuck here with you any more than you like me invading your little clubhouse. But it's done. Deal."

"Time out," Nick said, stepping between them. His voice was calm. "Everybody play nice."

Josie folded her arms across her chest. "I will if she will."

Madison stepped right up in Nick's face. "It's her mom's fault your brother is dead."

Josie gasped. Tony was dead?

"It's Tony's fault too," Nick said through clenched teeth.

Madison shook her head. "He wasn't the one operating the X-FEL. It's because of that woman locked away in that loony bin in Annapolis that Tony's dead. ZZ's aunt and uncle. Jackson's dad. *My* dad. All dead because of *her*."

"Wait," Josie said, turning to Nick. "A loony bin?"

"They're not dead," Jackson said through gritted teeth. "They're missing."

Madison swung around on him. "What, do you think a micro black hole swallowed them up? Our parents are dead, Jax, and if they're not they will be before we can get to them. You really think whoever has them will just let them go?"

"I . . . ," Jackson started. Clearly he had no answer.

"All we can hope for is answers. Answers that she"—Madison jabbed her thumb in Josie's direction—"might have."

"Nick, Dr. Byrne's in a loony bin?"

Nick held up his hand, signaling for Josie to wait. Madison turned her back on them and stood panting, her arms wrapped tightly around her chest. Josie was trying to process all the information she'd just heard—ultradense deuterium, micro black holes, Tony was dead, and everyone else was missing family members—and Dr. Byrne wasn't traveling for work or on vacation. She was in an asylum. One more thing Jo didn't tell her.

Nick laid a hand gently on Madison's shoulder. "Mads, calm down."

Josie's stomach clenched. The way Nick touched her, the way his hands lightly grazed the skin of Madison's bare arms, the softness in his voice. Josie recognized it right away. They'd been intimate, maybe still were. No wonder Madison hated Jo: she was in love with Nick too.

Madison sunk her head to her chest but didn't say anything as Nick continued. "I know this doesn't make any logical sense, but I saw the mirror with my own eyes. I saw it morph away at exactly three fifty-nine. Three fifty-nine," he added for emphasis. "Is that a coincidence? I felt the concrete wall with my own hands, and then . . . I felt something close in on me as the portal closed. I don't know how to explain it, but Josie's telling the truth."

"Don't defend her!" Madison erupted. "How many more people are going to disappear because of her family, huh? I'm done with this." She walked to the corner where the generator hummed away. Over the dull noise, Josie could just make out a sob.

Silence fell. Jackson still held the gun, but it hung limply in his hand, forgotten, as his eyes followed Madison to the corner of the room. The twins wandered back to a sofa and sat stiffly side by side. Nick shoved his hands deep into his pockets and stared at the floor, kicking at something in the dusty concrete with the toe of his boot. And Josie just stood rooted in place.

"Nick," she whispered. "What's going on?"

"We've all lost someone," he said in a hushed tone as if he were in a library. "Someone who was working on Project Raze. Jackson's and Madison's dads, ZZ's aunt and uncle."

"And your brother," Josie added.

Nick stiffened. "There was an explosion at the lab. Tony and your . . . ," he started, remembering who she was. "I mean Tony and Dr. Byrne were testing a way to eradicate the Nox. That's what Project Raze is, by the way. It's a joint project between the Grid and the government. Couple hundred scientists up at Fort Meade doing anything and everything they can think of to get rid of them."

"The explosion was an accident?"

Nick narrowed his eyes and scrutinized her face for the twentieth time that day. "It was ruled an accident stemming from the calibration of the X-FEL, but it was Dr. Byrne who set up the laser. My brother's body was vaporized and Jo's mom ended up shell-shocked. She's never been the same."

"And everyone else?"

"In the days after the explosion, they all disappeared." Nick shrugged. "One by one. No trace. No evidence of foul play. No . . ." His voice trailed off.

"No bodies," Josie said, completing the thought.

"Right," he said quickly. "Except Jo's mom, who's in a military hospital near Annapolis."

The loony bin. So that's why no one mentioned Jo's mom. "Oh."

"Yeah."

"But the thing is," Nick said, leaning closer to her. "The explosion? Happened at exactly three fifty-nine p.m. Six months ago. I'm not much of a scientist, but that can't be a coincidence, can it?"

Josie took a deep breath. "No," she said slowly. "No, it can't." There was no such thing as coincidence. Everything happened for a reason, and in this case it was as if a lightbulb had gone on in her brain.

"Nick," she said quietly. She didn't really want anyone else to hear. "You remember earlier when I said a massive explosion could have caused the portal between our worlds?"

Nick smiled. "Yeah?"

"I think . . ." She paused. "Six months ago, if your brother and Dr. Byrne were experimenting with ultradense deuterium and micro black holes at the same exact time my mom was doing the *same exact* thing . . . well, the explosion could have weakened the fabric of space-time, pinpointed at the moment of the explosion."

"Okay," Nick said slowly. He wasn't putting the pieces together.

"Then the train. You said it yourself: the fifteenth was six months to the day after the explosion. To the very minute. Two trains, in two different dimensions, carrying the same material."

Nick looked up sharply. "Boom." He made an exploding motion with his hands.

"It's a theory, at least." She shifted her feet. "Although there must have been a catalyst for the actual flash I saw. Deuterium on its own is highly stable. It would require some sort of trigger to explode like that."

"Like?"

Josie shrugged. "Not sure." An explosion caused by the X-FEL made sense, but Josie had no idea what would have caused the flash at the train tracks. "Maybe it had something to do with what your brother and Dr. Byrne were doing. Do you know the exact details of the experiment?"

"Tony was working on an injectable for the Nox that when zapped with a powerful laser would actually create a micro black hole and suck the Nox in."

"Wow," Josie breathed. "It would trap them beyond the event horizon of a micro black hole, which would then collapse under its own mass, destroying itself and the Nox. That's brilliant. Like the ultimate flu shot."

Nick smiled. "A black-hole flu shot. I like that."

"Any idea how it worked?"

Nick shrugged. "Not sure. The remnants of the injectable were destroyed in the explosion, and Tony was the only one who knew the formula."

And that died with him, Josie thought. Her eyes met Nick's and she hoped her face didn't reflect what she had just been thinking.

Nick stood up and passed a hand through his wavy hair. "Everyone who's missing had a hand in the experiment. Jackson's dad worked on the chemical aspects of the injection. Madison's dad constructed the X-FEL prototype. ZZ's aunt and uncle synthesized some of the ingredients. Years of work went into it, all leading up to one day."

"One clusterfuck of a day," Madison said, rejoining the group.

"Which was all your mom's fault."

Josie threw up her hands. "She's not my mom!"

"Whatever."

Josie tried to remain calm. Tony's and Dr. Byrne's experiment was somehow related to how Josie got there. Of that she was convinced. Maybe if she could help them figure out what happened in the lab, she'd also find a way to get home.

"Okay," she said, examining the board again. "Someone either wants to re-create the injectable or wants to make sure no one else does. That's the only way your relatives' disappearances make any sense."

The room fell silent. Josie looked from face to face as everyone avoided her eyes. She knew they were all reliving their own angst and anger over the loss of their loved ones. She felt the need to apologize, even though none of this had anything to do with her. Or did it?

Josie's mouth was dry and parched. She swallowed and continued. "And it's connected to how I got here."

"Even if you're telling the truth," Madison said at last. "Even if your batshit tale is true, how does it affect us?"

Josie shrugged. "If we know how I got here, maybe we can figure out what went wrong that day in the lab. Re-create it. If your family members are being forced to try and replicate the experiment, and we beat them to it, you have a bargaining chip."

"Exactly." Nick nodded. "And I don't know about you guys, but even if we can't get our families back, I sure as hell want to finish what they started."

Jackson kicked the sofa. "How? Seriously, we've been over every piece of their research, every note, every email, everything we could get our hands on. We can't make heads or tails of it. We'd need a couple of science geniuses to figure this out."

A slow smile spread across Josie's face. "Science geniuses? I think I've got that covered."

Madison snorted. "You? Oh, please."

"You didn't see her in physics today," Zeke said.

"It was kind of epic," Zeb added.

Nick grabbed Josie's arm. She could feel his excitement. "Could you? I mean, do you think you could figure it out?"

"Don't know." Josie shrugged. "Maybe. But I'm going to need help."

Nick tilted his head. "You got someone in mind?"

There was only one person who could handle it, and from what she'd seen, this Penelope was just as much of a science geek as her old friend back home. "Penelope Wang."

"Shit," Madison said with a roll of her eyes. "Why don't we just put a welcome sign outside."

Nick ignored her. "I don't know."

Josie's smile deepened. "You said I needed to trust you. Now it's time to return the favor."

THIRTY

"JOSEPHINE?" MR. BYRNE CALLED OUT FROM THE living room the second Josie closed the front door behind her, blocking out the floodlights from Nick's car that had lit her path up to the house. "Is that you?"

Damn. She'd been hoping everyone would be in bed. She was completely exhausted, and her mind reeled with a million new bits of information she needed to digest and process. She wasn't sure she had enough energy to masquerade as Jo for even a few minutes.

"Josephine?" Mr. Byrne repeated, this time more urgently.

"It's me," Josie said. "Daddy," she quickly added, remembering the way Jo always mentioned her father. She meandered over to the archway that led into the living room and leaned wearily against the wall.

"Oh, thank God!" Mr. Byrne exclaimed. He placed his tablet down on the coffee table. "I was so worried. Why didn't you answer your phone?"

Josie flinched. Her phone. She'd turned it off at the warehouse and totally forgotten about it. "I'm sorry. The . . . the battery died."

Mr. Byrne sighed and patted the cushion next to him on the sofa. Josie dutifully sat down, pulling the sleeves of her sweater down past her wrists so he wouldn't catch a glimpse of her bandages, and tried to look suitably ashamed.

"I was worried," Mr. Byrne repeated. "There have been elevated Nox sightings throughout the area. We got reports tonight of particularly large swarms between Baltimore and D.C., and there's a rumor going around that someone was attacked in our neighborhood just recently. Have you heard anything about that at school?"

Josie folded her arms across her chest, hoping he hadn't caught sight of her bandages. "No," she lied. "Haven't heard a thing."

He patted her knee. "Hopefully it's just a rumor, then. But please be careful. I can't bear the thought of losing my little girl after . . ." His voice drifted off. Josie looked up and saw that Mr. Byrne was staring across the room at a photo on the mantelpiece above the fireplace. A photo of his wife.

A wave of guilt passed over her. Here she was, an impostor pretending to be the daughter of this man who had been through so much. His wife was still alive, but in what state? She had no idea who she was or where she was. Was that better or worse than having her die in the explosion?

Mr. Byrne smiled weakly as he gazed at his wife's photo. For the first time, he reminded Josie of her own dad. "Maybe we should go see her," he suggested. "Try again."

Josie stiffened. Go see her fake mom in a mental hospital? That seemed like an incredibly bad idea. She'd been lucky with Mr. Byrne: he was distracted by work and grief over his wife, and hadn't noticed the girl pretending to be his daughter was really nothing of the kind. But a mom? Moms had a way of *knowing* things, of looking right through you and reading your mind. Even if Dr. Byrne wasn't quite 100 percent there, would she know the girl standing before her wasn't the one she gave birth to?

Still, the woman was suffering mental effects of a massive explosion. If she started ranting about how Josie wasn't really her daughter, they might not actually take her seriously.

Josie looked up from making her mental pros and cons list, and noticed Mr. Byrne watching her intently. He raised his eyebrows as if to say, *Well?*

"Whatever you'd like, Daddy," she forced herself to say.

Mr. Byrne laughed drily. "Josephine, who do you think you're kidding? You don't have to go if you don't want to. I won't force you to, okay? I know how hard it is to visit her when she doesn't know who you are."

For the first time in almost forty-eight hours, Josie felt sorry for Jo. No wonder she was so desperate to get through the mirror and find a mom who knew who she was. Josie could hardly blame her for not wanting to come back. Though maybe missing her dad would precipitate a return? He seemed like a great father and clearly cared for his daughter tremendously. Between him and Nick, maybe it would be enough to lure Jo home.

Josie smiled. "I'll let you know if I change my mind."

"Deal." He picked up his tablet and rose from the sofa, planting a light kiss on the top of her head as he did so. "Now how about you get to bed, young lady? Busy day tomorrow."

He had no idea.

3:59 A.M.

Her mom sits at the kitchen table. She rests her elbows on the laminate wood surface and holds a steaming cup of tea to her lips.

She closes her eyes and inhales deeply, relishing the aroma. "I dearly love a cup of tea," she says on a breathy exhale.

"I know."

"That woman only drank coffee. Bins of the stuff in the house, and not even a box of tea when I got here." She stares lovingly at the box of tea bags on the table.

"Oh."

"I can't tell you how many mugs of that slime I've had to choke down at the lab." She takes a long sip, then abruptly lowers the cup. "Speaking of, you'd better start making a list of what your other half did and didn't do. We can't have any suspicions if we're going to stay here."

"Stay here?"

Her mom arches an eyebrow. "Don't you want to? You don't really want to go back to all that, do you? The secrets and the lies. And the Nox."

She shudders at the mention of the Nox, then shakes her head hesitantly. "No." She pauses. "I don't know. Maybe?"

"Don't worry about your boyfriend," her mom says sharply. "He'll be fine."

Jo's stomach tightens up. "He's not my boyfriend." *Not yet,* she thinks to herself.

"We can't go back," her mom says with a nod of her head. "The mirror has to stay where it is. Besides"—her mom reaches across and pats her hand—"now that you're here, I don't have to worry about creating a new portal. That's all I've been working on the last six months, you know. A way to bring you here."

"Oh." Jo tries to hide her anxiety. She doesn't want to stay, not any longer than they have to. "Are you going to destroy the mirror?"

"I can't," her mom says. "Too dangerous. I have to find a way to close the portal first."

"Oh."

Her mom whisks away her hand. "It's not so bad here, Josephine. I promise."

Jo shivers. Her body feels suddenly cold.

"Get to know the other Nick," her mom says. It's like she can read her daughter's mind. "Maybe you'll like him."

"I suppose."

"Try," her mom says. "Because once I figure out how . . ." She pauses and stares Jo directly in the eye. "We'll destroy the portal. Forever."

Josie's eyes flew open and she pushed the sleep mask up over her head. They were still connected. She and Jo.

A hundred ideas flooded into her head at once. Her mom. The portal. *Her* mom.

Holy shit.

It had been Jo's mom she'd been living with for the past six months. Jo's mom who kicked Dad out of the house. Jo's mom who seemed so cold and distant and spent twenty-four-seven in the lab.

Jo's mom. Not *her* mom.

Which meant her mom was here.

THIRTY-ONE

4:06 A.M.

JOSIE PACED THE ROOM, JO'S SILK PAJAMAS SWISH-ing with every manic step. Excitement coursed through her body as the pieces of what happened six months ago began to organize themselves in her mind. Things were starting to make sense. There was an answer to her myriad questions lurking just beyond the horizon. She just had to focus and the solution would present itself.

The first piece was obvious. The connection between her and Jo was still strong. Jo could secure the mirror against the basement wall, but she couldn't close her mind against Josie. Good to know.

Second, the story Nick told her yesterday fit in perfectly with the changes Josie had noticed in her mom. Six months ago, at the same time as the explosion that killed Nick's brother and left Dr. Byrne supposedly insane, Josie and her dad noticed the change in her mom. Her personality had become harder, less tolerant, less kind. Things she used to love, she suddenly hated. She pulled away from friends. She pulled away from her marriage.

Because it wasn't her.

What if the explosion in the lab that day had the same effect as the flash from the passing train? What if Josie's mom and Dr. Byrne created a portal—an earlier portal—and accidentally switched places?

And the mirror. It had been in her mom's lab for years. What if it had been the portal then just as it was now? The explosion, the flash—the same event that happened to her at the railroad crossing. Maybe it happened that day because it had happened before, zapping Josie's mom and Dr. Byrne into different worlds? That exact moment in space-time had been weakened, connected to the mirror itself. The catalyst. And when it came in close proximity to trace amounts of ultradense deuterium on the train—the right place at the right time—*BOOM!* And in the lab in Josie's basement—*BOOM!*

The mirror was the catalyst. It wasn't affected *by* those explosions; it had been the cause of them.

Josie's pace quickened. She had to keep moving or she was going to burst.

The mirror was the portal, unstable at first, then strengthening after each explosion until it stayed open for one full minute every twelve hours at the exact moment space-time had been weakened. A hole through which first her mom and then Josie had traveled.

That would explain why her mom was so desperate to get the mirror back. And that would also explain the X-FEL her mom had been cobbling together in the basement. She was trying to re-create the events that led to her being switched in the first place. Her mom was . . .

Josie paused midstep. Not her mom. Jo's mom. Dr. Byrne.

Because her mom was trapped in this world, locked away in a mental hospital.

Dr. Byrne had been trying to reopen a portal to bring her daughter—her real daughter—through to Josie's world. And now they were plotting to stay there forever.

Josie took a deep breath. She had a purpose now. It wasn't just about finding a way home anymore. She had to help her mom. She had to stop Jo and Dr. Byrne before they could destroy the portal and trap Josie in a world overrun with the Nox. She had to re-create Dr. Byrne's experiment and open her own portal that would send her and her mom home.

She just had one problem. How?

Without thinking, she grabbed her cell phone and dialed Nick.

"Wh-what's wrong?" Nick said, his voice thick with sleep. "Are you okay?"

"Nick, something happened. A dream."

She heard rustling on the other end of the line and Nick sat up in bed. "You called me because you had a bad dream?"

"No. I was in Jo's head. She doesn't know." Josie was practically laughing. "She doesn't know I can still see her in my dreams."

"What did you see?" Nick said, instantly awake.

"Dr. Byrne."

"Jo's mom's in a hospital in Annapolis."

"No, she's not. Dr. Byrne is sitting in my kitchen. In my house. *In my world.* Nick, they switched places."

"What?"

"The explosion. Six months ago. Don't you see? That's why Dr. Byrne didn't recognize Jo or her husband. They switched places. It's my mom locked up in a mental hospital."

"Holy shit."

"I know."

"You're going to go see her." It wasn't a question.

Josie made the decision in an instant. "Tomorrow. After school."

"Do you want me to come with you?"

"But you have practice. Don't you have a big meet this weekend?" If this Nick was anything like hers, he wouldn't miss track practice a few days before a meet for anything short of the apocalypse.

"Regionals," Nick said. He made a sound somewhere between a yawn and a groan, and Josie could almost picture him stretching his long limbs out in bed. "But I can skip. This is more important."

A warm flutter spread from her stomach to her chest, and a smile broke the corners of Josie's mouth. She couldn't help herself. Nick barely knew her, and yet here he was anxious to help her, willing to sacrifice something that was important to him because he thought Josie needed help.

With a twinge of sadness, Josie realized that her ex-boyfriend would never have offered.

"That's sweet," Josie said softly. "But I think I need to see her alone."

"I understand." Nick was silent for a moment. "Call me, though, okay? When you're done? I want to make sure you're okay."

Josie's smile deepened and her heart raced. She knew this feeling only too well, the goofiness that threatened to swamp her rational mind every time she'd see Nick from afar in the hallway, or watch him running laps around the track after school. The impetuous way she wanted to launch herself into his arms when he'd look into her eyes and tell her that he loved her, that she was the only girl for him. The way her stomach would clench when she felt his touch against her skin. The way her body tingled when he pressed his lips to hers. The way she wanted to disappear into him whenever he held her close.

She knew the desperation of that love. She knew the horrific pain it brought.

And she wasn't going to let that happen again.

With a shake of her shoulders, Josie banished the growing attraction she had for this Nick. He would only hurt her, as his doppelgänger had done. Because regardless of which dimension he was in, Nick wasn't in love with her. She thought of the way he touched Madison in the warehouse, how intimate it had been. She wouldn't let him break her heart again, intentionally or not.

"I'll be fine," she said in a very businesslike manner.

"Oh, okay." Nick sighed. "But Josie?" he added quickly. His voice sounded anxious. "Be careful."

Josie swallowed hard. *He doesn't love you.* "I will."

THIRTY-TWO

6:33 A.M.

MR. BYRNE WAS ALREADY AT BREAKFAST WHEN Josie bounded into the dining room. There was an extra bounce in her step, a levity and excitement Josie hadn't felt since she first stepped through the mirror. She was going to see her mom today.

"Aren't you looking bright and happy this morning, princess," Mr. Byrne said, glancing up from his tablet. "Is it going to be a good day?"

"I hope so," Josie said with as much perkiness as she could muster.

"I'm glad." Mr. Byrne beamed as she took a seat and poured herself some coffee. Teresa was at her shoulder almost immediately with a bagel and cream cheese. She hovered near the buffet, straightening unused serving platters for a full five minutes before she silently slipped out of the room. Josie waited until she heard the swinging door to the kitchen whoosh into place before she opened a conversation with Mr. Byrne. It was a conversation she'd been rehearsing in her head all night.

"Daddy?" she said meekly.

Mr. Byrne never even looked up from his tablet. "Yes, princess?"

"I've been thinking. About what you said last night."

Mr. Byrne carefully laid his tablet facedown on the table and folded his hands in front of him. "About going to see your mother?"

Josie nodded.

"Why this sudden change of heart, princess?"

She'd been mulling it over in her head since she'd woken up from Jo's dream. Tell Mr. Byrne what's going on or not?

On the one hand, he deserved to know. Just like Josie, his life had been ripped apart. His wife and now his daughter were far away, replaced by doppelgängers he didn't know. Josie thought of her own dad, sitting in his apartment in Landover, wondering what had happened to his happy marriage. She wished she could contact him, let him know it was all a mistake and a misunderstanding. That her mom still loved him and was desperate to get home to him.

But she couldn't. She could, however, tell this man the same thing. Maybe he could help get his daughter and wife back, and send Josie and her mom home?

On the other hand, telling Mr. Byrne that she had been pretending to be his daughter might totally backfire. Would he freak out? Have her arrested? Or maybe think that the insanity her mom suffered from was spreading to his daughter? And how much more painful might it be for him if Josie and her mom were stuck there for good? Was it worth mentioning he might never see his wife and daughter again?

No. She couldn't risk it. As much as she wanted to trust Mr. Byrne, it was for his own good that she kept him in the dark as long as possible.

"I need to see her," Josie said simply. "Can I go after school today?"

Mr. Byrne smiled warmly. "Of course. I'll arrange it with the hospital. Do you want me to come with you?"

"No," she said quickly. The last thing she needed was for Mr. Byrne to witness this mother-daughter reunion.

"I understand." He reached out and laid his hand over hers. "I'm so glad you reconsidered. I think she'd really like to see you. I hope . . . " His voice trailed off and he swallowed, trying to maintain his composure. "I hope she recognizes you."

Josie did too.

"There you are," Josie said, descending upon Penelope in the science lab. "I need to talk to you."

Penelope jolted at the sight of Josie and launched the apple she was eating three feet in the air. It soared over Mr. Baines's desk and splatted onto the floor.

"Sorry," Josie said. "I didn't mean to scare you."

"I'm okay," Penelope said. Her voice shook ever so slightly. "W-what do you want?"

Josie looked around the abandoned science lab. It had taken her twenty minutes to find Penelope's lunch spot. She'd combed the cafeteria and all the hallways, and only started checking class-rooms as a last resort. "Why are you eating in here all by yourself?"

Penelope shrugged. "It's better than eating in the cafeteria all by myself."

"Good point." One Josie had learned only too well.

Penelope picked at one of her cuticles and refused to look Josie in the eye. "So, um, what do you want?"

Josie pulled out the stool opposite Penelope and sat down. "Look, I know you don't trust me."

Penelope opened her mouth as if to protest, then snapped it shut again. Apparently, it was too valid a point to argue.

"I know you don't trust me," Josie repeated for emphasis. "Or like me very much, for that matter. But I need your help."

"I'm only good at science and math," Penelope said. "If you need someone to do your homework in anything else you're asking the wrong girl."

"I don't need help in science or math," Josie said with a dry laugh.

Penelope's dark eyes flashed toward Josie just for an instant before resting on the table again.

"But I do need your help," Josie continued.

"Fuck you," Penelope said. Her voice was breathy and hoarse, and barely above a whisper.

Josie wasn't sure what she expected by way of a reaction from Penelope. Curiosity? Interest? Friendship? She didn't know. But not that.

"Huh?"

Penelope raised her eyes slowly, deliberately. "I said, 'Fuck you.'"

"I'm not playing, Pen," she said, using the nickname for her old friend. "I really need your help."

"Don't call me that," Penelope said. She wasn't whispering anymore. "We are not friends and I don't care what you do to me; I'm not helping you." Penelope snatched her bag off the ground and started for the door so quickly Josie barely had time to react.

Thankfully Josie was closer to the door. She headed Penelope off and wedged herself in front of the only exit. "Please, just hear me out."

"What do you want from me?" Penelope's voice cracked. "Are you going to threaten to cut our access to the Grid since my dad lost his job? Fine. Do it. I'd rather be eaten alive by the Nox than have to be your bitch for one more day." Her eyes welled up with tears.

"Jo did that?" Josie said.

"*You* did that," Penelope corrected. She pulled the sleeve of her sweatshirt across her cheeks.

"I'm not Jo."

She had already resolved to tell Penelope exactly what was going on, but she was hoping to do it at the warehouse or in front of the mirror right at one minute to four to prove to Penelope that she was telling the truth. But Penelope's violent reaction meant she'd have to play it from the hip.

"Have you lost your mind?" Penelope said.

Josie slowed shook her head. "I can't explain it now, but Jo and I sort of switched places."

"Twins?" Penelope sounded dubious.

"Um, kinda."

"I don't understand."

"I know." The warning bell rang. Any minute the room would start filling up for fourth-period physics. Josie needed to hurry it up. "Look, I can't explain it here, but I'm not Jo Byrne. You remember physics the other day, right? Did I sound like Jo?"

Penelope's eyes were still red and puffy, but she'd stopped crying. "Yeah, no. You don't know anything about physics."

"*Jo* doesn't know anything about physics," Josie corrected her.

"Riiiiiight," Penelope said slowly, like she was placating a crazy person.

"And I know you don't trust her, or me, for that matter, but you know Nick Fiorino, right?"

Penelope nodded.

"Well, he trusts me."

Penelope laughed. "Yeah, right."

"Ask him. After school. Find him and ask him."

Penelope shrugged. "Whatever." Not exactly a confident reassurance she was going to do what Josie asked.

"Pen," Josie said, grabbing Penelope's arm. "Please. Just ask him, okay?"

Penelope tilted her head. Her eye drifted down to Josie's hand, which gently gripped her arm, then back up to Josie's face.

"Fine," she said at last, just as the door opened and students poured into the room. "I'll ask him. But don't count on my help, okay?"

"Okay." Josie let go of her arm. "Thank you."

Now it was up to Nick.

THIRTY-THREE

JOSIE HAD A HARD TIME KEEPING JO'S BMW AT the speed limit as she raced down Route 50 to Annapolis. She'd managed to keep her mind occupied for most of the school day, focusing on boring classroom lectures and trying not to let her mind wander to inappropriate thoughts of Nick. He'd sought her out after school, just to make sure she was okay and knew how to get to the hospital and hadn't changed her mind about having some company on the trip because he could still bail on track practice and come with her. . . .

Josie sighed as she eased up on the accelerator and signaled for the off-ramp. She couldn't allow herself to have these feelings for Nick. No way. She had to stay focused on her mom and finding a way to get them home. Besides, it wasn't like Nick was going to come back with her. Once she created another portal, she and Nick would never see each other again. She had to remember that.

Had to.

Thoughts of Nick vanished the moment Josie turned her car into the parking lot for Old St. Mary's Hospital. A military facility housed in an old naval hospital outside Annapolis, it was a typical mid-Atlantic façade of brick and white columns, with parallel wings stretching out from either side. Three stories of barred windows gazed out onto the parking lot, thin slits in the moldering brick walls that looked more like the ramparts of a castle than a hospital.

Josie could almost feel the despair radiating from the hospital. Aside from a half dozen cars in the parking lot and a new wheelchair ramp added to the stone steps at the entrance, the building looked abandoned. She'd pictured it as more of a bustling hospital, doctors and orderlies rushing around, an ambulance parked out front. Instead, the only movement was the rippling of leaves from the large elms that flanked the south side of the building.

As Josie stared at Old St. Mary's, she tried to imagine her mom, confused and scared, staring out onto a strange world wondering if she'd ever see home again.

Nick had tried to warn Josie about what she might find when she got there. "Josie," he had said in that straightforward way. "You need to be prepared for what you might find."

Josie had looked up sharply. "Prepared?"

It was true. For six months she'd been locked away while doctors continually told her she was not in her right mind. Josie pictured Jo and Mr. Byrne visiting her. Her mom would have known right away that this wasn't her family, which would only have strengthened the claims that she was nuts. Maybe after six months she was beginning to believe it?

Or worse. Maybe her ordeal had changed her. Permanently.

Josie pushed her fears out of her mind as she walked up the front steps of the hospital.

The first odd thing about Old St. Mary's struck her the moment she walked through the door. Instead of a receptionist, two military guards greeted her. One sat at an enormous desk surrounded by security monitors. The other stood behind him, shouldering an automatic weapon. Neither of them looked at her.

"Do you have an appointment?" the seated guard asked. His eyes never left the monitors, and though Josie couldn't see what they showed, she watched his eyes bounce furiously around from screen to screen.

"Josephine Byrne," Josie said by way of an answer.

The guard clacked away at a keyboard hidden beneath the desk. Within a few seconds, a printer whirred into action. His eyes still fixed on the security monitors, he leaned back and whipped a preprinted ID badge out of the print tray, affixed an alligator clip, and handed it to Josie.

"Wear the badge at all times. Lieutenant Maynes will escort you back," he said.

The armed guard nodded. "This way."

The guard led Josie through a maze of corridors. He walked quickly, apparently uninterested in whether or not Josie managed to keep up. Josie felt like they'd walked in circles before they stopped abruptly at a glass security door. The guard placed his hand flat against a pad on the wall, and after a few seconds, a loud beep sounded from the door and it slid open.

A handprint security door in a hospital? That didn't seem right.

The guard, however, didn't enter through the open security door. Instead, he stood aside and flanked the doorway. She glanced at him but got nothing. He stared straight ahead of him at the wall.

"Am I supposed to go in?" she asked.

Silence.

Really? Not even a nod of his head? Sheesh, what *was* this place?

Josie took the hint and passed through the door. She found herself in a stark white room shaped like a giant semicircle, with eight or nine of the same glass security doors facing inward at her. No desk. No doctors. Just doors. She turned back to the guard, but the door immediately slid closed. Josie could see the guard outside, at attention. Not looking at her.

"Miss Byrne?" a voice said. Josie spun around and saw a woman in a white doctor's jacket smiling at her broadly. She was young, maybe thirty, with a short, dark bob and narrow brown eyes that seemed to disappear beneath the weight of her smile.

"Yes."

"I'm Dr. Cho," she said, her voice light and airy, like the way grown-ups speak to toddlers. "I've been working with your mom for the last few months."

"Oh."

"She's been remembering a little bit more as of late, so I'm

203

glad you've decided to come back. Maybe it will help her reconnect to her old life."

Josie smiled grimly. Dr. Cho's words held more truth than she knew.

"Let's see how your mom is feeling today, shall we?" Dr. Cho said. She placed her hand lightly on Josie's back and guided her toward the far side of the room. Like with the entrance, each individual door had a scanner pad in front, and as Dr. Cho approached one, she placed her hand flat against the pad. As before, a loud beep preceded the door sliding open, and Dr. Cho's smile deepened as she led Josie into the room.

It was a cross between a hospital room and a prison cell, the best Josie could figure. A bed with wrist and ankle restraints clearly visible stood on one side. There was a desk and a chair on the opposite side, and a small alcove in the back with toilet and sink. There were no windows, only overhead lights reflecting off the stark white and metallic surfaces in the room.

And it was empty.

"Dr. Byrne?" Dr. Cho said in her jingly voice. "Dr. Byrne, I've brought someone to see you."

No response.

Dr. Cho stepped into the alcove and crouched down. Josie could hear whispering. Then she stood up and held out her hand. From the space in the back of the alcove hidden by the wall, Josie saw a pale, shaky hand in Dr. Cho's.

Josie's mom shuffled into the room, head down, with lank, dirty hair obscuring any traces of her face. She didn't look up.

She didn't ask any questions. Just shuffled her slipper-clad feet forward without lifting them off the floor. She wore a light blue hospital gown that was at least two sizes too big. It hung off one shoulder, exposing the bony joint and pale white skin. Sickly pale. Her skin looked as if it hadn't seen the sun in years.

Josie had to fight to keep her face from reflecting the horror she felt. Her mom looked completely broken. Josie wanted to grab her and make a run for it, but she was helpless in that guard-infested hospital. And the thought that she'd have to leave her mom there made her want to cry.

Dr. Cho guided Josie's mom to the bed. She stood in front of it but didn't sit down until the doctor placed a hand on her shoulder and gave her a gentle nudge. Then she tentatively lowered herself and sat forward on the edge of the mattress, her toes just touching the floor. As she sat there, Josie could see how thin she was. Her knobby knees looked too large for her legs, and her mom's athletic frame, which had always been fit and healthy from her morning runs, now appeared frail and fragile, as if her bones would snap in half if Josie hugged her too hard.

Even worse, Josie caught sight of thick, purple bruises encircling her mom's wrists and ankles, and up and down her arms and legs, the remnants of deep cuts. Like long, harsh claw marks.

Her stomach lurched. Josie knew those marks only too well.

"Dr. Byrne likes to cut herself," Dr. Cho said. She watched Josie's face keenly. "So we have to keep her restrained. For her own good. Isn't that right, Dr. Byrne?"

Josie's mom gave an almost indiscernible nod but said nothing.

"I see," Josie said. Suddenly, Dr. Cho's sunny smile seemed ominous. Her mom wasn't cutting herself. Josie would recognize those marks anywhere. They were exactly the same as the ones on Josie's arms: red, jagged, and sliced deep into her flesh. They were from a Nox attack. How could she have gotten them in here, and why was Dr. Cho lying about it?

"Your daughter's here to see you," Dr. Cho said. "Don't you want to say hello to your daughter?"

"That," her mom said slowly, without looking at Josie, "isn't my daughter."

Her voice was parched and raspy, but Josie recognized it right away. The inflection, the intonation.

"Mom?"

Her mom flinched. Visibly. Slowly she raised her head and the dirty locks of hair fell away from her face, exposing the deep blue eyes Josie knew so well. There was fear in those eyes, and confusion. "Josie?"

Josie threw her arms around her mom's neck. "It's me," she said in a barely audible whisper. Her mom wouldn't know what was going on, and Josie needed her to maintain the illusion as long as possible.

"Excellent!" Dr. Cho cooed. "I'll leave you two alone for a bit." She turned toward the door. "But not too long. We don't want to overdo things." Her megawatt smile breezed out of the room, and the door slid shut behind her.

"Josie?" her mom breathed immediately. Her eyes darted around Josie's face. "How? Where?"

Josie hugged her mom again, tighter this time. Emotion clogged her voice and she fought to keep back the sob threatening to erupt from deep within her. This was her mom. Finally.

"I've seen you," she said, her voice tight with emotion. "In my dreams. You'd be at home doing your homework just like nothing had happened."

The nightmare Dr. Byrne had. At exactly 3:59. Dear God, they were sharing visions of each other's lives, just like Josie did with Jo. That must have been even worse for her mom than being tortured by the Nox.

"Mom, I'm so sorry."

"Oh, Josie. The dreams I've had . . ."

She wanted to tell her mom everything—the mirror, the flash, her and Jo—but something stopped her. If they had her mom locked away, it was for a reason. They had to be careful. "Call me Josephine," she whispered into her mom's ear. "They might be listening." Then Josie cleared her throat and spoke in a clear, loud voice. "I've missed you, Mom."

"I've . . ." Her mom paused, then Josie felt her arms encircle her back. "I've missed you too. Josephine," she added.

Thank God. Whatever they'd done to her, Josie's mom still had her wits about her. Josie gave her mom a squeeze, then sat back down. "I'm sorry I haven't come to see you sooner," she said. "I've been really busy. School. Daddy. You know." She spoke deliberately, in a slightly stilted manner and hoped her mom picked up on the fact that they were, in all likelihood, being watched.

"Of course." Her mom nodded. "I understand."

Josie sat down on the edge of the hospital bed and leaned her head against her mom's shoulder. "I've missed you, Mom."

A sob racked her mom's body. Suddenly, her arms were around Josie, frantically pulling her close. "You have to get out of here," she said. "This place is evil. There are things. Evil, horrid things." Her mom's voice got louder and louder, and she barely got the words out between sobs.

The door slid open immediately and two orderlies rushed in. They pried Josie's mom away, pinning her arms behind her back. Her mom stopped fighting and went limp almost immediately, but tears streamed down her cheeks and her eyes never left Josie's face.

"Don't come back," she said. "Don't. Don't come back here."

"I think that's enough for today." Dr. Cho stood in the doorway. She gestured for Josie to follow her.

She started to follow Dr. Cho out of the room as her mom sobbed quietly in the arms of the orderlies. It broke Josie's heart to have to leave her mom there, but she needed time to figure out a plan with Nick. And no one could guess their secret until then, which meant her mom was going to have to play along too.

She ran back to her mom, and threw her arms around her neck. "Play along," she whispered. "Give them what they want until I figure a way out."

She pulled away and looked her mom in the eye, trying to look and sound as confident as possible. For an instant, the fear drained from her mom's face. "I love you."

"I love you too, Mom." Josie turned to leave. "And I'll be back soon."

THIRTY-FOUR

4:10 P.M.

JOSIE COULDN'T CONTROL THE TEARS AS SHE raced back to Bowie. They poured down her cheeks, stinging her eyes and blinding her as she drove. She didn't care about the speed limit. She didn't care about her own safety. All she could think about was getting her mom out of that horrible place. Stat.

But a special agent she was not, and the security at Old St. Mary's Hospital was like breaking into Langley. There was no way Josie could just waltz in there, overpower a few armed military guards, and carry her mom out.

The image of her mom—emaciated, tortured, and desperate to keep Josie out of harm—was burned into her brain. Her mom had always been so strong, physically and mentally, and to see her broken like that was devastating. Josie wiped her eyes with the back of her hand and tried to calm down. She had to focus her mind. She had a problem; she needed to find a solution. It was that simple.

She had to find a way if she was going to save her mom.

Okay, so if she couldn't break into Old St. Mary's *Mission: Impossible* style, she'd have to find another way to get her mom out. Who was the most logical person to do that?

Dr. Cho.

Josie set her jaw as she thought of the fake kindness in Dr. Cho's face. She wanted to shove her into a room with the Nox and lock the door. A taste of her own medicine.

Still, Dr. Cho had the power to transfer Josie's mom out of the hospital. But she'd have to *want* to do so. That was the only way.

How could Josie make that happen? She had no idea. She needed help.

Josie hit the hands-free button on her steering wheel and scrolled through the address book to Nick's number. *Come on, Nick. Please answer.*

The phone barely rang before the voice mail picked up. "You've reached Nick's cell phone," his voice said. "You know what to do."

Josie hung up before the beep. He might still have been at practice, but Josie remembered the warehouse. No cell phones there. Ever.

It was worth a shot. Josie needed to talk to him. She couldn't wait.

It took some trial and error, but Josie was finally able to recognize the exit to the warehouse district. Nick's route the other day had been so erratic, Josie was surprised she could re-create it at all, but she remembered train tracks, and she remembered the lonely off-ramp with no other buildings in sight. And it wasn't too long before Josie found herself slowly driving down the abandoned street toward Nick's off-the-Grid home away from home.

The roll-up gate was locked, and unlike Nick, Josie didn't have a key.

So she knocked.

After a minute or so, she heard the sound of sliding metal. "Shit," someone said under their breath. The gate rolled up partway, and Josie found herself face-to-face with Madison.

"What are you doing here?" she asked coldly.

"Looking for Nick," Josie said.

"Nick's not here."

Yeah, like she was going to take Madison's word for it. Josie gazed over Madison's shoulder, trying to see if Nick's SUV was in the parking area. "Any idea where he is?"

"Maybe you should try calling him. Phones are magical like that."

Josie rolled her eyes. "He's not answering."

"Ever occur to you that maybe he just doesn't want to talk to you?" Madison said with a half smirk.

"Ever occur to you that you're a raging—"

"J-Jo?" Penelope shoved her head around the side of the wall.

"Damn," Josie said with a side glance at Madison. "You guys don't waste any time, do you?"

"Nick asked me to bring her over after school," Madison said drily. "If it were up to me, neither of you would be here."

Josie looked her straight in the eye. "Then I guess I'm lucky it's not up to you."

"Whatever." Madison shoved the door. It rolled up so quickly it clattered to a stop, bouncing against the top of the frame from the violence of her push. "Get your car inside before someone spots it."

Josie smiled as she climbed back into the black BMW. So Nick had overruled Madison on the issue of helping Josie get home. Considering what Josie assumed about their dating history, that was only going to make Madison hate her even more.

Madison relocked the gate but refused to acknowledge Josie's presence, let alone talk to her as the three of them walked to the living-room area of the warehouse. It was almost ironic, really. The same anger Josie felt toward the Madison who had betrayed her, this Madison seemed to harbor for Jo. Was it all because of Nick? Suddenly, Josie's and Jo's realities seemed more parallel than ever.

Madison curled up on one of the sofas, arms crossed over her chest, staring into the recesses of the warehouse. Her hatred seemed to taint the air, and the whole atmosphere felt heavy and unwelcoming. Josie had viewed the warehouse as a safe haven, the only place in this world where she could actually be herself and not Jo. Without realizing it, she'd actually been looking forward to coming back to that place where people, regardless of whether they believed her, actually knew her secret. There was a sense of comfort in it that had now vanished in the face of Madison's cold, impenetrable disgust, and despite herself, Josie yearned for Nick's presence.

"So do I have this right?" Penelope said, breaking the uncomfortable silence. "You're not actually Jo Byrne?"

"That's right. I'm Josie."

"Huh." Penelope wasn't quite convinced. She stood behind the table with a haphazard stack of books open in front of her, eyeing Josie with suspicion. Physics, quantum mechanics, string theory. Some were titles she recognized; some were completely foreign.

"Wow," Josie said, examining one of the spines. "You have Feynmann here too?"

Penelope tilted her head to one side. "Yeah," she said slowly, suspicion dripping from the long, drawn-out syllable.

Josie flipped through the book. "I'd never really thought about it before, but the laws of physics should—in theory—be uniform across both of our worlds. Which means the conclusions of science should be at least similar."

"Einstein?" Penelope said. "Relativity?"

"*E* equals *mc* squared," Josie recited.

"Quantum mechanics?"

"Copenhagen Interpretation or a many-worlds theory?" Josie asked quickly.

Penelope arched an eyebrow. "Unifying theories between the two?"

Josie smiled. "Too many to list. You want my favorite or should I give you the greatest hits?"

Penelope stared at her, eyes wide and gleaming in excitement, yet her face was still tense, her body closed off, and she stood angled toward the door as if she might make a break for it at any moment. She opened her mouth to say something, paused, then slowly scratched her cheek. Josie couldn't help but smile.

"What?" Penelope said sharply. "Why are you smiling?"

"You're scratching your cheek," Josie said. "My friend Penelope always does that when she's trying to figure out a problem."

"Your friend Penelope?" Madison said with a breathy laugh. "That's a good one."

"Why?" Josie asked.

"Give it a rest," Madison said. She shifted her position on the sofa to face Josie. "You've done nothing but bully Pen into doing your homework since sixth grade. Then when her dad lost his job last year, you promised you'd keep them off the No Access For Nonpayment list at the Grid, if she helped you pass physics. Not exactly the foundations of a friendship."

"The Grid actually cuts people off for nonpayment? With the Nox out there?" Josie asked, horrified. "I thought Jo was just bluffing. What do you do if you can't get power?"

Madison narrowed her eyes. "The shelters, duh. Like debtor's prison for people who can't afford to pay to keep the lights on."

"We cut back on everything to keep up our Grid payments," Penelope said softly. "Sold Mom's car, shut off the cable, even cut back on food. We're still barely making it."

Josie felt sick. "That's awful. Pen, I'm so sorry."

"Sure you are." Madison chortled. "Really sorry you have someone doing all your homework for you."

Josie set her jaw. "Do I sound like someone who needs help with their homework? Or perhaps you'd like to explain the differences between the Heisenberg uncertainty principle and Schrödinger's cat? Or riff on quantum field theory and how it might explain quantum gravity and, eventually, how the hell I ended up here in the first place?"

Madison shot to her feet. "I don't care what words you memorized or how you've managed to fool Jackson and Nick and even Penelope over there."

"Hey," Penelope said, sounding hurt. "I'm in the room."

Madison barreled on. "But you aren't conning me with your sci-fi bullshit, okay? So give it a rest."

"Just because you can't wrap your brain around complex physics," Josie said, "doesn't mean it isn't real."

Penelope slapped her hand against the table. "Enough. Both of you."

Her voice was so forceful it caught Josie off guard. She'd never so much as heard Penelope raise her voice, let alone snap at her. Madison must have had the same reaction. Both of them sat back and stared at Penelope.

"Good," Penelope said, slightly out of breath. "You didn't bring me here to referee, did you?" Her voice squeaked and her face was flushed pink.

Josie laughed. She couldn't help it. "No."

"That's what I thought." Penelope cleared her throat and took a deep breath. Josie watched with some amusement as Penelope muttered under her breath, as if she needed to calm herself down, then lifted her chin and smiled. "Now should we talk about quantum gravity?"

There was something inexplicably hilarious about Penelope's statement. Just the facts, plain and simple. Josie was trying hard to suppress her laughter, struggling to keep the giggling under wraps. She looked up and saw that Madison was smiling too, her body jerking every second as she tried to keep from erupting into laughter as well.

Madison caught Josie's eye and as the two girls looked at each other, Josie felt the tension between them ease. She wasn't sure if she'd earned a smidgen of respect or if Madison was just tired of fighting, but with an almost imperceptible nod of her head—a cease-fire in the heat of battle—Madison swung around and got to her feet.

"I guess quantum gravity it is."

THIRTY-FIVE

5:47 P.M.

PENELOPE PUSHED THE BOOK AWAY AND SANK her head into her hands. "Which still doesn't explain exactly how the portal was created."

Josie and Penelope had been at it for well over an hour, poring over a variety of books as they searched for anything that might explain how the portal had opened between Jo's and Josie's worlds. They'd covered everything from theoretical extra dimensions to pseudoparanormal studies, and still nothing quite explained the flash, the mirror, and the portal that opened every twelve hours.

Madison had been quiet, flipping through the discarded books, but she was far from disinterested. She watched Josie closely, listened to every word that came out of her mouth, and Josie couldn't help but wonder if her reticence to believe Josie's story had faltered in any way.

"Okay," Josie said, closing the book in front of her. "Let's start crossing things off the list, at least." Her mom always taught her that when faced with a seemingly unanswerable problem, the best tactic was to eliminate impossible answers first, and whatever you were left with, however improbable, had to be the truth. She picked up a book on time travel and chucked it onto the sofa. "It's not a time loop. Our worlds are too dissimilar to be replaying themselves."

"Right." Penelope grabbed two more books and walked them over to the sofa. "I don't think it's a holographic multiverse either. Same reason: our worlds are too different."

"A what-what?" Madison asked.

"It's a theory of parallel universes," Josie explained. "Based on the holographic principle. Meaning that every universe has a mirror image, exactly the same in every way."

Madison stood up and stretched her arms over her head. "I swear you two are speaking a foreign language."

"We are," Penelope said. "It's the language of geek."

Madison laughed weakly. It was the first time Josie had seen Madison let her guard down since they'd met. The harsh lines around her nose and jaw softened and Josie noticed the heavy circles under her eyes and the deep sagging at the corners of her mouth. The bitch-on-wheels attitude melted away and Josie saw a sad, exhausted girl.

Madison caught Josie watching her and turned quickly, but in that instant Josie had seen something else reflected in Madison's light brown eyes: fear.

She wandered over to the kitchen and opened the door to the mini fridge. "Dammit," Madison said. "Someone ate the half a sandwich I had stashed in here." Madison slammed the door. "I swear those boys will eat anything that's not nailed down."

Josie smiled. "Yeah, that sounds like Nick."

"Oh please," Madison said with a snort. "You barely know him."

"And you know him better?" Josie asked. She was pushing, she realized immediately, to see if Madison would spill the exact nature of her relationship with Nick. She was desperate to know, even though she kept trying to remind herself that it didn't matter. That her attraction to this Nick could never amount to anything. Still, she wanted to know what had happened between them. But before Madison could say another word, Penelope steered them back on course.

"I'm going to cross all the objective collapse theories off the list as well," Penelope said pointedly, still focused on the pile of books in front of them. "Since there's no way we can prove the Penrose Interpretation."

Josie sighed. "You would say that."

"What do you mean?" Penelope's eyes pinched together. She looked hurt.

"Sorry," Josie said. "I've just heard it from you before."

"Huh?"

"Back home. We're lab partners and we're doing our end-of-year project on the Penrose Interpretation."

Penelope arched an eyebrow. "I let you talk me into attempting to prove an unprovable theory? What the hell is wrong with me over there?"

"It's not unprovable," Josie said. Why did everyone keep telling her that?

"Okay," Penelope said. "But even if it's true, it doesn't explain how you're here. Superposition collapses at our mass."

"Fine."

Madison popped open a soda and rejoined them at the table. "Superposition? Is that like a superhero thing?"

"Quantum superposition," Penelope explained, "is the theory that a particle like an electron exists in all of its many property states simultaneously. But when you try to measure it, you only get one reading."

"Oh, I see," Madison said. She clearly didn't. "So where does that leave us?"

There were two books left on the table. Josie picked up one in each hand. "Brane multiverses and quantum gravity."

Penelope stifled a yawn. "So it must be one of them."

"I haven't read much on brane multiverses," Josie said, turning the book over in her hands.

"The core of the theory is that universes exist on these thin planes," Penelope said. Even though she was tired, she spoke quickly and her voice had a lifted inflection that Josie recognized. The science excited her. "An infinite number of them all existing very close together, but never intersecting. Some of them would be completely unrecognizable; some of them would be exactly like our own world. And everything in between."

Josie nodded. "Common multiworld theory."

"Right."

Josie skimmed through a chapter on phase shifting of brane multiverses. The idea was that these branes overlapped in space-time with a dimensional phase shift, which meant Jo and Josie and an infinite number of their doppelgängers could have been moving through the same space but on different planes of existence—literally out of phase—in their respective parallel dimensions, and totally unaware of each other. In theory, it could describe how their two worlds—and the people in them—existed. But how the portal was created between them? That was something else entirely.

Josie flipped through the pages when something caught her eye. "'While the branes overlap without connection between them,'" Josie read out loud, "'if the gravitons are disrupted from the brane on which they exist, they could attach themselves to another brane in close proximity.'" She looked up sharply. "So gravitons could connect two branes?"

Penelope slid the book over. "Looks like it," she said after reading a few pages. "It would take a massive subatomic explosion, but two universes could become attached to each other at a single point in space-time."

"A massive explosion like creating micro black holes using ultradense deuterium and controlled fusion?" Josie said.

Penelope's eyes grew wide. "Whoa. Does that work?"

"Yeah. Yeah, it does." Josie gazed at an illustration of a graviton connecting two brane universes. "The gravitons *are* the portal, the stuff that connects our two worlds. They're what's holding our universes together."

"So all we have to do is re-create the explosion," Penelope said, "and we'll have ourselves another portal."

"One problem," Madison said. "That explosion you're talking about killed Nick's brother. So unless you want to go down in a blaze of glory . . ."

Josie slumped back in her chair. "We're right back where we started."

THIRTY-SIX

5:57 P.M.

"SHIT." JOSIE SLAMMED THE BRANE MULTIVERSE book closed. What was the point in creating another portal if she or her mom might be killed in the process? They were so close to the answer. She felt like the rug had just been pulled out from under them.

"Do we know what caused the explosion?" Penelope said, scratching her cheek furiously.

Madison shook her head. "We have some of our parents' notes from the experiment, but the findings of the investigation are in a file somewhere up at Fort Meade. Jackson and I have tried a few times to get our hands on it. No dice."

"Too bad," Penelope said absently. "If we knew how the experiment was set up, we might be able to tweak it so there's no *BOOM*."

Josie laughed. She couldn't help it. All the science jargon in the last few hours boiled down to a good, old-fashioned *BOOM*. "If only Jo could show me *that* in one of her dreams."

Penelope tilted her head. "You share dreams with Jo?"

"Kinda. I can see through her eyes when the portal's open. Just for that one minute every twelve hours."

Penelope let the pen fall to the table. "Whoa. That's wild."

Josie shook her head. *Wild* wasn't the word she'd use. "I had another one last night. Dr. Byrne in my kitchen back home. Not my mom, see? Dr. Byrne."

"Are you telling me that it's your mom up at Old St. Mary's?" Madison said. For the first time, there was no hint of sarcasm in Madison's voice.

Josie nodded. "I was there. Today. It's her."

Penelope stared at her for a moment, then shrugged. "So you think your mom and Jo's mom have the same connection? That they can see through each other's eyes?"

"Definitely. Dr. Byrne had a nightmare last week. Woke up screaming in the middle of the night. I'm pretty sure she was experiencing the torture my mom's been going through at Old St. Mary's."

Madison sat up straight. "Torture?"

"Yeah." Josie tried to keep her voice steady and her mind calm as the image of her mother's scarred body flashed into her mind. "They're using the Nox on her."

"Shit," Madison said.

Josie pushed the image out of her mind. The panic she felt when she thought of her mom trapped there in that hospital room was not going to help.

"Okay, so let's summarize," Josie said. She had to stay focused if she was going to get her mom out of there, and find a way home. "We have a working theory as to how to create a portal, but without the findings of the investigation into Tony's death, we risk killing ourselves if we attempt it, right?"

"Right," Penelope said with a nod.

"Then there's only one thing to do," Josie said. She smiled as a plan formed in her head.

"Your smile is freaking me out," Penelope said, recoiling.

But Madison was intrigued. "What are you thinking?"

It was crazy, but it might work. "We'll just have to get those notes."

6:21 P.M.

A clanging noise from the back of the warehouse startled the girls, breaking the silence that had descended upon them. Josie jumped in her chair. "What's that?"

"Just the rats, I bet." Madison stood up and gazed into the back of the warehouse.

Josie snorted. "Yeah, I've noticed a lot of them around here."

Madison turned to her. "Really?" she said in exasperation.

Josie couldn't help herself. The words had just slipped out of her mouth. She was still having a hard time separating the two Madisons. "I'm sorry," she said. And she meant it. "Really. It's just..." Ugh. She so didn't want to explain the tragedy of her personal life to the doppelgänger of the girl who had caused it. She felt the heat rising up from her chest to her neck, spreading across her face like a big neon sign flashing, *There's something I'm not telling you*. She dropped her eyes to the notebook and pretended to examine equations, but Penelope didn't miss a thing.

"Who is she?" Penelope asked. To the point, as always. "Who is Madison in your world?"

Josie glanced at Madison out of the corner of her eye. "She was my best friend. Until I caught my boyfriend cheating on me. With her."

Penelope whistled. "Damn."

"Nick," Madison said. Her eyes were fixed on Josie. "Your boyfriend was Nick."

Josie nodded. But for the first time, the topic of Madison and Nick's betrayal seemed less painful, less vomit-inducing than before. She had bigger issues to deal with, and suddenly instead of anger, Josie just felt sorry for them both.

"What about me?" Penelope fidgeted with her fingers. Clearly the idea of hearing about her alter ego in another dimension made Penelope nervous.

Josie smiled. Just thinking about her old friend gave her a sense of comfort. "Penelope's the best," she said. "We've been friends since fourth grade. She's a lot like you, actually. Smart. Practical. Loyal."

"Interesting." Penelope gave herself a shake, as if tossing off a bad memory, then glanced at her watch. "It's late. We should get going."

Six thirty. Yikes. Mr. Byrne was expecting her for dinner.

"I have an idea. About how to fix our little *BOOM* problem," Penelope said simply, as she packed up her books and carried them to Madison's car. "In case you strike out with the file. I'm going to borrow Mr. Baines's laser rig from the lab. Can I set it up here?"

"Sure," Madison said, her old swagger returned. "Knock yourself out."

Josie paused at the door of the black BMW. "Thank you," she said. "Both of you."

Madison rolled up the door. She didn't exactly smile at Josie, but there was something like a nod of acceptance. Whatever. Josie took it.

As she backed out of the warehouse, she felt more hopeful than she had in days. Her mom was here. She had friends. She wasn't alone in this. She looked up as she turned the wheel to leave; something caught her eye. A shadow ducking around the side of the warehouse. She craned her neck as she drove around the building. She was sure she saw someone. Positive.

But there was no one there.

THIRTY-SEVEN

7:00 P.M.

JOSIE MADE IT JUST IN TIME FOR DINNER.

Mr. Byrne was already seated at the table when Josie burst into the house. "Perfect timing." He smiled at her warmly. "I'm glad to see you're finally making an attempt at punctuality."

So Jo was flakey with time. Good to know.

Teresa arrived the moment Josie sat down at the table with an enormous tray of homemade lasagna. A bowl of string beans was already on the table. She served both, silently as usual, then disappeared back into the kitchen.

"So?" Mr. Byrne asked. She could tell he was trying to sound casual. "How did it go?"

"Better."

"Yes?"

Josie nodded. "She knew who I was."

Mr. Byrne caught his breath. "I knew it. I knew she was improving. Dr. Cho said it was probably just false hope on my part, that her psyche was too damaged from the effects of the explosion, but I knew. I could just tell last time I saw her that there was something . . . more."

Josie's heart ached. He was so excited at the idea that his wife was getting better. The worry lines above his forehead instantly disappeared, and that pinched look around his eyes vanished. He looked ten years younger, and even more like Josie's own care-free dad. She felt guilty that she was hiding something from him, even if it was for his own good.

He leaned toward her. "Thank you, princess. We're going to get your mom back. I promise."

Speaking of . . . "Daddy?" Josie put down her fork and folded her hands in front of her. "That place she's in. Old St. Mary's. It's . . ."

"Awful," he said with a heavy sigh. "I know. But she was part of a Grid-sponsored experiment at the time of the accident, dealing with top secret information. They need to keep her at a secure facility for her own safety."

Josie was tempted to bring up the scars on her mom's arms and legs, but she didn't want to have to explain to Mr. Byrne how she knew what they were, and besides, the poor man really didn't need something else weighing on his mind. "Is there any way we can get her out of there? Moved somewhere closer to home?"

Mr. Byrne rubbed his chin. "It's not like I haven't tried, princess. But Dr. Cho feels like it's the best environment for your mom."

Best environment for them to get what they want out of her, more like it.

"But," he continued, "if your mom shows signs of improvement, I don't see why we couldn't move her close by. Heck, maybe even bring her home permanently." His eyes lit up at the idea.

"Awesome."

"I can definitely make a few phone calls tomorrow." He laughed softly. "What's the point of having all my connections at the Grid if I can't pull a few strings once in a while?"

Josie beamed. "Oh, and one more thing, Daddy."

"Yes?"

"You know how you offered Nick a job up at Fort Meade?"

Mr. Byrne laughed. "Of course."

"Well, he was thinking he might be interested." That would be news to Nick when she told him. "And we were wondering if maybe you could arrange a tour of the Grid? Maybe an interview?"

"Yes, of course. Absolutely! Tomorrow after school?"

"That," Josie said with a smile, "would be perfect."

3:59 A.M.

"Hello, Nick," Jo says. She's waiting by his car in the parking lot, leaning against the trunk.

Nick's eyes grow wide. He scans her from head to foot and back again.

"Oh. Hey, Josie."

Jo smiles. It has taken her days to put together a decent outfit in Josie's closet, and this is the first time she's felt as if she might actually catch Nick's attention. A tight, low-cut halter, hip-hugger jeans, and a pair of wedge sandals that look as if they've never been worn. Jo knows Nick has never seen his ex-girlfriend look quite like this.

"I've missed you," Jo says. She pushes off the car with a thrust of her pelvis and snakes her way over to Nick. He stands frozen, his eyes locked on to hers as she places a hand on his chest and slowly traces it down the front of him. "I've missed every part of you."

"Josie?" Nick says. His voice is husky. "Wh-what's gotten into you?"

Jo smiles. "Oh, you know. With all those unexplained murders recently, I've just been reevaluating my life. What I want. Who I want."

"Oh."

"Didn't you hear?" Jo says. She hooks a finger into Nick's belt loop. "Two more bodies found this morning. That makes six this week alone."

Nick takes a step toward her. "Yeah. Yeah, I guess that would make you question . . . things."

Jo leans forward, pressing her chest into his. "Do you want me to show you what I've been thinking about?"

Nick swallows. His head bends down to meet Jo's upturned face. She can feel his want and she smiles to herself. That was too easy. What was wrong with Josie that she couldn't keep him?

His lips graze her own when suddenly, his body stiffens.

"Nick!" Madison races across the parking lot and pulls Jo away from Nick. "What the fuck are you doing? Were you kissing her?"

Jo laughs hysterically, uncontrollably.

"This isn't funny," Nick snaps. He grabs Madison by the shoulders. "I wasn't doing anything, I swear. I was just shocked. But we're done." He glances at Jo, his face hard. "There's definitely nothing between us anymore."

Jo sobers up immediately. She's heard that before from Nick. But this time, she doesn't quite believe him.

"Whatever you say, Nick." Jo tosses her hair, casting an exaggerated wink at him as she turns to leave.

We'll just see about that.

THIRTY-EIGHT

2:43 P.M.

"ARE YOU SURE THIS IS GOING TO WORK?" NICK said. He fidgeted with the tie Josie had brought for him to wear for his fake interview. "I mean, do you even know what you're looking for?"

Josie reached over to the driver's seat and straightened his tie, just like she used to do for her dad—her real dad—on the rare occasion he had to wear one. "What, yes. Where, not a clue."

"Oh, that's comforting."

Josie smiled. "Isn't it?" She patted Nick's tie. "Just stick to the script, okay? You're a potential Grid employee, scouting out post-graduation jobs. We just have to act like stupid high-school kids, ask the right questions, and hope we get lucky."

Nick pursed his lips. "I thought you scientific types didn't believe in luck."

"We don't."

With a sigh of resignation, Nick stepped out of his car and into the afternoon sunshine. Josie followed, and together they stood side by side at the entrance of the National Headquarters of the Grid.

The building was unpretentious, all metal and glass in a utilitarian style popular in the 1970s. The entrance was unguarded, and employees came and went as they pleased with the use of security badges tethered to their clothes on retractable cords. But other than that, the headquarters for one of the most powerful companies in the world was oddly informal.

Four stories, lined straight across with windows showcasing a variety of mundane office tasks. In one window, a woman stood at a copy machine, staring out onto the lush grounds of Fort Meade. In another, two men sat at rapt attention while a woman in a lab coat diagrammed at a whiteboard. In a third, a man had his feet up against the window, his chair tilted back, as he gabbed away on the phone.

Where the government hospital at Old St. Mary's had been like gaining access to a maximum-security prison, as Josie and Nick strolled up to the main entrance to the Grid, it felt like they were walking into the DMV for a license renewal.

After a check-in at the receptionist's desk, which produced two visitor's badges, a young man in khaki pants and a tucked-in polo shirt hurried into the lobby.

"Nicholas Fiorino?" he said, extending his hand to Nick.

Nick flashed a giant shit-eating grin. "That's me."

"Richard Katz," the young man said, pumping Nick's arm furiously. "Director of Public Outreach for the Grid." His gaze drifted to Josie. "And you must be Josephine Byrne," he said in somewhat reverential tones.

Now it was Josie's turn to fake-smile. "You can call me Jo."

Richard took her hand in both of his and shook it delicately, as if he was afraid she might break. "It's lovely to meet you, Miss Byrne."

"Jo," Josie corrected.

"Right." Richard gingerly let go of Josie's hand, but his eyes never left her face. "And you may call me Richard."

Josie caught a glimpse of Nick rolling his eyes, and fought hard to suppress a giggle.

"Well, now that introductions are complete, shall we begin the tour?"

Nick cleared his throat and launched into the speech Josie had painstakingly coached him on during their drive to Fort Meade. "Absolutely. I'm most interested in the recent developments in free-electron—"

"How about you, Miss Byrne?" Richard said, crossing right in front of Nick without so much as acknowledging his presence. "What can I show you here at the Grid that might pique your interest?"

Josie wasn't used to getting hit on, especially by grown men who could spend thirty to life in state prison for so much as laying a hand on her. The thought of playing up to Richard Katz, Director of Public Outreach, kind of turned her stomach, but if it could get them the information they wanted, she was all for it.

"Actually," Josie said with a soft smile, "I'm most interested in the recent developments in free-electron lasers. Particularly in their applied usage for Project Raze."

Richard's eyes grew wide. "I'm not authorized to escort tour groups through the upper laboratories. Technically, they are government facilities, sponsored by the Grid but not directly controlled by us, and they've clamped down on access since . . . er, I mean . . ." His voice trailed off and his eyes shifted back and forth uncomfortably.

"You mean since the explosion that killed Nick's brother and sent my mom into a mental hospital?" Josie tried to sound as innocent as possible while still pressing her advantage. Maybe if she made Richard feel like a big enough douche, he'd show them what they wanted to see.

"Um, yes."

"Please?" Josie said, laying it on thick. "Just a quick look? It would mean a great deal to me."

Nick was having a hard time controlling himself. Standing just out of Richard's line of sight, he was going into convulsions as he tried to keep himself from laughing out loud.

"Well . . ." Richard checked the time on his watch. "I suppose we could do a quick walk-through of the fourth floor." He glanced up at Josie. "But perhaps it would be best if you didn't mention this to your father?"

Josie smiled. "I wouldn't even think of it."

Richard obligingly guided Nick and Josie up to the fourth floor. He prattled on about how the Grid isn't just a power company, but a philanthropic research facility as well. He preened over the importance of the research they conducted, its lasting impact on humanity, his own crucial position within the organization. When the elevator opened on the fourth floor, he walked briskly down the halls, throwing out the occasional factoid about one or another ongoing project while his eyes scanned the hallway, anxious lest someone find them up there.

Josie was only half listening as they blew past closed door after closed door. She kind of wanted to ask him about the shelters Madison had mentioned where poor people who couldn't afford extravagant power bills from the Grid were forced to relocate, but she didn't want to antagonize him. Besides, she had more important things to think about. Security, for instance. While the main entrance of the building displayed a pointed lack of it, on the fourth floor, each and every door was barred by an access-card reader. Even the restrooms. Some had a doctor's name stenciled onto the door; others just a department label. Josie had no idea what she was looking for; only in Saturday-morning cartoons did secret bad-guy headquarters have "Secret File Rooms" conveniently displayed for meddling kids.

They paused at one door, unmarked, and Richard dropped his voice. "This was, er, *is* Dr. Byrne's office," he said.

Josie perked up. "My mom's office?" So it had been left untouched. That could be promising.

"Yes," he said. "We've kept it pretty much intact if she—" He paused again, visibly flustered. "I mean *when* she returns."

Dr. Byrne's office. Like all the others, it had an access-card scanner to unlock the door. Which meant she needed to get her hands on a card.

Suddenly, Josie had an idea. "I need to use the ladies' room," she said.

"Now?" Richard asked.

Josie nodded.

"I can let you in with my access card," Richard said with a touch of consternation. "All the doors on this floor require an access badge."

So Josie had noticed.

Richard marched her down the hall and let her into the ladies' room. As soon as the door closed behind her, Josie searched the stalls, making sure she was alone, then stashed her purse behind one of the garbage cans. After running the water as if washing her hands, Josie emerged from the ladies' room with a sweet smile, and followed Richard and Nick downstairs.

Josie waited until Richard was halfway through his tour of the more innocuous second floor—which included his own semiprivate office—before she put phase two of the plan into motion.

"Ask to see the cafeteria," Josie whispered in Nick's ear.

He nodded. "Richard," he said, interrupting the Director of Public Outreach's monologue about the various tasks that made up his job. "I was wondering if I might be able to see the cafeteria? Getting kind of hungry."

Josie piped up. "Me too."

"Oh," Richard said. He sounded deflated. "I suppose, if you want. It's on the concourse level. Follow me."

"Oh no!" Josie said a few minutes later, as the elevator door opened on the basement level.

"What is it, Miss Byrne?"

Josie smiled sheepishly. "I've lost my purse! I'm so careless like that."

"Where do you think you left it?" Richard asked. His patience, even so far as it extended to the daughter of Mr. Byrne, was wearing thin.

"In the ladies' room. On the fourth floor."

"The fourth floor?" Richard asked. "Are you sure?"

"Positive." She eyed the access badge on Richard's belt. "If you just lend me your badge, I can pop upstairs and get it." Richard hesitated. "Or I can just tell my father where I lost it and he can find it for me?" she added.

"No," Richard said quickly, and handed over the badge.

Josie grabbed it before he could change his mind, and pressed the elevator button. "I'll grab it, then meet you guys in the cafeteria."

As the doors closed, Nick gave her a quick wink. She just hoped he could stall long enough, and that she'd actually find something.

THIRTY-NINE

3:22 P.M.

WALKING INTO DR. BYRNE'S OFFICE WAS LIKE walking into a tomb.

It wasn't the lab where she and Nick's brother had conducted the experiment, of that Josie was sure. It wasn't big enough, for starters, and lacked a full lab setup. This was strictly an office: desk, chairs, bookcases, file cabinet, framed diplomas on the wall. All perfectly normal.

Josie didn't have much time before Richard might get suspicious. There was no way the findings of the investigation would be locked away in Dr. Byrne's office, but maybe Josie could find something else that might hint at what happened to the X-FEL that day? It was her only shot. She had to think: Where would Dr. Byrne keep important information about her projects?

The locked file cabinet was the obvious choice. Six feet tall with four enormous drawers, it probably had experimental notes going back a decade or more. But that would be more of a reference for Dr. Byrne. Not an easily accessible source of information.

No, that would be in her desk.

Josie sat down and opened the large bottom drawer. It was lined with hanging file folders containing the most recent notes and findings. Okay, this was a start. But what exactly was she looking for? A filed marked "How to openly sabotage an X-FEL" was probably a stretch.

Josie flipped through a few files. The names were all innocuous: "calibrations," "beam tests," "Jo's school projects."

"Jo's school projects?" Josie said out loud. That didn't sound right. Josie glanced at the framed photo of Jo and Dr. Byrne on the desk. As far as Josie could tell, Jo wasn't exactly an academic.

With a trembling hand, Josie pulled the file from the drawer.

The first thing she noticed was that the file was full of chat transcripts. Printed out conversations between two anonymous screen names: xa929 and drtr000. There were no personal references—no names, no genders, no job descriptions—and as Josie read through them, she quickly understood why.

> xa929: $200 million is the final offer
>
> drtr000: Accepted
>
> xa929: When can we expect delivery of the product?
>
> drtr000: After the first test, I shall deliver the product the following day as soon as I have confirmation that the money has been wired into my account
>
> xa929: How will you obtain the product?
>
> drtr000: Not your concern

Holy shit.

A "product" sold to the highest bidder.

Had Josie just stumbled across proof that Tony Fiorino's experiment had been sabotaged?

4:45 P.M.

Nick loosened his tie as he sped back to Bowie. "And you're sure that's what you saw?"

"Positive."

"Two hundred million dollars." Nick whistled. "That's enough to kill for."

"I wonder who they were selling to?" Josie wondered out loud.

"A foreign power, a private company." Nick ran his fingers through his hair. "Hell, maybe even the Grid. Everyone and their mom would want exclusive ownership of a way to get rid of the Nox."

Josie nodded. "A traitor. There was a traitor working on Project Raze." She paused, and looked right at Nick. "It could be anyone," she said. "Anyone with access to the laser."

"Even Dr. Byrne herself," Nick said.

"Would she really keep transcripts of her own illegal activities in her desk drawer?" Josie asked. Seemed like a bonehead move.

"Maybe." Nick shrugged. "If she felt like she was about to get caught, she could always pretend to be a whistle-blower."

Josie nodded. "Yeah, that could make sense."

Nick set his jaw. "If it's true," he said slowly, "if she's responsible for my brother's death, she'd better pray she never comes back here."

"NO!"

There's a crash and a bang from the kitchen, then the violent sound of breaking glass. Jo runs down the hall to the kitchen and stops short at the door.

Her mom is ripping the kitchen apart. She opens every cupboard, every drawer, and pulls their contents out. She examines everything, then drops them on the floor. She dumps boxes of cereal and pasta on the counter. Canisters of flour, sugar, and who knows what else are poured unceremoniously on the table. Plates and silverware, condiments and tea bags—she's tearing the room apart.

After every inch of the kitchen has been ravaged, her mom leans on the counter, her back to Jo.

"Mom?" Jo asks.

She doesn't turn around, just continues to lean on her elbows, head hung low, panting.

"What's wrong?"

"It's gone," she says, her voice little more than a croak. "I've lost it."

"What?" Jo asks gently. She's never seen her mom like this.

"I put it in the one place no one would look for it. But now . . ." Her mom babbles on like she doesn't hear anything. "If it's back

there, I . . . we have nothing. It was our future here."

"Um, okay," Jo says. "Then we'll just go back and get it." She tries to keep the excitement out of her voice.

Her mom swings around suddenly and storms up to Jo, grabbing her fiercely by the shoulders. "We can't go back. Do you hear me?" She shakes Jo violently. "We can never go back."

Jo breaks free. "Why not?"

"The explosion," she says. "Tony's dead. You said it yourself."

"Mom, I don't understand."

"The experiment was sabotaged and I disappeared with the last of the formula. See?"

Jo stiffens. This is why Nick hates me.

"There will be a warrant out for my arrest," her mom continues, a panicked look in her eyes. "And the Grid will be after me as well."

"We'll fix it. We'll have him fix it." I have to go back. I have to explain this to Nick.

Her mom releases her grasp and turns toward the window, planting her hands on the counter. "We cannot go back. Ever."

Josie was smiling before she even opened her eyes. Short of a dream showing her the way home, this was the best thing that could have happened. She pulled off the sleep mask and calmly climbed out of bed. She knew what Dr. Byrne had lost. And more importantly, she knew where to find it.

For the first time in days, Josie could see the light in the darkness.

FORTY

"AND IT WAS JUST THERE?" NICK ASKED.

Josie smiled. "Yep."

"In the coffee bin?"

"Smell it."

Nick held the vial up to his nose and took a guarded sniff. His eyebrows shot up. "Yep, in the coffee bin."

"Crazy, right?"

"More like amazing. Do you know how many people would kill to have this? The only specimen of my brother's injectable left in existence?"

Josie looked around the cafeteria to see if anyone was paying attention, then reached out and covered the vial with her hand. "Then let's keep it on the DL, shall we?"

Nick grinned sheepishly, and slipped the vial into the hip pocket of his cargo pants. "Sorry. I'm a little excited."

"I know."

"This is my brother's legacy. And he died trying to prove it could work." Nick stared at the table for a moment, fingering his uneaten sandwich, then looked up at Josie. "You're amazing, you know."

Josie's heart hiccupped, but she forced herself not to give in, to let her heart go. "No, I'm not."

"Yes, you are. Remembering that the canister in your kitchen had tea not coffee? Putting the pieces together. Not many people would have been able to figure out that Dr. Byrne hid the vial in your own kitchen."

Josie felt a blush creep up her neck and dropped her head to camouflage her embarrassment. "I'm sure anyone would have known. Penelope. Madison."

At Madison's name, Nick cocked his head to the side, opened his mouth to say something, then thought the better of it. He picked up his sandwich and took a monstrous bite.

Way to go, Josie.

"Talked to Penelope in first period," he said, his tone very businesslike as he changed the subject. "She's going to borrow Mr. Baines's laser rig and set it up tonight. She wouldn't tell me what she's planning, only that it required some 'tweaking.' Any idea what she's working on?"

"Nope."

Nick shrugged. "Guess we'll have to just wait and see. Also, I thought I'd take you to Old St. Mary's after school today."

Josie dropped her head so Nick couldn't see her smile. "You don't have to."

"I know. I'll wait in the car if you want, but I thought . . . I don't know. Maybe you'd like to see her again."

"Thank you."

"Besides, maybe she can tell us something about her work that can help. We need to do everything we can to get you home."

Home. Right. She wanted to go home. And Nick wanted her to go home. Sitting there across a cafeteria table from Nick, she'd momentarily forgotten that little fact.

Nick leaned across the table. "You . . . you do want to go back, right?"

"I need to get my mom home," she said without actually answering the question.

"Then there we go." Nick stood up, his face serious. "I'll see you after school."

3:05 P.M.

Josie's mom was sitting up in bed this time when Dr. Cho ushered Josie into her room.

"She's *much* improved in the last twenty-four hours," Dr. Cho said when she greeted Josie. "Your visit made a world of difference."

Josie forced a smile, hoping her face looked benignly happy. "Hi, Mom!" Josie said with an abundance of enthusiasm. Her mom scooted over and Josie sat down on the edge of the bed. "I hear you're feeling better?"

"Much." Her mom's smile was genuine, but her eyes lingered suspiciously on Dr. Cho.

"You two have a good visit," Dr. Cho said, closing the door as she backed out of the room. "I'll be back soon."

Josie was all smiles until she heard the security door click into place, then her Mouseketeer persona vanished. She leaned close to her mom and dropped her voice to little more than a whisper. "Are you okay?"

Her mom let out a deep breath. "Better. They seem excited with my 'progress.'" She used air quotes.

"Good; let's keep it that way. Dr. Byrne needs to have a miraculous recovery. I'm pretty sure that's the only way I can get you out of here."

"A recovery?"

"Pretend it's all coming back to you. From what I understand you were conducting an experiment, using laser-generated micro black holes."

Her mom laughed drily. "That's ironic. That's almost exactly what I was doing when I ended up here."

"Really?"

"Controlled creation of micro black holes using ultradense deuterium and laser-generated fusion." Her mom shook her head. "Apparently not so controlled. We had a small explosion in the lab. I blacked out for a moment, and woke up here. In this world."

"That would explain it. If you and the other Dr. Byrne were doing the same experiment at the same time." Josie made an explosion motion with her hands. "Boom."

Her mom nodded. "Any idea what composition of deuterium they were using?"

"No, only that it was an injectable compound."

"An injectable? That's amazing. I'd love to see the formula."

"Do you think it would help?" Josie asked. "If you knew what was in the formula, maybe how it caused the explosion that sent you here, do you think we could figure out a way to get home?"

Her mom thought for a moment. "Maybe. Do you have the injectable?"

Josie bit her lip and gave an almost imperceptible nod of her head. Then she cleared her throat. "No. No, I don't," she said loudly, in case anyone was listening.

There was a commotion outside the cell and Josie heard hurried footsteps clicking across the floor. They didn't have much time.

"We're trying to figure a way to get you out of here," Josie said quickly.

Her mom's face went blank. "We?"

"Some friends of mine."

Josie's mom gripped her arm tightly, digging her fingers into Josie's flesh. "Don't trust them. You can't. Josie, you can't trust anyone here, do you understand me?"

Dr. Cho rushed into the room. "I'm sorry," she said breathlessly. "I'm afraid your mother is due for her medication now. We'll need to cut your visit short."

Josie forced the sunny smile back onto her face. "Oh, that sucks."

"Hospital regulations," Dr. Cho replied.

More like prison regulations.

Josie stood up, but her mom pulled her back, wrapping her

arms tightly around her neck.

"You can't trust anyone," she whispered frantically.

A cold sensation spread down Josie's spine, like an ice cube melting against her skin. All of her hope in getting her and her mom home rested in the trust she'd put in people: Nick, Penelope, even Mr. Byrne in his ignorant way. Had she been wrong? Was she placing them in even worse danger?

"I love you too, Mom," she said out loud, pulling away. The image of her mom's haunted, bloodshot eyes followed her from the room.

3:59 P.M.

Jo tiptoes down the hallway, careful to avoid the creaking floorboard right outside her mom's room. She can't wake up. Her mom would have a fit if she knew what Jo is about to do.

She opens the door to the basement a centimeter at a time. Her heart pounds in her chest. She has to hurry. It's already time.

Jo flips on the desk lamp in her mom's makeshift lab and squints against the light. The darkness is so lovely, but she needs to see what she's about to do.

The mirror faces the wall with a heavy wood beam leaning against it, securing it to the concrete. Jo crouches under it, pushing up with her legs and lifting the beam with her shoulder. She pivots a few inches, then lets the beam come to rest against the wall itself, freeing the mirror, if only temporarily.

Jo pulls the letter from her pocket as she eases the mirror away from the wall. The mirror's surface is smooth, reflecting Jo's old bedroom. But Jo doesn't waste any time. She reaches through the portal and drops the letter on the floor of her room, then lowers the mirror....

"Wait!" Josie screamed.

The car swerved. "Whoa," Nick said, both hands firmly gripping the wheel. "What the hell?"

She'd fallen asleep in the car. "Jo," she said breathlessly.

Nick's head snapped in her direction. "Did you have another dream?"

"She opened the portal."

"What?"

"She put a note through." Josie pounded on the dashboard. "Fuck! Why wasn't I there?"

It was too much. The portal, her mom. Too much. Josie hung her head in her hands and cried.

FORTY-ONE

4:21 P.M.

"HEY," NICK SAID SOFTLY. HIS HAND CARESSED her shoulder. "It's okay. It's going to be okay."

Josie wasn't sure how long she'd been crying, but apparently Nick had pulled the car off to the side of the road and killed the engine. She looked at him, his face sad and calm, and tried to control herself. After a few moments, her sobs, though still erratic, were less frequent, but she felt weak and helpless.

"If only I'd been there," she said, wiping tears from her cheek. "I could have—"

"You could have what? Beaten the crap out of Jo?"

Josie smiled. "Maybe." The thought was appealing.

"But it wouldn't have done your mom any good. She'd still be in that hospital, and it's not like you could force Dr. Byrne to go back and clear everything up."

The boy had a point.

"You said it yourself: your best chance is to replicate the experiment that landed your mom here in the first place."

Josie nodded. He was right. She knew he was right.

"And I'm going to help." His eyes swept over to her face, down to her neck, and fixed on something there. The necklace. He shook his head, as if snapping himself out of a dream, and quickly sat up straight. He started the car and pulled back onto the highway. "Let's see what Jo had to say, huh? Now I'm curious."

4:40 P.M.

Josie,

> *I'm sorry about all this.*

> *There's more going on than you know. Even if I could tell you, I doubt you'd believe me. I'm sure you hate me right now, but believe me when I say I didn't have a choice.*

> *But maybe I can make it up to you.*

> *I need to find something. I thought it was here, but I don't know if you noticed all the strange items that were switching back and forth between our worlds for the last couple of weeks? I had been missing a pair of shoes that miraculously reappeared a few days after I'd torn the house apart looking for them. Things like that. Back and forth without any warning.*

The thing I'm looking for? That's what happened to it. I think.

You need to search the house when Teresa and Daddy are gone for a black kitchen canister filled with coffee. Yes, I realize that sounds totally bizarre, but I need that canister.

In twenty-four hours I'll reopen the portal and then, if you have the canister, we can both go home. Deal?

—Jo

Nick lowered the note to the bed and shook his head. "Yep," he said. "This totally sounds like Jo."

"Does it?"

"The tone. The way she tries to make you feel that she's sharing with you when really she's playing everything close to the vest. Just like her mom."

Josie was intrigued. "Yeah?"

"My brother said she was single-minded about her job. Like a sociopath, practically."

"I noticed," Josie said with a dry laugh.

"Which made her a good scientist, but a crappy colleague."

"I can see that." Dr. Byrne was utterly and completely obsessed with her work. "Do you think she did it? Do you think she's the one who sabotaged the experiment and was going to sell your brother's formula to the highest bidder?"

"I wouldn't be surprised," Nick said. "I mean, she was

cold-blooded enough, clearly hiding something. And you did find the chat transcript in her office. If she was suspicious that someone else was the traitor, wouldn't she have gone to the authorities? She definitely would not have continued the experiment if she thought it was sabotaged, you know?"

Josie shuddered, thinking about the woman she'd been living with for the past six months. A woman who apparently had no compunction about letting people die in exchange for a hefty payday.

"Jo's like that too," Nick continued. "Single-minded. When she decides on something she wants, she doesn't stop till she gets it."

Josie smiled. "Like you?"

He steadily met her gaze. "And you."

"Wish I'd known that four days ago."

Nick leaned toward her. "Wish I'd known *you* four days ago."

Josie wasn't exactly sure what that meant, but it made her feel all warm and fluttery inside. She picked up the letter and lay back on her bed, propping her head up with a pillow as she read through it again. The note was so calculated. Josie could see that now—the cool, collected machinations of the Jo that everyone here seemed to know and loathe.

Why hadn't she seen it before? Hard to say. Josie had seen what she wanted to see: a perfect family and a boyfriend who adored her.

But now, Josie had the upper hand. It was what Jo omitted from her note that was the most interesting. No mention of

Josie's mom at Old St. Mary's. No explanation as to why she'd tricked Josie into switching places. She didn't want Josie to know that she'd reunited with her mom.

Because Jo and her mom had no intention of switching back.

"What are you thinking?" Nick asked softly, lying down next to her.

"They don't want to come back," she said. "Jo and her mom. I've seen it in my dreams. Dr. Byrne is terrified. She's lost the vial of the injectable formula, which was her only bargaining chip. She knows she'll be blamed for sabotaging the experiment and for your brother's death. And I think she's more scared of the Grid than anything."

"She should be." Nick inched his body toward her. "And what about Jo? Why doesn't she want to come back?"

"Jo's got her sights set on . . ." Josie stopped. She almost said, ". . . on my ex-boyfriend." But she hadn't told this Nick about his doppelgänger in her world, and her relationship with him. Nick gazed at her as he lay on his side next to her, his face so close to her own she could feel his breath against her cheek. She couldn't tell him. Not now.

"Got her sights set on what?"

"Nothing." Josie quickly changed the subject. "What I don't understand is why."

Nick tilted his head. "What do you mean?"

She propped herself up on one arm. "I mean, why risk opening the portal? Why risk the exchange? For an injectable they have no use for? It doesn't make sense."

Nick pushed himself up on one elbow so his face was even with hers once more. "You're right. If there aren't Nox in your world, the antidote is useless."

"Right," Josie said. "And there aren't any . . ."

Her voice trailed off. She remembered something, a glimpse of a wing outside her kitchen window, something moving in the darkness, and a far-off scream that sounded like metal grating against a chalkboard. She'd passed it off as an eagle or an owl at the time, but now after what she'd seen of the Nox, the horrible realization dawned on her.

"Oh no," Josie said, flopping back onto her pillow. "I'm such an idiot."

"Hardly," Nick said with a short laugh. "You're like the smartest person I've ever met."

Normally the compliment would have made Josie all goo-goo, but the mysterious deaths that had plagued her hometown suddenly all made sense. She'd been so stupid not to see it before.

"Dr. Byrne wants the vial," she said, her mouth suddenly dry, "because there *are* Nox in my universe."

"Wait," Nick said. "I thought you said there weren't any?"

"There *weren't*," she said. "Were not. As in past tense." She gave Nick a rough sketch of the dead bodies that had been turning up in the woods outside of town. Victims of animal attacks, partially eaten, always killed at night.

"It's the Nox," Nick said. "No doubt about it. But how?"

Josie shook her head. "The same way the vial got here?"

"Hm." Nick scooted closer to her on the bed. "Well, if it's just one, you probably don't need to worry much. Then it can't breed. But if there's more than one, it could be catastrophic."

"The deaths have been getting more frequent," Josie said, remembering what Jo said in the last dream. "It went from sixteen in six months to like six in a week."

Nick lowered himself to the bed again, resting his head on her pillow. "Then that's exactly why Dr. Byrne wants the formula. If the Nox are breeding, she'd be the only person who knows how to get rid of them."

"And in my world I bet that would be worth a hell of a lot more than two hundred million."

"Yeah," Nick said softly.

Josie rolled over to face him. Nick was so close to her, lying there on her bed. He stared directly into her eyes and smiled, so sweet and adorable. She wanted to sink into his arms. Screw the antidote. Screw the Nox. She could stay here, with Nick, forever. No one would know. She leaned her body closer to his, and closed her eyes.

A knock on the door sent Josie and Nick scrambling to different sides of the bed. "Princess?" Mr. Byrne asked. "Are you in there?"

Nick stood by the window while Josie grabbed a pillow and hugged it to her chest so Mr. Byrne couldn't see her blushing. "Yes, Daddy."

The door swung open and the smiling, good-natured face of Mr. Byrne sauntered into the room. "Nicholas!" He walked right up to Nick and shook his hand. "It's good to see you again." Mr.

Byrne glanced around the room, looking for something. "Were you two studying?"

"No, sir," Nick said. "I just drove Jos . . ." He swallowed. "I just drove Jo back from Old St. Mary's."

"Ah, I see." He smiled at Josie, sad and understanding. "Well, I'm glad my Josephine had a friend with her today. How was she?"

"Better," Josie said enthusiastically. "It's kind of amazing, actually."

Mr. Byrne nodded. "Well, in that case, I'm sure I'll have an easier time convincing Dr. Cho to let her come home."

Josie's face lit up. "Really?"

"I have a conference call with her doctors set up for tomorrow." He winked at Nick. "At least my position is good for something, eh?"

"That's fantastic news, Mr. Byrne."

"Speaking of jobs," Mr. Byrne said. "Nicholas, how was your tour of the Grid?"

Nick shuffled his feet. "Excellent. Very, um"—he cast a quick glance at Josie— "enlightening."

Mr. Byrne patted Nick on the back. "Good to hear. Care to stay for dinner?"

"No, thank you. My mom's expecting me." Nick pulled his car keys from his pocket as if ready to go.

"I see. Well, give my love to your parents, and I hope"—he cast a knowing glance Josie's way—"we get to see more of you."

Josie could have died from embarrassment, made no less horrific by the fact that Mr. Byrne wasn't actually her father.

"Yes, sir," Nick said. "Thank you, sir." He paused next to Josie as he passed by. "See you at school tomorrow?"

"Of course."

"Good night, Josephine."

She didn't even mind her full name.

3:59 A.M.

"We should go back for it then," Jo says. "If it's that important."

"I can't go back." Her mom sits on the sofa, her head cradled in her hands. "They'll know I have it."

"Had it."

"Same thing."

"No, we have to assume no one has found it, and leave it at that."

"But what if—"

"Don't say it." Her mom holds up her hand for silence.

Jo pauses, mustering her courage. Her mom is not going to like this. "What if I told you," she begins, "that someone's taking care of it?"

Her mom's head snaps up, her eyes enormous, wild. "What do you mean?"

"I mean, I have someone looking for it. Someone we can trust."

Her mom launches to her feet and grabs Jo by the shoulders. "What have you done?"

Jo forces a laugh. "It's fine. We can trust her."

"We can't trust anyone," her mom whispers.

FORTY-TWO

12:35 P.M.

JOSIE WAS JUST SITTING DOWN AT HER SOLO lunch table when she got the text from Penelope.

Meet me in the lab. Stat.

She didn't need to be told twice.

Penelope bounced excitedly on her stool as Josie rushed into the classroom.

"Well?" Josie asked.

"I was there all night," Penelope started. She spoke in quick, disjointed phrases, the hallmark of caffeine-fueled sleep deprivation. "At the warehouse. Set up the laser and did some modifications. Nothing big."

"You modified a free-electron laser?" She knew Penelope was a wiz, but this bordered on genius.

"Yeah, yeah," Penelope said. "It's just commercial grade. No biggie. I couldn't figure out, you know, how the laser and the contents of the vial were going to work to create a portal. I thought maybe a rapid cycling of photons might disrupt the gravitational field, but realized that the laser would have to be like a bazillion times stronger."

"Crap."

"Wait," Penelope said dramatically. "My cousin works at Goddard. For NASA."

Josie snorted. "Figures." Between Goddard and Fort Meade, suburban Maryland in either universe was packed with scientists.

"She has access to an X-FEL," Penelope continued with a smile. "I don't think we can take it to your house, but maybe I can figure out how to control the beam so we don't get another *boom*." She made the same explosion gesture with her hands.

"Let's stay away from the *boom*s, okay?" Josie'd had enough explosions to last a lifetime.

"Right." Penelope laughed. "If I can figure out how to control the beam, maybe we can just move the mirror to the lab, and try to open another portal to send you home."

"Awesome," Josie said.

"And there's something else," Penelope said. She scratched her cheek.

"Yeah?"

"You know that injectable you found? The one that's supposed to suck the Nox into a black hole?"

Josie nodded.

"Any idea how it works? I mean, it seems to me that the Nox

would actually have to be inoculated with the formula first. In order for it to work."

Again, Josie nodded. "That makes sense."

"Which seems kind of difficult, considering we can't actually catch them."

Josie hadn't really thought about it before, but Penelope was absolutely right. "So the formula is actually useless?"

Penelope shook her head. "Not necessarily. But I was thinking, since I'm already messing around with cycling the laser blasts, there might be a way to create the same effect with the micro black holes without actually having to inoculate the Nox."

"Crop-dusting the Nox with the formula and then cycling the beams like scattershot. You could literally eradicate hundreds at a time." Josie's eyes grew wide. "Penelope, that would be unbelievable."

Penelope shrugged. "We'll see if I can make it work."

"When can you go?"

"I'm bailing on fourth period and driving up to Greenbelt to check it out. Hopefully we can aim for tomorrow night."

Josie placed her hand on Penelope's shoulder. "Thank you," she said. "Without you I'd be stuck here."

Penelope shrugged. "It's nothing."

"Well, in this universe or any other, I officially owe you a favor."

Penelope turned bright red and started gathering up her things. "I've got to get out of here. You and Nick will meet me tonight? At the usual place?"

"I wouldn't miss it."

Nick was right on time to pick her up. Just like she'd asked.

"Nicholas!" Mr. Byrne exclaimed as he opened the front door. He'd been two seconds ahead of Josie when the doorbell rang. "Good to see you again so soon."

Nick took the hand Jo's dad offered and shook it warmly. "Mr. Byrne."

"You're here to pick up Josephine?" There was a playful quality to his voice.

"Yes, sir. We have a school project we need to work on."

"Somewhere well lit, I hope?"

"Of course, sir. We'll be at a friend's house, and my car is equipped with dual-mounted megawatt LEDs on the roof."

Mr. Byrne stepped aside. "Very well, son. Very well. Take care of my princess for me." He bent down and kissed the top of Josie's head.

"Thanks, Daddy," she said as she followed Nick out to his car.

The sun was barely hanging above the horizon as Nick backed his SUV out of the driveway. "Thanks, Daddy," he mocked in a high falsetto. "You've really got this Jo routine down."

Josie rolled her eyes. "I have to. Poor guy's been through enough, don't you think? Last thing he needs is to know his daughter is hiding out in a parallel universe with his estranged wife."

"I guess you're right."

Josie shifted in the passenger seat to face him. "You guess?"

Nick shrugged. "His job is closely linked to the Grid, you know. I mean, in theory, he's one of them."

"Yeah, okay, Madison."

"Hey!" Nick said, hitting the brakes a bit too fiercely as he approached a stop sign. Josie whipped forward as the seat belt tightened across her chest.

"Be careful!" Josie snapped.

"Madison's heart's in the right place, okay? She may be a bit abrasive—"

"That's the understatement of the century."

Nick sat at the stop sign. "Yeah, but it doesn't mean she's wrong."

Josie pursed her lips. For some irrational reason, she was ticked off by the way Nick defended Madison. "Your girlfriend's been nothing but a bitch since I got here, so excuse me if I don't jump on the 'rah-rah, Madison' bandwagon, okay?"

Nick gritted his teeth. "She's not my girlfriend."

"I don't know," Josie said, attempting to sound as flippant and disaffected as possible. "You two seem pretty simpatico."

Nick turned his eyes back to the road and continued the drive. "We dated. Briefly."

"I knew it," Josie said under her breath.

"Look," Nick said sharply. "We went on a few dates last year, but Madison's . . . intense. About everything. It didn't work out." He paused, then shook his head. "And she was *never* my girlfriend, okay?"

"Whatever."

"What do you care anyway? It's not like you're sticking around. As soon as we find a way to get you home, you're out of here. Right?"

That was the reality. Ever since she'd tried to get back through the mirror and found a concrete wall in her path, Josie had been singularly focused: find a way home. This wasn't her world. This wasn't her life. And yet for some reason the idea of leaving here—of leaving *him*—made Josie instantly sick to her stomach.

Nick stopped at a light and turned to her. "Right?" he repeated.

His face was drawn, taut like a boxer anticipating a blow to the face. Josie wanted to grab him, to hold on for dear life and never, ever let go.

She'd come here hoping for one day in a perfect life, one day to make amends. A happy family and loving boyfriend, a school full of friends. She'd known it would all be an illusion and a lie, but she hadn't cared. For one day, everything would be perfect.

Then everything had gone wrong.

But as she sat in the car gazing into Nick's eyes, she realized that something had happened to her. Nick Fiorino, the great love of her life. Except this wasn't Nick. Not really. He was a completely different person. Smart, brave, considerate. He took care of his friends, was trying to help save the people they loved. Unselfishly, since he knew his brother was already dead. Even Josie, someone he'd just met. He'd gone out of his way to help her. He'd been the one person she could trust, and the idea of leaving *this* Nick made her physically ill.

She wanted to tell him. All about her Nick and Madison and how they'd betrayed her, about how she'd come to his world for a fantasy, and about how somewhere along the way he'd become more important to her than she could have predicted.

She wanted to tell him everything.

But she couldn't.

"Right," she said, dropping her eyes.

Nick slowly turned back to the road. "That's what I thought."

7:41 P.M.

The sun had completely dipped below the horizon by the time Nick pulled his SUV into the warehouse. It was dark and empty.

The only light was from the floods on the top of Nick's car. He cut the engine, and Josie strained her ears, listening for the telltale flapping and shrieking of the Nox.

It felt strange to be in the near-darkness as Josie slipped out of the car. Nick had pulled a giant flashlight from the backseat of his car and walked off, presumably to fire up the generator, but as Josie stood there beside the car, she had the distinct feeling that she wasn't alone. She could have sworn she heard a shuffling noise like someone darting around in the dark recesses of the abandoned space, and her eyes must have been playing tricks on her. She thought she saw something move. A shadow in the blackness, darker than the dark, if that was even possible.

"Hello?" she called into the shadows.

No answer. Josie shook her head. It had been so many days since she'd experienced actual darkness, her ocular membranes were no longer capable of adapting to the lack of light.

The generator whirred to life, flooding the warehouse in artificial glow, and Josie jumped.

"There's no one here," Nick said. He pulled the chain, rolling the gate back into place.

"Oh." Josie peered into the back of the warehouse, now bathed in the orangey overhead lights. Nick was right. No one there.

After he secured the door, Nick wandered over to the fridge, mumbled something to himself, then closed the door without taking anything. Josie watched him, unsure what she should do next. He was clearly annoyed with her, angry almost. She felt like she was to blame, and yet how could she be? What did he want from her?

Nick plopped himself down on a sofa and picked up one of the books on interdimensional travel Penelope had left there. He flipped through the pages quickly, and kept his eyes focused on the book. The signal was loud and clear: *I don't want to talk*.

Josie shrugged and sat down on the sofa opposite him. Suddenly, she was exhausted. The excitement at Penelope's discovery had long since evaporated, and Josie was left feeling fatigued and sore. Every muscle in her body ached as if she'd run back-to-back marathons in stilettos. She leaned her head against the armrest and closed her eyes, wishing she had a sleep mask with her. The orange glow beyond her closed eyelids only enhanced the dull ache emanating from the back of her head. Never in her life had she craved the darkness so desperately. Josie's breath began to slow. Sweet, calm black . . .

Josie didn't realize she'd fallen asleep until she felt a hand over her mouth.

"Shh!" Nick hissed in her ear.

Josie's eyes flew open and panic immediately welled up inside her. It was completely silent in the warehouse; the gentle, ever-present whir of the generator was gone. And though Josie could feel Nick's breath against her cheek as he held his face close to hers, she couldn't see him.

The warehouse was completely dark.

Josie lay there frozen, Nick's hand still covering her mouth, his body pressed tightly next to hers on the sofa. She couldn't see any movement in the warehouse, but as before she had the sensation of motion. A shuffling sound. A breath. Was she hearing things?

Nick made no move for the car. He was listening intently. He held his breath and didn't move a muscle.

That's when Josie heard it. In the distance.

The shrieks.

"Come on!" Nick yelled, all pretense at subterfuge evaporated. He grabbed her hand and hauled her off the sofa. She stumbled over the coffee table as Nick dragged her forward. The shrieks of the Nox intensified quickly, like they moved at light speed. Josie and Nick didn't make it halfway to the car before the windows at the top of the warehouse exploded.

A coordinated attack, bursting in through several windows at the same moment, as if directed to do so. Screams filled the warehouse and in an instant Josie was surrounded by the sensation of flapping. The air beat around her as countless leathery wings swooped at them. Glass rained down from the roof, and though Josie could feel the broken shards crunching beneath her feet as Nick feebly dragged her toward the car, she could hear nothing but the deafening roar, the piercing screams of the Nox.

Josie felt Nick trip in the darkness, his hand ripped from hers.

She dropped to her knees, desperately searching for Nick as the wings continued to swarm around her. Her hand caught hold of his leg, motionless on the ground. As she blindly felt upward toward his face, she touched thick, leathery skin.

The Nox flinched when she touched it, but the monster didn't move. It felt smaller than she'd imagined: about the size of a pit bull. It sat there, perched on Nick's chest.

A predator claiming its prey.

She lashed out at the beast, punching at it fiercely with her fists.

The Nox shrieked, not the ferocious war cry that filled the rest of the warehouse, but a cry of fear and surprise. As if it didn't know she was there.

Josie paused in confusion. Instead of attacking her, the Nox beat its wings desperately and flew away.

Josie had no time to contemplate her strange encounter with the Nox. She crawled on top of Nick, feeling for his face. Her fingers touched something wet and slick. Blood. She tried to feel for a heartbeat, for movement from his lungs, but the swarm whipped up to a frenzied pitch. The air whistled around her as if the Nox were circling above, preparing for a final attack. Just like in the woods that night. In the chaos, she'd completely lost track of where she was. Could she carry Nick to the car? Could she find it in the blackness? She heaved his shoulder, desperate to move him away from the attacking swarm of invisible beasts that seemed to fill every inch of space in the warehouse. She got to her feet, looping her arms under his, and lifted with every ounce of strength she had left. She staggered backward, dizzy and disoriented. She had to make it to the car. She had to. They were going to die if she didn't. . . .

Suddenly, the weight of Nick's body was gone. She felt him lifted upward by an unseen force. She grasped at his arm. The Nox had him. They were carrying him away.

"No!" she screamed. She clung to Nick's arm, desperate to keep him away from the Nox.

A hand grabbed her wrist, prying it off Nick's arm.

A *human* hand.

"Nick?" Josie yelled. He was alive. They were going to get out of there together.

"Quiet," a voice said close to her ear. "Follow me."

Josie stopped. It wasn't Nick's voice, but it was familiar. Harsh and raspy. She'd heard it before, whispering in her ear amid the chaos of a Nox attack.

The man in the woods.

FORTY-THREE

9:05 P.M.

"WHO ARE YOU?" JOSIE REMEMBERED THE SHAD-
ows she'd seen in the darkened corners of the warehouse ever since
Nick had first brought her there. A trick of the eye, an overactive
imagination. Not so much. But where had the man come from?
Materialized out of thin air? Magically risen out of the ground?

"Quiet!" he barked.

Josie shook herself from her daze. She reached out and felt his
shoulder, tall and strong in front of her. He held Nick cradled in
his arms.

"This way."

Not that she had a choice. Stay in the warehouse and be eaten
alive by monsters that live in the darkness or follow the mysterious stranger down the rabbit hole.

Mysterious stranger it was.

He led her across the warehouse to what must have been the
far corner beyond the parking area. He moved slowly, unhur-
ried, which seemed odd considering the swarm of creatures that

continued to circle just above their heads. It took Josie a few moments before she realized they weren't being attacked. It took her even longer to realize that while Nick had been viciously overcome within seconds of the Nox bursting into the warehouse, she didn't have so much as a scratch on her.

The Nox left her alone.

What was going on?

The stranger paused, and Josie felt him bend down. Or so she thought. He continued to move forward and as Josie followed, she realized he was going down a set of stairs.

The steps were rickety wood, judging by the way in which each step sagged ever so slightly under her weight. Only a dozen or so, and Josie landed on a firm dirt floor.

"Wait here," the stranger said. He squeezed past her in the passageway. He was tall—Nick's height, at least—but broader and heavier. Josie's eyes strained against the blackness of the space, trying to get a glimpse of the stranger, but other than an outline of a body disappearing up the stairs—even blacker than the blackness around her—she couldn't make out anything.

She heard a distant thump, and the shrieks of the Nox were instantly muffled. A trapdoor. He really had come through the floor.

"Who are you?" Josie asked again, now that she could actually hear her own voice. Above in the warehouse, the shrieking intensified, punctuated by thumps on the floor.

"They can hear you," the stranger said, ignoring her question. She could hear him breathing in the darkness. "They get angry when deprived of prey. We should keep moving."

Josie took a step back. Her foot nudged something on the ground. Nick's leg where his body lay motionless. "We're not going anywhere with you," she said. Her voice sounded small in the darkness.

"*You,*" he said firmly, "don't have to go anywhere. But *he's* coming with me. He needs medical attention."

"Is . . . is he . . ." Josie felt the weight of Nick's motionless body behind her on the ground. She pressed against his lifeless form, afraid to ask the question on the tip of her tongue.

"He'll be fine. I think."

She felt a figure move past her in the darkness. She stepped aside as the stranger grunted against the weight of Nick's body. "This way."

Josie placed a hand on either side of the narrow passageway and slowly followed the sound of the stranger's shuffling footsteps. She stooped, worried she'd clock her head against a low beam, and picked her way cautiously across the uneven ground. The floor was soft dirt, dry and powdery; their footsteps kicked up small clouds of the stuff that tickled Josie's nose and made her eyes water. It was significantly warmer in the passage than the late spring evening above, and the heat accentuated the stench of mold and damp cardboard that permeated the space.

They hadn't gone far before a creak from in front of her stopped Josie in her tracks.

"Watch your step," the stranger said. "They're rotting away on this end."

Great. Josie felt with her foot for the first step, then tentatively tested her weight. It was bouncy, but sound, and clearly the stranger had gone ahead of her carrying Nick. Without a second thought, Josie climbed the stairs.

Like the passageway through which they'd just come, the room Josie stepped into was almost completely dark. Almost. Unlike the metal walls of the warehouse, this room had been constructed with wooden beams, and slivers of grayish-blue moonlight filtered in through the weathered slats. A hint of light in the utter blackness, but it was enough to show the dimensions of the space—no more than ten feet in any direction, windowless with a low roof and a thin outline of a door on the opposite wall. She wrinkled her nose as an acrid, chemical smell wafted toward her, mixed with the stale stench of unwashed bodies.

There was only one place they could be.

"We're in the storage shed," Josie said out loud. "Next to the warehouse."

"Yes."

Dust billowed up in amorphous clouds as the stranger shuffled across the dirt-layered floor. He grunted, then the metallic creak of ancient mattress coils signaled that he had deposited Nick on a bed of some kind. More shuffling, then a single flame burst to life, strong and unwavering, from a table in the middle of the room. Not the feeble flickering of a candle—this was the powerful, gas-fueled light of a Bunsen burner, which illuminated a bedlam of beakers and cylinders, test tubes and flasks cluttered around a low-grade laser rig on a large metal table. The orange light of the burner barely permeated the darkness, but Josie could see a shadow moving around on the far side of the table. The shadow of a man.

He walked quickly, purposefully back and forth from the table to a cot. Josie tentatively stepped around the table toward the body that lay unconscious on the bare mattress. Nick was motionless, and his thick, wavy hair looked matted and sticky with blood. She stared at him, desperate to catch a glimpse of movement from his body. A shudder, a slight expansion of the chest to prove he was still breathing. Anything.

The stranger remained cloaked in shadow even as Josie drew closer to him. She could see his outline, a dark silhouette that seemed to absorb the feeble moonlight streaming in through the tiny fissures in the wall. He sat on the edge of the cot and rolled Nick onto his side, then dabbed at the back of his head and neck. The stranger was utterly consumed with his task, seemingly unaware that Josie stood within arm's length.

"This wound is deeper than I thought," he mumbled to himself. "Going to have to stitch it."

"Shouldn't we take him to a hospital?" Josie said.

The stranger jumped as if he'd completely forgotten her presence. He turned to her, stared her straight in the face as the light from the burner illuminated his features, and suddenly all the life seemed to drain out of Josie.

There was no face.

The man had no face. At all.

From where she stood, Josie should have seen the articulated facial features of a human being: the sunken eye sockets, protruding nose, lips, chin.

Instead she saw nothing but a flat, featureless sea of black.

FORTY-FOUR

9:21 P.M.

JOSIE BEGAN TO TREMBLE. SHE WANTED TO FLEE and yet this man, this thing, had saved her life—twice—and currently held Nick's life literally in his hands.

"We can't take him to the hospital," he said calmly. "The people who sent the Nox to attack you will know you're still alive."

"Someone sent them?"

"It was a coordinated attack. Contrary to popular belief, the Nox can communicate with one another. And with humans."

"Those things can talk to us?"

The shadow man stared at her for a moment—or at least she assumed he did—then without answering her question, he slowly turned back to Nick. "He's going to require stitches to close this kill wound," he said. "I'll need your help."

The shadow man stood up and walked across the room to the table, and Josie heard rattling and scraping as he dug around in his clutter of science equipment. Help stitching up Nick's head?

Was she really going to let this *thing* near Nick with a needle and thread?

He returned to the cot, but Josie stepped in front of him. "Who are you?" she asked again, feeling the futility of her repetition. Then added, "*What* are you?"

A breathy, humorless laugh came from the shadow. "I might ask you the same question."

Josie straightened up, squared her shoulders, and held her head as high and mightily as she could, in her best Jo-like pose. "I'm Jo Byrne."

This time, the laugh was genuine. It burst from the shadow in a violent explosion, as if his body was unused to the expression. "Sure you are," he said at last. "Just like the woman locked up in Old St. Mary's is Dr. Byrne."

"It *is* my mom," Josie said truthfully. This shadow knew way too much about her.

He sobered up immediately. "I didn't say it wasn't your mom." He stepped right up to her, the movement a blurred shade in the dimly lit shed. Josie backed up instinctively until her legs were pressed against the edge of the cot. There was something terrifying about the flatness of the shadow man, like a thinking, living black hole that might suck her past the event horizon of his emptiness if she got too close.

He sensed her fear and backed away. "I'm not going to hurt you," he said. His raspy voice ached with indignation.

"I know." Much to her surprise, Josie actually meant it.

"Then can you step aside and let me save him?"

Josie gazed into the void that should have been his face. The darkness was impenetrable. If she shined a light directly onto his face, she doubted it would illuminate anything. It would be sucked into the darkness, where even the individual photons of light couldn't escape its pull. She was afraid, and yet she needed to trust this thing who had saved her twice from a gruesome death. She stepped aside. "What can I do to help?"

He knelt down beside Nick. "Hold his head. Keep it steady and still, especially if he starts to wake up. I don't have any anesthesia."

Josie's stomach did a backflip as she crouched at the top of the cot and took Nick's head firmly in her hands. *If he starts to wake up. Oh crap.*

The stranger got to work right away. Josie could see his hands moving in the dusky light, dark flashes that swirled around Nick's head. He worked quickly and confidently despite the dim conditions, as if he had absolutely no trouble seeing in the dark.

"They go for the brain stem first," the stranger said casually. Just making conversation while he sewed Nick's head back together. "Kill you or paralyze you. Doesn't matter. They've learned it's the fastest way to render us incapacitated."

Josie wasn't sure if she should respond, but the stranger rattled on, speaking ever more quickly.

"Most people don't know that. The fact that they learned how to hunt us. That's the part that should scare people the most. Not the claws."

"Or the beaks."

The shadow man tilted his head to the side. "You've seen them?"

Josie paused. She thought of the glimpses of wing and the flash of a beak that she'd seen in the darkness. Never distinct, never for longer than a split second, but . . .

"Yes. I've seen them."

"I see." He didn't seem surprised. "They're not quite beaks," he continued. He drew his arm up, pulling the thread taut, then dove back down. "More like a pickax. They skewer prey, then feed on it."

For a moment, Josie forgot her fear. "You can see them too?"

"Yes, I see them," he said. Bitterness dripped from every word. "I see them every night."

"Oh." It made sense, in a way. They were both beings of darkness. Two inhabitants of a strange world. But that still didn't explain why Josie could see them.

He pulled his arm up one last time, then with a flourish, tied a knot in the thread. A flash of metal scissors, a sharp snip, and Nick's wound was closed.

Josie stroked Nick's stiff, matted hair. "Will he be okay?"

"Yes," the stranger said. "I think so." He sat on the floor and watched the rhythmic heaves of Nick's breath. "You're in love with him."

It was so direct. Not a question at all. "Yes."

"What will happen when you go back?"

How the hell did he know so much about her? "Go back? I don't know what you're—"

"Save it," he said. "I know. I know about the mirror and the portals."

The portals. With an *s*. Plural. He knew it wasn't Dr. Byrne in Old St. Mary's. He knew that Josie wasn't Jo. There was only one person Josie could think of who could have known both of those things.

"You're Tony," Josie gasped. "You're Nick's brother."

He sighed. A slow intake followed by a sharp, almost painful exhale. "Yes."

"You've been here all along, keeping an eye on Nick." The missing food. It had been Tony.

"Yes."

"But you're supposed to be dead," Josie blurted out. "How . . . I mean, why?" Crap, what did she mean?

Beneath her hands, Nick stirred on the bed. He twitched like a man jolted awake by a horrific nightmare, then moaned.

Josie stroked his hair, careful not to touch the recently stitched-up wound. "Easy," she said softly.

"Josie?" He pushed himself up on his elbows and lifted his head to look at her. Even in the dim light, Josie could see the pinched look of pain wash over his face. His elbows slid out from under him, and he hung his head. "What happened?" he said, his voice muffled by the thin mattress.

"The Nox," Josie said. "They attacked the warehouse."

"Right."

"We . . ." Josie glanced at the shadow that was Tony Fiorino. "We barely made it out alive."

"My head." Nick reached his hand around and tentatively

tapped the back of his head. He took a sharp breath.

"We had to stitch you up," Josie said. "After the attack."

Nick grabbed Josie's hand. "We?" His eyes darted back and forth. He squeezed Josie's hand so tightly she thought her fingers might burst as he hauled himself into a sitting position. "Who's here?"

"Um . . ." Josie looked at Tony. How was she supposed to break this news?

"Hey, Nicky," Tony said, saving her the effort.

Nick stiffened. "That's not possible."

Tony tried to sound light and easy. "I'm afraid it's true."

Nick dropped Josie's hand. "I don't believe it."

"He saved us," Josie said. "He carried you out of the warehouse."

"Tony's dead. My brother is dead."

"I wanted to tell you earlier but . . ." Tony paused. "It's complicated."

Nick turned his whole body to face Tony. Josie scooted around to the side of the cot and watched as the harsh, set lines of Nick's jaw bulged and rippled. His eyes scanned the storage shed, looking for signs of his brother. They passed right over the shadow of Tony once, twice.

"I'm right here, Nicky."

Nick started. He hadn't expected the voice to be so close. Still, his eyes couldn't focus on the outline of Tony's body. "Tony?"

Against the dusky glow of the Bunsen burner, Josie watched as Tony reached out and touched Nick on the arm. Nick's eyes flew to the spot, then grew wide as they distinguished the shadowy outline of Tony's hand on his. Nick traced the shadow with his eyes: up the arm to the shoulder, then around the head and down the front of the body, encompassing his brother's entire form. "Oh my God," he whispered.

FORTY-FIVE

9:35 P.M.

"I KNOW," TONY SAID. "BELIEVING I WAS DEAD might have been better than this."

"How?"

"It's a long story."

Nick reached his hand behind his back, groping blindly for Josie's hand. When his fingers found her own, he laced them together. "We're not going anywhere."

Tony walked to the far side of the table. He turned up the flame on the burner, which shifted hues from orange to bluish white, casting a brighter light across the room. For the first time, Josie really saw Tony. His outline was sharp and defined against the lit interior of the shed, and though there were no defined features to his form, there was depth to the shadow, an infinite void that was there but not there. To say that he was dark or black didn't do justice to the intensity of what he was. His body was like the absence of light, the opposite of light. There wasn't a surface for light to reflect off or illuminate, and judging by the fact that there was no shadow cast by his body on the floor or walls, it was as if the light was absorbed by his very being.

"Something happened that day in the lab," Tony started. The voice sounded so real and normal, like a regular human body was in the room talking to them instead of a wraith.

"The explosion," Nick said. He squeezed Josie's hand.

"Project Raze had exhausted almost every possibility: vaccines with killed Nox cellular matter, toxoids, live viruses that were supposed to infect the Nox population, DNA and photon therapies, genetically engineered bacterial proteins. Nothing worked. The Nox themselves seemed immune to everything we threw at them."

Tony leaned his arms against the table. It creaked in protest as it accepted his weight, which seemed so odd to Josie since his body appeared to have no depth.

"Then last year, we made a breakthrough. The reason we can't affect the Nox? *They don't exist in this universe.*"

Josie sat straight up. "What?"

Tony tilted his head to the side. "I thought you'd appreciate that. Just like you, they come from another place."

"Is that why I can see them?" Josie said.

"Yes."

Nick stared at her. "You can see them?"

"Er, kinda," Josie said. "Just for like a second."

"Like a flash? Tony asked. "As if the Nox were illuminated by a spotlight for an instant?"

Josie's eyes grew wide. "Yeah. That's exactly what they look like."

"Interesting." Tony paced back and forth. "We'd always believed that the Nox were accidentally brought to our world through some sort of dimensional portal," Tony continued. "Which was only partially true. Their universe and our universe have somehow gotten stuck together, like two pages in a book. You're supposed to flip them separately, but suddenly you're going from page forty-eight to fifty-one."

"Brane multiverses," Josie breathed. "Just like Penelope suggested. That's how the Nox are coming into my world. Instead of two pages stuck together, now it's three. You're turning from page forty-eight to fifty-three."

"Smart girl." Tony continued to pace aimlessly behind the table, his shadow eating the light as he moved from point to point.

"But why can't we catch one?" Nick asked. "If they can attack us, kill us, feed on us, why can't we do the same to them?"

Tony laughed. "Who says we can't catch one?"

"But I thought . . . ," Nick started.

"That's what the government wants you to believe. The last thing they need is heavily armed lynch mobs tracking incredibly dangerous prey. They have government hit squads that are barely able to accomplish that. It would be a bloodbath if your average neighborhood watch tried to take matters into their own hands."

"Why is it so difficult to catch them?" Josie asked.

"They exist in a complex quantum state, without a fixed superposition," Tony said. "And they can shift between universes at will." He turned to Josie. "I think that's when when you can see them, in the instant that they phase shift, like they're cycling through the dimension you belong to."

"Wow," Josie said. "That blows the rules of quantum properties out of the water."

Nick shook his head. "I don't understand."

"They're like me," Tony said simply. "I mean, I'm here and I'm not. You can feel me and hear me and smell me when I choose to shift my mass into this universe. But as you can tell, I'm not quite of this world anymore. And not of any other. I'm something in between, the glue that's holding the pages of the book together."

"So the Nox are the same?" Nick asked, rubbing the circulation back into his wrists.

"Yes," Tony said. "They can shift their mass at will between our world and their own. And they've adapted to it relatively quickly, just like they adapted to a penchant for humans as dinner."

"The space in the portal," Josie said. She thought of the darkness that seemed to engulf her, the weight of an entire universe trying to squeeze the life out of her. She tugged on Nick's hand. "Remember when you were checking out the portal that day you tried to kill me?"

Nick flinched. "I wasn't going to kill you."

"Whatever. But remember the inky blackness that oozed all around you when the portal started to close?"

"Exactly," Tony said. "That's exactly what I am."

"*What* you are?" Josie asked. The viability of Tony's experimental antidote being a way home was quickly diminishing.

"I *am* the stuff of the portal now."

"How?"

"My first attempt at an injectable was an inoculation, designed for humans. Like the eventual formula, it was deuterium-rich, and the idea was to phase-shift humans ever so slightly so we could coexist in the same universe with the Nox without them even knowing we were there.

"The problem was that it was too dangerous to attempt a phase shift. I even injected myself with the antidote last year, in the hopes I could get the green light to attempt the experiment on myself, but I was shut down."

"I had no idea," Nick said. He sounded hurt.

"Sorry, Nicky. Sharing my work around the dinner table would violate about a half dozen nondisclosure agreements. We had a few Nox in captivity to experiment on—again, not dinner-table conversation—and I'd spent a year adjusting the formula to use it on *them* instead of *us*."

"Amazing," Josie said.

"We had injected two Nox, and Dr. Byrne was attempting to create a micro black hole to suck them beyond the event horizon before it collapsed on itself."

"So what happened?" Nick asked.

"The explosion. I was in the other room, testing the controls that would raise and lower the blast glass to expose the Nox to the beam. Dr. Byrne was in the main chamber, finishing the last calibrations. We hadn't even started the process when a blinding flash tore through the room. I'd never experienced anything so intense. It actually threw me to the ground."

"I remember," Josie mumbled.

"When I came to, your mom was sprawled on the floor and the Nox were gone."

"So that's how they got into your world," Nick said. "Two Nox, already breeding. That's not good."

Tony whistled. "No, not good at all." He shook his head. "Anyway, I helped who I thought was Dr. Byrne get to her feet and realized something was wrong. Her lab coat. Her hair. Her shoes. Physically she looked exactly like Dr. Byrne, but it wasn't her."

"My mom."

Tony sighed. "She was disoriented, confused. The lab was different, and then she saw me." He paused. "I didn't know yet what had happened to me, how the explosion had reacted with the antidote in my system. She completely freaked out."

Nick placed his hand gently on Josie's shoulder. "Your poor mom."

"I could hear boots pounding down the hallway outside the lab. I only had a few seconds to make a decision. I'm sorry I had to abandon her. I didn't know what else to do. I had to find out who wanted us dead, and I figured the best way to do that was to actually *be* dead."

"Because someone sabotaged the experiment?" Josie asked.

"Exactly. The security and medical teams arrived within moments of the blast. Once I realized what had happened to me, I literally disappeared into the shadows of the room and waited. The blast had knocked out the security cameras, so once they removed your mom from the lab, I had a few seconds to examine the blast radius. The laser itself exploded, not the deuterium."

"So anyone could have tampered with the laser," Nick said.

"In theory, yes."

"Even Dr. Byrne." Josie recalled the conversation she'd overheard in one of Jo's dreams. Jo's mom seemed anxious to get her hands on the vial that contained the antidote. Desperate, even.

"It makes the most sense," Nick said with a glance at Josie. "She could have had access to the equipment, and we know for a fact there was an insider willing to sabotage the experiment and sell your formula at a massive price tag."

"I suppose," Tony said. He sounded unconvinced. "But Dr. Byrne was a scientist. She was just as invested in the outcome of the experiment as Dr. Cho and I."

Josie's eyebrows shot up. "Dr. Cho?"

"Yes, she worked on my team."

Josie was on her feet in an instant. "Nick, Dr. Cho is the one 'treating' my mom at Old St. Mary's. I assumed she was a psychiatrist or something."

"Geneticist," Tony corrected. "She specialized in mapping the genetic code from the unstable tissue samples we'd managed to retrieve from the Nox."

"What are the odds it's the same Dr. Cho?" Nick asked.

"High." Tony began pacing again.

Nick turned to Josie. "What would she want with your mom?"

Tony walked faster this time, his dark silhouette a metronome's pulse between the two walls of the shed. "The antidote.

They'd want the formula for the antidote."

"But Dr. Byrne didn't develop it," Nick said.

"Yes, but she was the last one with it. There were two vials of it on her desk when we began the experiment. After the explosion, only one."

"It passed through the portal," Josie said. "With Dr. Byrne."

Tony caught his breath. "How do you know?"

Nick pulled the vial out of his pocket and handed it to Tony. "Because it passed back through."

"Amazing," Tony said.

"Yeah," Josie added. "And Dr. Byrne is desperate to get it back."

"With two breeding Nox, a swarm large enough to threaten the human existence could exist in just a few years." Tony handed the vial back to Nick. "There, as here, whoever controls the antidote would be very powerful. That's why I've been trying to re-create it here, in secret. I figured that way, no single government entity would have control over it. I'm only missing a powerful enough laser to make a real test. If it works, it would be enough to kill for."

Something clicked in Josie's brain. "Enough to kill for? Enough to send a swarm of Nox to attack?"

Tony stared at her, the faceless black giving no hint of emotion. "Yes, absolutely."

"They were sent after us?" Nick asked.

"Like I said, it was a coordinated attack," Tony said. "The generator was disabled. Someone knew where you would be and when."

Nick touched the back of his head and winced. "But how could they . . ." His voice trailed off and he turned suddenly to Josie.

She came to the same realization at the same time. The three of them were supposed to meet at the warehouse that night: Nick, Josie, and Penelope. "If they came after us, then they'll go after Penelope too."

Nick sprang to his feet. "Then let's get there first."

FORTY-SIX

10:15 P.M.

THE ONE GOOD THING ABOUT HAVING A POPULA-tion terrified to go out at night was that there was no traffic after the sun went down. Not that there would have been an abundance of joyriders out for a late-night drive in Josie's version of Bowie, Maryland, but in this world, there weren't even cops on the street. No all-night gas stations, no twenty-four-seven convenience stores with their bright red-and-green neon signs warming the night sky. Nothing. Even the streetlights were dimmed in areas with a low density of houses, or perhaps just areas that weren't as affluent. Money was power. Literally.

Nick raced through the suburban landscape, blasting through stop signs and blackened traffic lights. He hit a drainage ditch and the SUV jumped with such violence Josie's head smacked the roof. But she didn't say a word. She wished he could make the car go faster.

If anything happened to Penelope, it would be all Josie's fault.

Nick screeched to a halt in front of a large, well-lit tract home just a few miles south of town.

"Lights are on," Josie said. "Good sign." She started to open the door.

Nick laid a hand on her knee. "Maybe you should stay here."

"Why?"

Nick didn't even blink. "Just in case."

Josie jerked her leg away from his hand. "If something happened to her, it's my fault. I got her into this mess."

"This isn't all on you," Nick said firmly.

Josie looked away. She couldn't help thinking of her own friend Penelope back home. How, in the end, Penelope had been the only one there for her. This Penelope had done almost the same thing, and how did Josie repay her? By making her a target in a very dangerous game.

"Come on." Nick reached across Josie and unlatched the passenger door. He practically lay on her lap as he pushed the heavy door open just an inch, and held it there. The wound on the back of his neck—the price of his own role in helping Josie—was still red and swollen from the makeshift stitches. "Hurry up," he grunted. "Can't hold it all night."

Josie kicked the door open with her foot. "Thanks."

"Don't mention it." Nick sat up straight, wincing as he tossed his hair out of his face. "Let's go find her."

Everything seemed normal at Penelope's house. All the lights were on, including the one over the front porch. Nick rang the doorbell and waited. After a few seconds he tried again. They could hear the soft melody of the bell echoing through the house, but no one answered the door.

He tried the handle in case it was unlocked. No luck. "Come on," he said, grabbing Josie's hand. "Let's check the back."

Light streamed out of the kitchen and dining-room windows that faced the back of the house, and Nick and Josie had no difficulty staying in the bright swath of safety they provided. Josie could see dirty dishes in the sink—cleared from dinner, no doubt. But no one was home.

"Try her cell," Josie suggested.

Nick had called her a dozen times on the way over, but no one had picked up. "You think it'll be any different now?"

"If she's inside, we might hear it."

"Good point." Nick pulled his phone out of his jeans pocket and hit redial.

They stood still, ears straining against the deafening silence.

"Listen!" Nick heard it first. The harsh electronic ring of Penelope's phone. He turned to his right. "Over here."

He followed the ringtone around the corner of the house to the garage. The light from the windows ended there, and Nick and Josie had to backtrack around to the front of the house. He dialed again, and this time they could clearly hear the phone ringing from inside the garage.

"Maybe she left her phone in the car?" Josie said hopefully.

"Maybe."

Nick tried lifting the roll-up garage door, but it wouldn't budge. Without a word, he opened the rear door of his SUV and rummaged around in the back, emerging with a wire coat hanger. He unwound the hanger, and then stood on his tiptoes in front of the garage door. Gazing through one of the windows, he threaded the hanger up through the top of the door and used the hook to pull the emergency release lever.

"Voila!" he said, pulling the door free. It rolled up easily. "There's no door I can't—"

Nick froze midsentence, staring straight ahead into the garage.

There, huddled beside the car were two corpses, arms linked around each other. They were little more than skeletons, splattered with bits of gore. Their faces were unrecognizable; the flesh had been ripped off, exposing their skulls and empty eye sockets. Clumps of hair still clung to their scalps, and Josie could easily recognize Penelope's long, thick black mane. The body beside her, skeletal arms wrapped around her in an act of futile protection, was larger and heavier. Her father.

Josie tried to look away, but her eyes were locked in place.

The Nox had left very little. A hole in Mr. Wang's skull where they'd ripped into his brain matter. The clothing had been shredded in the mad frenzy to pick every last ounce of flesh from their bones. Blood splattered the side of the white minivan and pooled around the bodies, streaming down toward the driveway by the sickening force of gravity. It threaded its way toward Josie, who stood rooted in place. Her eyes followed the stream of blood as it seemed to have an intelligent route in mind: right to her. Like Poe's tell-tale heart, it pointed out their killer.

"Don't look." Nick slipped a strong arm around her waist and pulled her away from the garage.

She turned on him fiercely. "Don't look? How can I not look? How can I not picture their last moments, clinging to each other as the Nox overwhelmed them?" She pounded on his chest with both of her fists. "How can I not think of that? How can I not hear their screams?"

She was sobbing, hysterical, and uncontrollable. Her breaths came spastically, like her body was fighting against itself to continue to function properly. She wanted to run into the darkness and scream for the Nox to come at her, to take her. She didn't care what they were. She didn't care where they came from. She'd rip them limb from limb if she had to, just as they had done to Penelope and her dad.

"There's nothing we can do," Nick said. He held her firmly to his chest, as if he was afraid he was going to lose her.

"It's my fault," Josie sobbed. "It's all my fault."

"No, it isn't."

Josie pushed away from him. "How would you know?" Why wouldn't he let her have this moment of suffering and blame?

"Okay, enough." It wasn't an angry statement, but the totality of it made Josie instantly pay attention. "Who is she?" Nick said softly. "Back in your world?"

She calmed herself almost by sheer force of will, and met Nick's steady gaze. "She was my friend. She was the only true friend I had. When my world fell apart, she was the only one there."

"Sounds like our Penelopes have a lot in common."

"Yeah."

"What happened?" he asked. "How did your world fall apart?"

Josie swallowed. Her mouth was oddly parched. She'd been avoiding this since the first moment she met Nick. It was this selfish, ugly secret she'd hidden from him, either out of shame for her own motivations in coming through the mirror in the first place, or because her feelings for the old Nick seemed somehow shallow in comparison to what she had grown to feel for this one. Which was utterly and totally ridiculous. Not only did she barely know him, but the majority of their time together had been spent actively trying to return Josie to her own world. Not exactly the foundations of a long, healthy relationship.

But now, with her world crumbling around her once again, Josie felt like she had nothing left to lose. She might as well tell him the entire truth. Maybe he'd be disgusted by what he learned, and any affection, any feelings he'd developed for her over the last few days would evaporate entirely. At least then it would be easier for her to leave.

"Madison," she said, staring at her shoes. Then the words flowed so quickly she couldn't have stopped them with a concrete wall. "Madison was my best friend." She looked up at Nick, his face deeply shadowed by the harsh high beams from his car. "Until I caught her sleeping with my boyfriend." Josie's stomach backflipped as she opened her mouth to drop the ultimate bomb. "She slept with you."

"The other me." Neither his face nor his voice reflected any emotion. "He cheated on you with your best friend."

"Yes."

"I see."

I see. Josie tried to guess what he was thinking, but his expression was vacant. The slack muscles around his face looked more like the complete and total absence of emotion, the stereotypical blank slate. Either he was totally unable to process the weight of what Josie had just told him, or he was so horrified by the realization that Josie had come through the mirror with the intention of reliving her broken relationship with her boyfriend's doppelgänger, that his mind had curled up into some sort of protective fetal position. Neither possibility was a good thing, and suddenly Josie felt like crawling inside her own skin, just to escape the empty, dark stare from Nick.

BRRRRRRRRING!

Josie screamed as a cell-phone ring ripped through the silence.

FORTY-SEVEN

11:49 P.M.

JOSIE AND NICK SPUN TOWARD THE GARAGE, momentarily forgetting the vomit-inducing sight before them. The ring was close by.

"Penelope's phone," Nick said.

Josie stared inside, eyes glued to the far wall of the garage in a futile attempt to avoid the corpses. But they were there, clasping each other on the cold, cement floor, leaning precariously against a car, and no matter how ferociously Josie willed her eyes not to glance down and to the left, they did. Just a flicker. But enough to refresh the sick feeling in the pit of her stomach.

Josie tried to focus on the bright, insensitive ring of Penelope's phone. "It's in there," she said.

Wow. That might have been the dumbest observation in the history of this universe, or any other.

The phone stopped. Just as suddenly as it had pierced the uncomfortable silence of the night, it ceased, and the lack of sound felt even more oppressive. Josie and Nick stood still. For what, Josie wasn't sure, but for some reason, she felt like she shouldn't move an inch. She even held her breath. Waiting.

As if on cue, the ring started again. This time, Nick didn't hesitate. He took a deep breath, then marched right into the garage.

Josie followed, her desire to help Nick outweighing her terror of the macabre scene inside. He paused near the bodies and Josie crept up behind him, cowering behind his frame as they listened intently for the ringing phone. It sounded nearby, but not directly in front of them, and the ring wasn't muffled by layers of clothing but sliced through the silence of the night with its clear, loud toll, cutting off abruptly.

Josie's eyes scanned the ground. No sign of the phone. She crouched down on her knees and peeked under the car. Nick knelt next to her and together they peered into the ominous darkness beneath the Wangs' station wagon.

The ringing started again, and immediately a dull blue light glowed from the inside of the wheel.

"There!" Josie cried.

Nick scampered around to the front of the car and reached behind the wheel for the phone. Josie was at his shoulder as he flipped it around and read the name of the incoming caller. Josie's stomach knotted up.

"Mads!" he said, answering the phone.

No answer from the other line.

"Madison?" Nick said. "Can you hear me? Something's happened. Where are you?"

Still no answer.

Nick glanced at Josie and his face tightened. "Who is this?" he demanded.

The line went dead.

The color drained from Nick's face. He tossed Penelope's phone to Josie while fishing his own from his pocket. He hit a speed-dial button, and they both waited while the phone rang.

"Come on," Nick said under his breath. "Answer."

"This is Madison," said a characteristically flat voice. "Not here. Leave a message."

Nick ended the call. Then dialed again.

"This is Madison. Not here. Leave a message."

Again.

"This is Madison. Not here. Leave a—"

"Dammit!" Nick roared. He scrolled back to his call screen and dialed another number. This time, the phone didn't even ring, just went straight to voice mail. "Jackson's not here." He dialed another number. "Is this Zeke or Zeb? Doesn't matter. Leave a message."

Nick stood there panting, staring vacantly into his phone. Josie didn't know what to say. *I'm sorry? I'm sure it's okay?* None of it was true. None of it was appropriate. Penelope was dead. Maybe Madison too.

"They're dead," Nick said. "All of them."

Josie gripped his arm. "You don't know that."

"Don't I? You said it yourself: the Nox were sent to attack us. Just like they were sent to attack Penelope."

The nagging voice in the back of her head. Something had

been off about the whole evening. "I don't—"

"And Penelope and her dad? The lights are on, Josie. Were on when we got here. So how do you explain both of them dead from a Nox attack?" He threw up his hands. "Don't you see? The Grid. They cut the power and used the Nox. This was intentional."

Josie squeezed her eyes shut. "They must have happened at the same time."

"Exactly," Nick said. "If they targeted us and Penelope, it's only logical everyone else was on a hit list too."

"Why would the Grid do this?" Josie said. The idea that the shadowy, nebulous corporation that Nick and Madison blamed for everything was somehow using Nox as hit men against a group of high-school students seemed so fantastical, Josie couldn't quite wrap her brain around it.

"I don't know," Nick said. He shook his head, defeated. "I really don't. We were just looking for our families, for the people we cared about who'd gone missing. My brother . . ." He paused. "Well, we know how that turned out. But the rest, we just wanted answers." He turned and gripped Josie's arms. "And honestly? We hadn't gotten anywhere before you showed up. So I have you to thank for helping me find Tony. And for getting me out of that warehouse." His eyes trailed down her face to her neck, then down to her arms. He paused, and his brows drew together. Again, his eyes scanned her face, but this time he wasn't looking at her so much as he was examining her. He looked around her head, to her ears and her neck. He lifted her hair off her back, then froze.

Suddenly, his hands gripped her again. Fiercer this time. The look of confusion vanished from his face, replaced by hardened features and a cold, dark stare.

"What's wrong?" Josie asked. She could feel his fingers digging into the soft flesh of her arms.

"Your neck. Your face."

"Yeah?"

"You weren't attacked. In the warehouse. There are no wounds on you anywhere."

It was true. She'd realized it after Tony led her down through the passage, but she'd put it out of her mind. The Nox hadn't touched her. Moreover, when she'd been trying to protect Nick, she'd touched one of them, and its reaction had been surprise and fear. Like it didn't realize she was there.

"How is that possible?" Nick growled.

"I don't know," she said, trying to stay calm. "But I'd think by this point, you'd actually trust me."

Nick's gaze faltered. "I—"

Brrrrrring!

Penelope's phone. Josie still gripped it in her hand. She glanced down and saw the name of the incoming caller. Madison.

Nick snatched the phone from her hand and put it on speaker. "Who is this? What have you done with Madison and—"

"Listen carefully," a woman said through the speakerphone. Her voice was familiar. "Are you ready?"

Nick glanced at Josie. She leaned in next to him and listened. "Yes."

"Your friends are safe. For now. Whether or not they stay that way is up to you."

Nick set his jaw. "What do you want?"

"You know what we want."

"You killed Penelope," Nick growled through gritted teeth.

"She wouldn't tell us what we wanted to know."

Josie realized how she knew the voice. "Dr. Cho," she said out loud.

Dr. Cho was silent a moment. "I seem to have both of you on the line. How convenient."

"You didn't have to kill her," Nick said.

"She didn't give us a choice."

Josie clenched her fists. First her mom, now Penelope. If she ever got her hands on Dr. Cho, she'd make a Nox attack look like a playground catfight.

"We're wasting time," Dr. Cho said. "You have the antidote. We are willing to exchange it for your friends."

Nick covered the mic with his hand. "How did they know?" he whispered.

Josie cringed. "I told my mom. In her cell at Old St. Mary's."

"Damn."

"Are you listening?" Dr. Cho said.

Nick scowled. "Yes."

"Bring the vial to your warehouse. Tomorrow."

"Bring my mom," Josie blurted out. Nick looked at her. *What are you doing?* he mouthed silently.

But Josie realized this might be their only chance to get her mom out of the hospital. She had to risk it. "Bring my mom and all the others. Our friends *and* their families."

Again, silence on the other end. Would Dr. Cho argue the point? Try to negotiate?

"Fine," she said at last. "Tomorrow at nightfall. Do not be late."

FORTY-EIGHT

12:05 A.M.

NICK SLOWLY LOWERED THE PHONE. "IT'S A trap," he said simply. "No way they'd just let us all waltz out of there."

"I know."

Nick handed the phone to Josie and pulled down the garage door. Then he slowly walked around to the door of his car and climbed in. Josie followed, and they sat in Nick's SUV, silently lost in their own thoughts.

Josie's eyes were fixed on the phone. Something wasn't right. How had it gotten inside the rim of the tire? Even in the chaos of a Nox attack, it couldn't have bounced off the concrete and into the tire, especially since Penelope was right there, huddled against that side of the car.

Unless she put it there.

Of course. Penelope had been trying to hide her phone, a last act of defiance. But why? Josie clicked on the phone and scrolled through the recently opened applications. Phone. Messaging.

Camera.

Josie caught her breath.

"What?" Nick asked.

Josie opened the photo gallery on Penelope's phone. There were three new photos, all of equations. "Holy shit," she said.

Nick leaned over her shoulder and squinted at the photos. "Math equations. Any idea what they mean?"

Josie scrolled through the photos, a lump rising in her throat. "Yeah," she said hoarsely. "Yeah, I do. This is what she was killed for."

"I don't understand."

"We were trying to figure out a way to use the X-FEL laser to open a new portal, and Pen had an idea of how we could get it to work without killing us all. Then she had another idea. Long story short, she thought we might be able to apply the same principle to the antidote, using it to phase-shift the antidote itself, *before* the subject's been inoculated. Which would make it about a million times easier to get rid of all the Nox." She looked at the equations again and laughed. "It's like crop-dusting on an epic, quantum level. And the only way the injectable might actually work. I can't believe no one thought of it before."

Nick whistled. "That's enough to kill for."

"Yeah." Josie paused, thinking about the various pieces of this conspiracy: Dr. Byrne and the Grid, Tony's formula, everyone's missing family members. A plan was forming in her mind. "If we go to the warehouse, we're dead, right?"

"Pretty much."

"Nox again, would you guess?"

Nick nodded. "Most likely."

"So what if," Josie said slowly, "what if we're ready for them?"

Nick looked at her sidelong. "What do you mean?"

"We have Penelope's equations. We have the formula. Why not just zap the Nox right out of the universe?"

Nick scratched the back of his neck. "We'll need a laser," Nick said. "You heard my brother. The one in the storage shed isn't powerful enough."

"Then we get him a laser. There's one up at Fort Meade?"

"Josie," Nick said, eyeing her cautiously. "We cannot break into Fort Meade. No way."

"Of course not." Josie smiled. "But Mr. Byrne has security access, right? You two can go borrow it."

"Mr. Byrne?" Nick looked skeptical. "I don't know if we should get him involved."

"What choice do we have?"

Nick was silent for a moment, mulling over the idea. "We don't," he said at last. "Make the call."

Josie pulled out her phone and powered it up. She'd turned it off at the warehouse and completely forgotten about it. As soon as the network connected, the phone beeped a dozen times in rapid succession. Voice mails, all from Mr. Byrne.

"Dammit," she said. "He's probably scared out of his mind wondering where I am."

"Well," Nick said with a sly grin, "maybe he'll be so relieved you're alive he'll do whatever you ask?"

Josie dialed Mr. Byrne's cell phone. "Or ground me for the rest of my life and ban me from ever laying eyes on you again."

"Josephine!" Mr. Byrne gasped, picking up a half second into the first ring. "Are you okay?"

"I'm fine," she said.

"Oh, thank God. I had no idea where you were." His tone changed from relief to anger. "Why was your phone off? Do you have any idea what time it is?"

"Daddy, I'm so sorry. Something happened and—"

He gasped. "Something happened? Where are you? Where's Nicholas?"

"Is he pissed?" Nick whispered.

"He's here with me," Josie said, smiling weakly at Nick.

"Well," Mr. Byrne said, his voice stern. "I'm seriously questioning his decision to keep you out this late. I thought he was more responsible than this. My phone has been ringing off the hook tonight with reports of elevated Nox attacks, and I can't get a hold of you; I don't have Nicholas's phone number. We're going to have a long talk when you get home tonight."

Josie looked up at Nick. "Yeah, he's pissed."

"I have every right to be pissed," Mr. Byrne said, laying special emphasis on the last word.

"I know. Daddy, let me explain."

"Where are you right now? Where are you calling from?"

Nick made a circle movement with his hand, motioning for Josie to get on with it. Right. They were running short on time.

"Daddy," she said, her voice crisp and businesslike. "I need your help."

"I knew something was wrong. Where are you?" She heard a jangling of car keys on the other end of the line. "I'm coming to get you."

"Daddy," she said slowly, trying to calm him down. "Daddy, you need to listen to me, okay? This is important."

Something about her tone must have struck a chord with Mr. Byrne. He paused, and when he spoke again he seemed calmer. "What is it, princess?"

Josie took a deep breath. She wasn't exactly sure how to say it gently, so she just blurted it out. "Mom needs our help." Well, at least that wasn't a lie. "But what I'm going to ask you to do could get us all in a lot of trouble."

"Princess, what is going on?" Mr. Byrne said slowly.

"It's about Project Raze," she said. Nick nodded, encouraging her to go on. "And the experiment Mom was working on when the accident happened."

"Okay."

"Well, long story short," she said, glancing over certain details like *your real wife's in a parallel dimension* and *she might be a traitorous fugitive*, "the explosion wasn't an accident. It was sabotage and . . ." Oh man, was she really going to lie to Mr. Byrne about this? The truth was stranger than anything she could make up.

"Yes?" Mr. Byrne prompted.

"And she needs us to prove that she didn't do it."

"Princess, how do you know all this?"

"Tony Fiorino," she said.

"Dr. Fiorino passed away," he said slowly, like he was talking to a three-year-old. "Remember?"

"No, he didn't." Time to go for broke. "Okay, I know this sounds crazy, but Tony isn't dead. He survived the explosion, but he's altered. Atomically altered. We saw him tonight, Nick and I. He saved us from a Nox attack and—"

"A Nox attack?" Mr. Byrne roared.

"Yeah, we're fine. I promise. But Daddy, I think the Grid sent the Nox. I think they knew we were going to try and help Mom. Tony saved us and he says he knows a way to help Mom too."

Silence on the other end.

Nick gave Josie a thumbs-up, but guilt ate at her conscience. Here she was, asking Mr. Byrne for help with something that might get him into a ton of trouble, and she was lying to him. She'd told him part of the truth. The important parts, more or less. It was true that they needed his help to save Josie's mom, and it was true that the experiment had been sabotaged. It was even true that Tony was still alive. Leaving out the other details was just her way of saving him a tremendous amount of confusion and grief. Wasn't it?

"What do you need me to do?" Mr. Byrne said at last.

"We need to use the X-FEL laser. The one up at Fort Meade."

"When?" Mr. Byrne asked.

"As soon as possible."

She heard Mr. Byrne let out a slow breath. "All right, princess. Whatever you need. I can probably get them access for a few hours."

"Actually," Josie said, wincing at what she was about to ask, "we need to get the laser out of Fort Meade."

Mr. Byrne cleared his throat. "You want me to *steal* the X-FEL prototype from a highly secure military base?"

"Um, yeah." It sounded so awful the way he said it.

"You realize I could be charged with treason if we're caught."

Josie sighed. "It's the only way to save Mom."

More silence. Josie bit her lip. Her entire plan hinged on whether or not Mr. Byrne could help them. What was she thinking? There was no way in hell he was going to help them smuggle a top secret laser out of Fort Meade. This was the stupidest idea she had ever had and now they'd have no way to—

"Okay, princess. Just tell me when."

Josie's heart raced. "We'll be there in ten minutes. I . . ." She hesitated. "I love you, Daddy."

And she meant it.

3:57 A.M.

JOSIE GRIPPED THE VIAL IN HER HAND. SHE wasn't sure what to expect. Clearly, Jo and her mother had no intention of letting Josie just waltz back into her own life. They wouldn't be going back to their own world willingly, so Josie was just going to give them no other choice.

She checked the time on the bedside alarm clock. Another minute clicked by. Any moment now. Josie curled her toes inside her reclaimed pink tweed Converse. She took a deep breath and tried to calm her racing pulse. This was it.

By now, Mr. Byrne, Nick, and Tony were smuggling a multi-million-dollar experimental laser out of Fort Meade.

But Josie wasn't with them. Mr. Byrne had insisted she stay behind out of fear for her safety—which was just fine. She had no intention of going up to Fort Meade that night.

Josie had a date to keep.

She stared at her reflection in the mirror as it began to ripple. The portal was opening. She had to play this perfectly, not let Jo suspect what she was really up to. She knew from experience that Jo was an excellent manipulator, but Josie wasn't the same girl she was a few days ago. She was smarter, wiser, and most important, she had something to fight for.

All she had to do was keep track of the seconds. Sixty of them. If she timed it perfectly, she'd have the advantage. Finally.

As soon as Jo's face came into focus, she gestured for Josie to pass through the mirror. Perfect. Much easier to stall when you could actually have a conversation. Josie reached her free hand before her and forcefully pushed her way through the gelatinous substance of the portal.

"Where is it?" Jo said the moment Josie's feet were firmly planted in her old bedroom.

Josie pursed her lips. "I'm doing well, thanks. How are you?" *Ten, eleven, twelve.*

"Funny," Jo said.

Josie surveyed the room. She'd expected Dr. Byrne to be there with her daughter, but instead, Jo stood alone in Josie's old bedroom. It looked pretty much the same, though Josie's eye immediately noticed that the objects on top of her bureau had been rearranged: perfume bottles aligned by height, unused jewelry organized by type and size, and the loose photos that had been shoved into a dresser drawer had been put into an array of matching frames, clustered together.

"So do you have the vial or not?" Jo tried to sound harsh, but there was a tremor in her voice, and she shifted her weight back and forth between her feet. *Twenty-three, twenty-four, twenty-five.*

Josie flashed a view of the vial in her hand, then clenched it firmly behind her back.

Jo's hand shot forward. "Give it to me."

"You said I could come home," Josie said, taking a step back. Her hand grazed the heavy, viscous surface of the portal.

Jo held up her hands. "No!" she squeaked. She glanced to her left, took a slow breath, and regained her usual composure. "I mean, not now."

Not exactly a surprise answer. "Why not?" *Thirty-three, thirty-four.*

Jo's eyes shifted to her left again. "Because . . ."

"Because we can't allow it." Josie knew that voice, only the version of it that she knew was more like a jingly domed bell, while this voice was harsh and staccato and lacking anything even remotely considered hospitable. Dr. Byrne stepped into the room from the hallway. She held a gun clasped tightly in her left hand, only it wasn't pointed at Josie but off to the side. With a violent yank, Dr. Byrne pulled someone into Josie's view. The straight, black hair. The watery dark eyes.

Penelope.

Josie clenched the vial even tighter. "What is she doing here?"

Penelope gasped. "Josie?" she said. Her eyes flitted back and forth between Josie and her doppelgänger. Josie could pinpoint the exact moment Penelope realized she wasn't in Kansas anymore. "Wait, which of you is Josie?"

"It's me, Pen," Josie said.

"But . . ."

"I know." Josie's voice choked off. She'd lost Penelope once and to have her here, in danger again—it was too much. Josie swallowed hard, forcing the emotion back into the pit of her stomach. She had to focus, now more than ever. Penelope's life depended on it. *Thirty-nine, forty.*

Penelope stared at the mirror, taking in all the details of Jo's room. She turned and took a quick look at Josie's bedroom, then back to the mirror. "Wow," she breathed.

"Enough," Dr. Byrne said, tugging at Penelope's arm. The gun wavered. "Give me the vial," Dr. Byrne said coldly. "And I'll let her go."

A new plan began to take shape in Josie's mind. A laser, right there in her house. Penelope would know how to use it, if only Josie could get her out of there. She could get Josie's dad, explain what she saw. Together, maybe they could force Dr. Byrne and Jo to switch back. . . .

"You can't come home," Jo said, in that soothing you-can-trust-me voice that had at one time been so seductive. "Okay? We can't both be here. Someone will find out the truth. But I can give you something else."

"Josephine, hurry."

Forty-seven, forty-eight. Josie shrugged. "Like what?"

"Nick. We can exchange them."

Josie practically laughed out loud. The idea of exchanging her old boyfriend for the Nick she'd grown to care for was ludicrous. "Not a chance."

Jo tilted her head to the side, her expertly waxed brows drawn together. She must have thought the idea of delivering Nick would have Josie salivating, and Josie's lukewarm reaction threw her for a loop. Her pinched face reflected confusion, but her eyes reflected something else. Something more like suspicion. "Why is that funny?"

Fifty-three, fifty-four, fifty-five.

The five-second countdown. Time to act.

Josie tossed her head. "I'll give it"—she nodded at Penelope—"to her."

"Fine." Dr. Byrne shoved Penelope. She stumbled forward, unable to take her eyes off Josie. Jo crept up behind her and stood at her elbow almost as sentry.

Josie caught sight of the mirror just as the image began to blur. Time was up.

She spun around and threw her arms around Penelope, enveloping her in a massive bear hug. "Tell my dad," Josie whispered directly into Penelope's ear. "She's not my mom. You've got to get the mirror free at exactly three fifty-nine p.m."

Penelope stiffened, unused to the physical contact. "Huh?"

Fifty-nine, sixty.

"Do it," Josie hissed.

"O-okay."

"Run," she whispered. "Now."

FIFTY

WITHOUT ANOTHER WORD, JOSIE BROKE HER embrace and tossed the vial toward Dr. Byrne, who lunged for it, dropping her aim momentarily. Josie had timed it perfectly. Just as the image muddied, she gripped Jo's arm as tightly as she could, then with all of her strength, she yanked Jo toward the mirror.

Jo was caught off guard, focused on her mom's attempt to catch the vial. She lost her balance, stumbled forward, and tripped on the bottom edge of the mirror. Josie gave one final heave, and Jo careened with her through the mirror.

She landed on top of Josie, momentarily knocking the breath out of her. Josie rolled onto her side and just caught sight of the distorted image of Penelope dashing out the bedroom door before the mirror only reflected Josie and Jo.

Finally, something had gone right. Josie prayed that Penelope made it out of the house safely, and that Josie's dad would listen to the bizarre story she told him with an open, objective state of mind.

"What did you do?" Jo screamed. She sounded winded, taking labored breaths between each word. "What the hell did you do?"

Josie pulled herself up on the side of the bed; her legs were wobbly and weak. But with one look at Jo, she felt a shot of adrenaline racing through her. She reared back her arm and slapped Jo across the face.

"Me?" Josie roared. "What the hell have *I* done?"

Josie braced herself, prepared for Jo to lunge at her. Instead, Jo collapsed onto the floor and dissolved into tears.

Okay. Josie wasn't expecting that.

"Why are you crying?"

Jo didn't answer, just continued to sob.

Josie was torn between incredulity and offense. Shouldn't *she* be the one crying? Wasn't *she* the one who had been lied to, manipulated, and stranded in another world?

"Stop it," Josie said, more harshly than she realized. "This is all your fault."

"I know," Jo wailed. "I know it is."

Dammit. She's not supposed to admit to being wrong. How was Josie supposed to continue to hate her if she admitted this was all her fault?

"Calm down." Josie grabbed a wad of tissues from the dresser and shoved them in Jo's face. "Here."

Jo stopped wailing and took the tissues, dabbing gingerly at her eyes while she tried to control her sobs. "What," she started, "what are you going to do with me?"

"Do with you?" Josie had no idea what she was talking about.

"I needed you as a hostage."

Jo's eyes grew wide and her bottom lip trembled. *Shit, wrong choice of words, Josie.*

"Not like that," Josie said quickly. "More like collateral. I needed to make sure I had a way home."

Jo shook her head. "It's no use. She won't go."

"Your mom?"

Jo nodded. "Not after what happened."

"Look, I don't care where you guys end up. Your mom sabotaged an experiment and tried to sell state secrets to the Grid? Whatever. Don't care. As long as my mom and I get to go home." The idea had never occurred to her that Jo and Josie, Dr. Byrne and Josie's mom could all stay in the same world at the same time. It would be weird, but whatever. "So your mom doesn't have to go back if she doesn't want to, okay?"

"She doesn't?"

"I don't see why not." Another idea flashed in her mind. If Jo and Dr. Byrne could stay in her world, why not Nick?

"We just have to make sure everyone is safe." Josie slipped the real vial out of her pocket. "I've got the injectable, so that's something to bargain with."

"You kept it?"

Josie shrugged. "You're not the only one who can lie. The one your mom has is a fake."

"Oh."

"With any luck, your dad and Nick are working out a way to

322

use this to get rid of the Nox for good."

Jo straightened up, her tears forgotten. "Daddy?"

"Yeah." Josie turned her back so Jo couldn't see her smile. "He's with Nick."

"What do you mean?" Jo snapped.

Oh, Josie was going to enjoy this. "They're breaking into Grid headquarters at Fort Meade to steal a laser."

Josie expected to see jealousy reflected in Jo's face. Instead, all the color had drained out of it and Josie could see that she was trembling.

"My . . . my father?"

"Yes!" Josie said, exasperated. She felt oddly protective of Mr. Byrne. The way his wife and daughter had abandoned him, lied to him. Like Josie, all he wanted was his family back, and Josie would do everything in her power to make that happen for both of their sakes. "Maybe if you'd bothered to trust him, we wouldn't be in this mess."

"Trust him? Trust my father?" Jo looked confused, uncomprehending, as if Josie had spoken her last words in Swahili.

"Duh," Josie said. "He wants what's best for you both. Hell, he's been trying to get my mom out of Old St. Mary's for the last few days just because I asked him to. And he never even questioned me when Nick and I asked for his help."

"Getting her out of Old St. Mary's?"

Why was Jo suddenly so slow in putting all these pieces together?

"Yeah, that's what I said."

Jo shook her head back and forth. "He's not going to help your mom."

There was something in the slow, metered way in which Jo said the words that made every hair on the back of Josie's neck stand at attention. There was fear in Jo's voice, combined with a kind of resignation that made Josie's mouth go instantly dry. "What do you mean?" she croaked.

"Josie," Jo said simply. "He's the one who put her there."

FIFTY-ONE

4:21 A.M.

SCIENCE MAY NOT BE ABLE TO PROVE IT, BUT there are moments when time actually slows down. The exact second you cross the event horizon, for example. Due to the tremendous gravitational pull of the black hole, once you passed the point of no return, time would elongate to such an infinite level that a second might last a year, and if you looked back toward the lip of the black hole, you'd actually be able to see yourself as you crossed into oblivion.

Theoretically, of course. No one had ever experienced the inside of a black hole firsthand. But what Josie felt at that moment was as close to time standing still as she would ever get. It was as if she felt every nanosecond of time from the instant Jo dropped the bomb. Her brain tried to come to terms with the information she'd just heard. The room faded into the background, the mirror and the vial a distant memory. All she saw was Jo, who stood before her tense and edgy, a wildebeest in a Sahara full of cheetahs and lions, ready to bolt at the slightest hint of danger.

"What do you mean?" Josie repeated.

"He sent your mom there. He knew right away she wasn't his wife."

Panic gripped Josie's stomach, twisting and turning it like a wrung-out dishrag. "I don't understand," she said lamely.

"You weren't supposed to trust him," Jo said. "He's known about the portal all along. About you and about my mom. He's the one who made me switch places with you, to try and find the injectable my mom supposedly brought with her when she accidentally zapped into your world. What he wants more than anything"—she pointed to the vial on the bed—"is that. He'll do anything to get it."

"He was the traitor. He sabotaged your mom's experiment. He was going to sell the formula to the Grid."

"Exactly. He'll kill anyone that gets in his way," Jo said. "Anyone."

Josie's mind whirled. She could go to the authorities with what she knew, show the antidote, and hope someone would actually listen to her, but that seemed unlikely at best.

No, there was only one way to get her friends and family back. One thing Mr. Byrne wanted more than anything else.

The vial.

"Jo," she said. "Would your father really kill anyone who got in his way?"

"Without blinking an eye," she said.

"Even you?"

Jo looked confused by the question. "I—I don't know."

326

"Do you want to save Nick?"

The mention of Nick's name seemed to brace Jo's courage. "Yes."

"Then let's find out how far Daddy would really go." She pulled out her cell phone, dialed Mr. Byrne's number, and handed it to Jo.

"What are you doing?"

"Just act like you're on his side. That you've caught me and have the vial. I'll prompt you."

Mr. Byrne answered on the first ring. "Princess!"

"Save it, Daddy," Jo said. "It's me."

"Jo?" He sounded genuinely surprised.

"Of course." She glanced up at Josie and covered the mouthpiece.

"Tell him you came back to find the injectable," Josie whispered.

"I came back," Jo started. Her acting skills were impressive. She sounded cold and confident. "Like you told me. Mom doesn't have the vial."

Josie gave her the thumbs-up.

"Doesn't matter now," he said. All the fake warmth had vanished from his voice. "I've got everything I need."

"Not everything," Josie whispered.

Jo echoed her. "Not everything."

"What do you mean?" Mr. Byrne snapped.

Josie held up the vial.

"Josie had the original vial," Jo said. "I've taken care of her. I have the antidote now."

"Well, well, well," Mr. Byrne said. "I guess you're my daughter after all."

"Ask to exchange it for Nick," Josie whispered again, lower this time.

Jo nodded. "More than you know. I have what you want, and you have what I want."

Mr. Byrne laughed. "The boy?"

"Yes."

"I thought I taught you to think bigger than that."

Jo didn't take the bait. "Do you want to make the exchange or not?"

There was a pause before Mr. Byrne spoke again. "Where did I take you for your seventh birthday?"

Jo winked at Josie. "That's a trick question. You never took me anywhere for my birthday. Parties make you weak."

"Very well," he said slowly. "If you want the boy, you can have him. Meet me at my office at dawn."

FIFTY-TWO

6:15 A.M.

THE PLAN WAS RELATIVELY SIMPLE. JOSIE WOULD pretend to be Jo and confront Mr. Byrne in his office, and Jo would try and find the hostages and lead them to safety. It wasn't a great plan, but at least the blush of sunrise was starting to spread its way westward across the sky. That meant they wouldn't have to worry about the Nox. Point in their favor.

"There's a massive lab complex on the third floor," Jo said as she drove her BMW to her dad's office, proving to be more helpful than Josie could possibly have imagined. "If he's got them working on the antidote, that's where they'll be."

"Perfect." Josie handed her Nick's gun. "You get them out of there, and I promise I'll save Nick for you."

Jo looked at the gun in her lap, then up at Josie. "For me?"

Josie's heart felt like it was being squeezed by a vise. "He's part of your world, Jo," she said, her mouth dry. "Not mine."

Jo nodded but didn't say a word.

They pulled into the brightly lit parking lot where Nick's SUV was parked between two large, black Suburbans. "Any idea who that might be?" Josie asked.

"They're company cars," Jo said. "One might be my dad. Not sure about the other."

Josie sighed. She'd known this was a long shot, but she'd been hoping to find Mr. Byrne alone. Oh well. If she was going down, she was going down fighting. She just prayed her dad and Penelope had managed to free the mirror. At this point, it might be their only way home.

"My dad's office is on the fourth floor," Jo said. "Northeast corner."

Josie nodded. "You go first. If he's watching security footage, hopefully he'll stop once you enter the building. I'll follow right behind. You head straight for the lab and I'll deal with your dad."

"But how am I supposed to fit all those people in this car?"

Josie had no idea. She didn't even know if there'd be anyone in there to save. Instead of answering, she gave Jo a weak smile. "Good luck. I'll meet you back at the house."

Josie watched from inside the car as Jo walked to the front door. Blood thundered in Josie's ears. They were walking into a trap—that she knew. But even if she didn't make it out, she hoped the others—Madison and Jackson, the Kaufman twins, even Josie's mom—might make it to safety.

Jo had a conversation with someone over the intercom, the door buzzed, and she pushed it open. As she walked through, she jammed a wad of paper into the locking mechanism as she and Josie had discussed.

As soon as Jo was out of sight, Josie sprinted across the parking lot to the front door, praying the wad of paper had prevented the lock mechanism from latching back into place. She tensed as she pushed the handle.

The door swung open without a sound.

Well, at least that had worked.

Josie held her head high and tried to look as arrogantly sure of herself as possible as she pushed the elevator button, just in case anyone was watching. Maybe having two Jo Byrnes in the building would at least confuse people long enough to give Josie a chance to get away. Maybe. The door slid open immediately, and Josie stepped inside, pressing the button for the fourth floor just as Jo had told her.

Mr. Byrne's office was at the end of the hall. Josie had half expected him to meet her at the elevator door, but the hallway was deserted. She walked slowly down the hall; the squeak of her Converse against the highly polished floor echoed through the deserted corridor. At least she wasn't trying to surprise anyone. That wouldn't have worked out so well.

She knocked on the door at the end of the hall and waited. No answer. She was about to knock again when she realized that Jo wasn't exactly the polite type. And she was Jo, after all. Josie took a deep breath, threw her shoulders back, and marched into the office.

Josie wasn't sure what, exactly, she thought she'd see in Mr. Byrne's office. An oversized wooden desk with a leather executive chair, awards and degrees mounted on the wall, and photos of

Mr. Byrne with dignitaries and celebrities displayed on a book-case. That seemed like standard high-powered executive digs to her. But what she found was a laboratory, all high-tech and stainless steel, with a modest architect's desk facing the window and a cluster of white armchairs in the corner, set up around a short conference table.

Mr. Byrne was a scientist? That seemed so out of character.

She scanned the room, looking for any sign of Mr. Byrne or Nick. She stepped farther into the room. "Daddy?" she said forcibly. "Where are you?"

A sound from the back of the room made Josie turn. There were three doors, and beside each was a large viewing window. Two of the windows were completely dark; the third was lit from within. Through the window, slumped forward in a metal chair, she saw Nick.

Josie wasted no time. She sprinted down the length of Mr. Byrne's lab-slash-office and yanked at the door. She hadn't expected to find it unlocked, but the door whipped open.

Nick's face was scratched and bruised. His right eye was already half-closed with heavy swelling, and his lower lip was cut in two places. Blood stained his shirt, but when his head snapped up as the door opened, Josie saw that his face was defiant and angry. As soon as he saw Josie, a look of fear washed over him.

"Josie," he said. "Get out of here. It's a trap. It was Mr. Byrne all along."

A lump rose in Josie's throat. He'd been beaten and tortured, all because she insisted they trust Mr. Byrne. She ran to him, caressing his cheek, then ducked behind him to try and untie the ropes that bound him to the chair.

"I'm so sorry," she said, struggling with the knots.

"Leave me," he said. "Just get out of here. He's got Nox in the other rooms. He likes to watch through the windows while they torture and kill people."

"Almost got it."

"He can't catch you here, Josie. He can't. I couldn't bear it."

With a final tug, Josie loosened the ropes and Nick tipped forward in his chair. She grabbed him around his waist and held him back, keeping him from falling on his face. He was so weak. Whatever Mr. Byrne had done to him, it was all Josie's fault.

Nick sat there panting for a moment, then caught his breath. "I'm okay." He pushed himself into a standing position, and grabbed Josie's hand. "Come on. Let's get out of here."

They stepped out of the cell and froze.

Mr. Byrne stood in the doorway, blocking their only exit. He held Nick's gun in his hand, pointed right at them.

FIFTY-THREE

6:37 A.M.

MR. BYRNE'S ENTIRE DEMEANOR HAD CHANGED, and Josie wondered how she had ever seen kindness in that face. The soft eyes and sad smile had been replaced by a steely glare and lips pressed firmly together in a determined line. There was a gauntness about his cheeks, sunken and sallow; yet far from appearing tired or drained, he had an uplifted energy about him, as if the death and destruction he'd put into motion in the last twenty-four hours actually invigorated him.

The silence of the room was oppressive as Mr. Byrne stood before them, coolly assessing the situation. The hum of the overhead lights seemed louder now, more intense. Everything was heightened around her. Even the sound of Josie's own breathing sounded like it was amplified through a loudspeaker.

"It was a nice try," Mr. Byrne said at last. "Using my daughter as a decoy. For a moment, I almost thought she was you."

Josie tried to sound brave. "Where is she? What have you done with her?"

Mr. Byrne clicked his tongue. "I'll deal with her later." He nodded at Nick. "And your brother. Right now it's your turn."

Nick stepped to his right, attempting to shield Josie from the gun pointed at her. For a moment, Josie almost laughed. It hadn't been that long ago that Nick had been the one holding her at gunpoint with that exact same weapon.

"What do you want?" Nick said. He reached behind his back and grasped Josie's hand firmly.

Mr. Byrne smiled without a hint of mirth. "That's funny."

Nick squeezed Josie's hand. "We're just trying to get Josie home. That's all."

"Of course you are." His words dripped with sarcasm. "You're not trying to smuggle the vial out of here at all, right?"

Nick squared his shoulders, as if preparing for a blow. "I don't know what you're talking about."

"Sure you don't." Mr. Byrne reached his free hand to the wall and pressed a button. Above the exterior windows, a blackout curtain slowly descended. "I can just shoot you both and rifle through your bodies later. Or let the Nox have at you like I did with your friend and her father." There was a cold-bloodedness in his voice that made Josie's skin crawl. "Her death was anything but quick and painless."

Josie started, but Nick tightened his grip on her hand. If Mr. Byrne was going to shoot her, she at least wanted to get a running start and maybe get one decent swipe at his face before the life drained out of her body. That would almost be worth it.

A shriek from the windows behind them made Josie and Nick

turn. In the darkness of the other two cells, she could just see a swirling of movement, a chaos of wings and bodies nebulous in the shadowy night.

"My army," Mr. Byrne said with a nod toward the window. "I've promised them fresh meat."

Nick sucked in a breath. "You communicate with them?"

Mr. Byrne laughed again, but this time with genuine enjoyment. "Oh yes. Our research is quite advanced. The Nox are significantly more sentient than we give them credit for. More like a dolphin than a dog in their ability to intuit our intentions. As soon as they discovered that we could come to a mutually beneficial arrangement, they naturally got on board."

Nick tilted his head. "Mutually beneficial arrangement?"

"Of course. We have to work together, you know. They provide certain services to the Grid as required. Like your little friend. And I make sure they are healthy, prosperous"—he paused and shrugged—"and plentiful."

The intensity of the shrieking increased, almost as if the Nox were getting impatient. Something bumped against one of the windows. Then another, harder. The Nox were trying to get out. Josie remembered the way they'd come tearing into the warehouse—a fierce, merciless attack—and shuddered.

Mr. Byrne pressed another button on the wall and this time Josie heard the sounds of two deadbolts being thrown. Her stomach flip-flopped. He'd just unlocked the two doors behind them. "Now the lights are the only things keeping them at bay. So I suppose the choice is yours. You can play nice and I'll make sure to kill you both quickly and cleanly before I let them in. Or not, and I'll shoot you both in the kneecaps, feed you to the Nox, and pick through your bones."

Josie glanced around the lab, desperate for a means of escape. Bare tables, dormant lab equipment, a desk, some chairs. Her eyes drifted upward to the overhead light illuminating the room, its humming made dormant by the shrill cries of the Nox behind them. It was a single, massive fluorescent bulb that ran practically the length of the room. But just one, and it was the only light in the lab.

Josie bit her lip. They'd come so far, were so close to the finish line. Her mom, Jo, Penelope, not to mention the entire human population of both their worlds—so many people were counting on her. She couldn't let them down. Not if she could help it.

That night in the forest, the Nox hadn't directly attacked her—more like accidentally found her in the darkness when she cried for help. And in the warehouse, when Nick had been the focus of the attack, the Nox barely touched her—even seemed surprised and scared when she lashed out at one. It was as if they didn't know she was there.

Like she wasn't in their world at all.

It was a hypothesis only. A theory developed from a logical examination of the facts. But Josie was about to bet her life—and Nick's—that she was right.

"Well?" Mr. Byrne said.

Nick squeezed Josie's hand and turned to face her. His eyes were sad, defeated. "I'm sorry," he whispered.

Josie smiled. "We're not dead yet."

Nick's brows drew together with a question he never got a chance to ask. Without warning, Josie spun around, grabbed a Bunsen burner off the table, and heaved it at the overhead light.

"No!" Mr. Byrne screamed.

Nick gasped. "What are you doing?"

For an instant, nothing moved. The burner seemed to hang in midair, locked onto the long fluorescent bulb above them. There was no sound, just a frantic blinking that happened in slow motion as the fixture swung violently back and forth on its moorings. Josie held her breath. She wasn't sure if she wanted the light to go dark or not. If she was wrong, she and Nick were in for a horrific death. But at least they'd be taking Mr. Byrne with them.

The room went dark for a split second and Josie heard repeated thuds as the Nox propelled themselves against the cell doors. The light blinked back on, bathing the room with its sterile blue-white glow for a half second, then with a crack that Josie could feel more than hear, the bulb broke free of the fixture and plummeted to the ground, submerging the room in total darkness.

Without warning, life kicked into regular speed. She grabbed Nick by the arms and pulled him to the ground just as the muzzle of the gun flashed. But Mr. Byrne and his handgun were the least of her problems.

The sound of a crash pierced the room and suddenly the shrieks of the Nox were twice as loud. Josie felt the rush of air as they swooped into the lab.

Nick wrapped his arms around her to try and shield her from the Nox, but this wasn't the time for chivalry. "Curl up into a ball," she whispered.

"What? Why?"

"Stay quiet." She didn't have time to explain. "Trust me."

Without waiting for him to comply, Josie forced him onto his side, then climbed on top. She wrapped her arms tightly around him, resting her head directly on top of his. Maybe, just maybe, they wouldn't be able to sense Nick with her covering him.

A scream tore through the chaos. Not an animal this time—human. It was close to them, just on the other side of the table, and Josie could feel the terror of it seeping into her bones.

"No!" Mr. Byrne cried. "Not me. Not me!"

His screams shifted, less pleading and more pain. Excruciating pain, the kind of cries Josie imagined from a fourteenth-century witch burning at the stake. The air beat around her, faster and faster, a torrent of ecstasy in the kill.

Josie hugged Nick tighter. So far she hadn't felt as much as a wing graze her body as they lay on the floor in some kind of bizarre spooning pose.

Suddenly, Mr. Byrne's screams choked off. There was an abatement in the shrieks of the Nox, and Josie could hear sputtering, like a man drowning. She heard a crash, and felt the reverberations through the floor. A table falling over as Mr. Byrne made one last, desperate attempt for the door.

Without warning, the Nox exploded into a frenzy. The noise of their screaming was so loud Josie was sure her ears were bleeding. But she didn't move her hands to her ears to try to mute the noise; she kept them wrapped around Nick. She had to protect him. The screeching intensified, at once joyful and horrific, and Josie realized it was the bloodlust as they ripped Mr. Byrne's body to pieces. The table bounced, pushing up against them from one side, and Josie could feel the vibrations of the Nox as they attacked Mr. Byrne's body again and again and again. . . .

Then as suddenly as it began, the room went silent.

Josie didn't move. Her head throbbed, her ears rang from the sheer decibels of the noise that had inexplicably ceased, and her breaths came fast and deep, like after line sprints in PE. Beneath her, Nick didn't stir. She could feel him breathing just as heavily as she was, but neither of them felt brave enough to move.

Nick was the first to break the spell. "I think they're gone."

"Where?" Josie whispered.

"Wherever they go during the daylight?"

Josie nodded, even though Nick couldn't see her in the darkness. "They must have phase shifted. Like Tony said."

"What happened?" Nick asked breathlessly. "I mean, why aren't we dead?"

Josie continued to straddle him. "I think . . ." Her voice was trembling. "I think it's like with Tony, where he's not quite in our world but not quite out of it? I think that's what's happened with me. When I came through the portal."

Nick shifted, and she sat back on her heels, freeing him from the weight of her body. In the pitch darkness, she didn't realize he was sitting up until his nose grazed her cheek.

Nick froze, and Josie heard him suck in a quick breath, then slowly he drew his cheek against her own. His skin was rough with stubble. It scratched her face, but Josie didn't care. She inhaled deeply and caught the spicy traces of aftershave long since applied. She wanted to bury her face in his neck and take gulping breaths of him.

Fingers against her face. Just the tips, deliberately outlining her jaw, the contours of her face. Nick's touch was soft, yet assertive. She could sense his want, his need to touch and feel her, but with a gentleness that Josie had never encountered in his predecessor. His fingertips traced down her cheeks to her chin, and his thumb swept lightly across her lips, causing a fluttering thrill deep within her.

Josie's heart thundered in her chest. She reached a tentative hand forward and pressed it against Nick's body. Through the thin cotton of his shirt, she could feel the strong, rapid beat of his heart. He was just as excited as she was.

Her touch gave Nick the green light. His hand snaked behind her neck and pulled her to him. The feel of his lips against hers was electric.

Josie pressed her mouth to Nick's and kissed him greedily. She'd fantasized about this moment so many times, but it had never been like this. In her dreams, she was using him as a substitute for the boy who had broken her heart. But that pain and loss had passed, and now Josie found herself yearning for this Nick of his own merit. He was not her ex-boyfriend. He was different. He was better.

And she was in love with him.

Nick moaned softly into her mouth as he wrapped both of his arms around her. He rolled over, cradling her head in his hand so she wouldn't clonk it on the tile floor, and slid his body on top of hers. She arched her back as she deepened their kiss. The darkness that had been a thing to be feared, a place where nightmares lived, had lost its menace. Josie couldn't see the outline of Nick's face and body, though they were just inches from her own. She couldn't tell where his hands were, where he would touch her next.

Nick gently glided his hand up beneath her shirt, then kissed the soft part of her neck just below her ear. Josie trembled as he inched his hands upward toward her chest. So slowly it was almost torture. Her body ached for him in a way she'd never felt before. She wanted to feel his hands on every inch of her skin, to revel in the warmth of his body sliding against her own. Just as his hand swept over her breast, she reached her arms up over her head.

Her hand touched something in the darkness.

A shoe.

Josie pulled her lips away from his; the spell of Nick was broken in an instant.

"What's wrong?" Nick panted.

Josie didn't answer. She felt up the smooth, leather of the shoe to a sock. A sock clothing the hard bone of an ankle. A sock that was sticky and damp.

She yanked her hand away, realizing what it was, but the foot came with her, sliding several inches closer to where she lay on the floor. It was easy and light, as if it was no longer attached to a body.

"Oh my God!" Josie pushed herself up, cracking her forehead against Nick's in the process. Nick grunted, fell back, and Josie scrambled after him, desperate to get away from the body on the floor.

"Are you okay?" Nick said, reaching for her in the darkness.

"It's . . . it's . . . ," she started. Her brain felt paralyzed and all she wanted to do was wash the hand that had accidentally touched Mr. Byrne's severed leg.

"Oh my God."

Nick rocketed to his feet and fumbled around in the darkness, swearing under his breath as he bumped into tables and crunched on broken glass in his sneakers. After a few seconds, she saw the weak but steady beam of the flashlight a moment before Nick shined it in her face. "Are you okay?" he asked again.

Her face must have answered when her voice couldn't. Nick sprinted to her side and lifted her to her feet. She felt his strong arm around her waist, and she let her body sag into it. But she couldn't enjoy the sensation, not even for a moment. The beam of Nick's flashlight traced a slow trail across the lab floor, sweeping back and forth, looking for the remains of Mr. Byrne. He spotted the shoe first, black and unmarred, as if its owner had just come from a shoeshine.

Knowing Mr. Byrne, he probably had.

As Nick traced the shoe up to the ankle and beyond, Josie

saw what she'd feared: the leg was severed at the knee. Shreds of the dark dress slacks Mr. Byrne had been wearing still clung to the leg, gathered down by the blood-soaked ankle. But the rest of what had been his lower leg was little more than a skeleton. Thick puddles of blood spilled out in every direction, splattered across the floor by the frenzy of the attack. Bits of ripped and shredded flesh still clung to the bones, but for the most part, the Nox had picked it dry.

Josie couldn't help but wonder how long he'd remained conscious during the attack. Judging by the horrific screams she'd heard above the clamor of his attackers, it was long enough.

His army. His allies. Only so far as he could control them. In the end, he was just another meal.

Nick turned Josie around and raised his flashlight beam to the wall. "We don't need to see any more."

FIFTY-FOUR

7:06 A.M.

JOSIE FOLLOWED NICK AS THEY RACED DOWN the hall. He kept his gun, retrieved from beside the body of Mr. Byrne, poised, expecting to see a security guard at any moment. People would be arriving for work, which would hopefully provide a distraction of some kind as they tried to get their friends out of the building.

Nick barreled into the stairwell, Josie close behind him.

"She said there was a lab on the third floor and that's where they'd be."

Nick glanced back at her. "Who said that?"

Oh yeah, she'd forgotten to mention that part. "I brought Jo back with me."

Nick screeched to a halt at the third-floor landing. "You trusted Jo Byrne."

"Yeah."

"After everything she did to you?"

It sounded like such a bad idea when he said it like that. "I didn't have a choice."

"Shit." Nick checked the gun cartridge, then cocked the barrel. "How many times do I have to tell you, you can't trust her?"

Just then, the door to the third floor flew open and Jo Byrne popped into the stairwell. "Can't trust who?" she said with a huge smile.

Nick vaulted back, holding his gun out in front of him. "Where are they?" he barked. "Where are my friends?"

"It's okay, Nicky." A shadow slid into the stairwell and Josie recognized the raspy voice of Tony Fiorino. "It's all good."

Madison followed him. "Tony slipped out of the lab when Mr. Byrne brought Jo in."

Tony laughed. "Easy when you're a shadow."

Zeke and Zeb were the next through the door. "He got the keys," one of them said.

"From Dr. Cho," said the other.

Jo smiled. "And here we are."

Jackson slipped into the stairwell last. He carried a thin figure in his arms. She was wrapped in a blanket and her dark hair hung over her face.

Josie's voice cracked. "Mom?"

"I'm okay," her mom said weakly. "I'm going to be okay."

Josie turned to Jo, grabbed her by the shoulders, and hugged her. "Thank you."

* * *

"Do you think your mom will agree to come back now?" Josie asked.

Jo laughed. "With Daddy gone? Yeah, she'll be cool."

Josie smiled.

"I really am sorry," Jo said simply. "About everything."

Josie caught sight of her mom sitting on the edge of Jo's bed. "It worked out."

"I suppose I could have told you," Jo continued, speaking in a very calm, deliberate tone. "About our moms, and about what my father was." She looked up at Josie. "He told me one day that he'd tried to kill my mom. And if I didn't do exactly as he said, I'd be next. He was deranged."

"I'm so sorry, Jo."

Jo shrugged, and her carefree attitude immediately returned. "Oh well, he's dead. Too bad, so sad."

Jo may have been totally unfazed by her father's gruesome death, but the thought of Mr. Byrne's mangled body made Josie shiver. As happy as she was that he was gone, it was a death that would haunt her for the rest of her life.

Jo glanced at Nick, then back to Josie. "So you're really going back?"

Josie's stomach clenched. The time was rapidly approaching when she'd have to make a decision: stay or go. She honestly wasn't sure which it would be. "I think so."

Jo stared at her for a moment, assessing; then her eyes drifted

347

down to Dr. Byrne's necklace that still hung around Josie's neck.

"Oh," Josie said. "Right. You probably want this back." She reached up and placed her hand on the necklace, two entwined hearts. Josie and Nick. He hadn't given it to her, but somehow it had come to symbolize all that they'd been through together, and the idea of taking it off was almost as painful as the idea of leaving Nick forever.

Jo continued to stare at the necklace. "You really thought Nick gave that to me."

Josie nodded.

"You're in love with him, aren't you?"

Josie nodded again. "Yeah."

Jo's face was blank and impassive. "But you were going to give him up. Back at Fort Meade, you said you'd save him for me."

"Yeah." She had said that. And she'd meant it, realizing at the time that the odds of her and Nick actually being together were very slim.

"You know, he's the only guy that ever said 'no' to me. I think that's what made me want him so badly." Jo pointed to the necklace. "You keep it. As if he gave it to you." Then she turned on her heel and walked to the window.

Josie's mom sat on Jo's bed staring at the mirror. "I can't believe it's all come down to that wretched mirror."

Josie sat down next to her and squeezed her hand. "Think of it this way: if the initial explosion hadn't established a connection between the two mirrors, I never would have known you were gone, never would have been able to come here and find you."

Her mom sighed. "That's one way of looking at it."

"Personally," Nick said with a smile, "I kinda love that mirror."

Josie looked at Nick. Despite his smile, his eyes were sad. Her heart ached at what was coming, and when Nick twitched his head toward the hallway, Josie stood up and followed.

"Stay," Nick said as soon as the bedroom door closed behind them. "Stay here with me."

"I can't. My mom needs me."

"I need you."

Josie swallowed. "Come with me, then."

Nick reached up and cupped her cheek with his hand. "But my brother . . ."

"I know." Josie dropped her eyes. She leaned forward and rested her head against his chest, listening to the rapid beat of his heart. Could she stay? Her mom was going home to her dad, and hopefully they'd be able to reconcile once Dad knew the whole story. With Tony completing the Nox injectable and Dr. Byrne there to oversee the eradication, this universe would be safer. She could send her mom home with the formula to help do the same in her world. And besides, maybe she could contribute something here, explore the physics of this universe with a different perspective. It was an enticing possibility.

But the only thing that really mattered to her was Nick.

"Okay."

They said it in unison, both Josie and Nick. Josie looked up and Nick's head was tilted to the side. "Did you say 'okay'?"

"Yeah." Josie laughed. "Did you?"

"Yeah."

That was it. They needed each other, were desperate to be together no matter whose universe they chose. Josie's heart ached from happiness. She'd never felt this way with her ex-boyfriend. This was something different. Something deeper. Even though they had only known each other a few days, Nick knew her better than anyone else, and loved her even more because of it.

Nick wrapped his arms around her, pulling her body to his. When his lips touched hers she reached for his neck, grasping frantically at his wavy hair. Nick pressed her against the wall, kissing her cheek, her jaw, her neck. She'd do whatever he wanted her to, stay or go. She'd never believed in fate, thought it was something for the weak-minded to find comfort in. But in that moment, she knew that fate did exist. Because Nick—this Nick—was her fate.

Just then the house shook violently. Nick broke away, bracing himself against the wall with one arm, the other still laced behind Josie's back. It felt like an earthquake, or at least how Josie imagined an earthquake would feel. Only it didn't weaken. After a few seconds, the shaking was getting stronger, so violent Josie had a hard time standing upright.

Jo flung the bedroom door open. "Something's wrong."

Josie and Nick ran into the room. The portal had opened and on the other side, Josie could see Penelope and her dad standing in front of the large X-FEL rig in their basement.

Dr. Byrne had already come through the portal. She stood in the middle of Jo's bedroom, a look of panic on her face.

"I didn't know," she said to Josie's mom. "I thought my husband had Jo. I thought he'd be here when the portal opened. I . . ." She looked up at Josie. "I didn't know what to do."

The rumbling intensified. Inside the mirror, a massive hole was forming. The thick substance of the portal swirled around it, picking up speed as the hole grew larger.

Josie grabbed Dr. Byrne by the arm. "What's happening?"

"I calibrated the X-FEL to hold the portal open," Dr. Byrne said. "Until I could figure out what happened to my daughter."

"To hold it open?"

Dr. Byrne nodded. "Only it's growing too quickly. The gravitational field is accelerating beyond the bounds of its force."

Josie stared at the widening hole in the portal. "At this rate, the field will collapse in on itself."

"Isn't that what we want?" Nick said. "To close the portal?"

Josie shook her head. "This will close the portal, all right. And destroy both of our worlds in the process."

Josie's mom staggered to her feet. "Oh dear God."

"Can we stop it?" Josie said. "Shut the laser down?"

Dr. Byrne shook her head. "It's too late. Turning off the laser won't stop the process."

"Wave interference," Josie's mom said. "A wave-interference pattern will cancel out the beam."

Dr. Byrne's face lit up. "If it's of equal strength, it should disrupt the field completely, breaking the portal for good."

"Equal strength?" Nick said. "I don't suppose you've got another X-FEL lying around the house?"

Josie shook her head and smiled, remembering her science experiment in AP Physics. "But we've got some mirrors."

Josie's mom passed through the portal first to explain to her husband and Penelope what they needed. Penelope dashed upstairs and Josie watched with a fluttering heart as her dad lifted her mom into his arms and hugged her.

On her side, Jo and Nick had retrieved the large mirror from above the fireplace downstairs and lugged it into Jo's bedroom. Once Penelope was on the other side with a similar mirror, Josie began directing their placement.

It had to be exact, which was easy when you had a variety of instruments with which to measure distance, angles, and other environmental variables. Not so easy when you were eyeballing it in a room that was literally being shaken apart.

Dr. Byrne and Nick struggled to keep the angle steady, reflecting the beam of the laser directly back onto itself. Penelope stood behind the X-FEL, her mirror catching the split photons as they passed through the portal. Together, it should be enough to create a powerful interference pattern that would disrupt the portal.

If only they could keep the mirrors from moving.

"Higher," Josie yelled. The rumbling was so intense she could barely hear her own voice. "Ten degrees."

Jo's room was literally falling apart around them. Chunks of plaster loosened by the violent shaking crashed to the floor.

The bookcase pitched forward, falling face-first onto the bed like a diver doing a belly flop. The window rattled so fiercely she thought it might explode.

"It's not working," Jo screamed.

Josie didn't lose focus. She stood right next to the mirror. They were so close. "Just an inch more."

Suddenly the shaking stopped. The mirror had hit its target and Josie watched with rapt attention as the hole in the middle of the portal fluctuated, then rippled as the particle waves began bouncing against one another. Dr. Byrne and Nick held the mirror firmly, the angle perfect.

In an instant, the hole in the portal was gone. The surface blurred and the image of Josie's parents distorted. The portal was closing. This time for good.

"Let's go," Nick said, grabbing her hand.

"Are you sure?"

Nick smiled. "Hurry up."

Josie plunged into the portal, her hand clasped tightly in Nick's. Only this time the substance around her felt heavier. Less like pudding and more like setting concrete. She could barely move. Her legs strained against the portal but she wasn't getting anywhere. Her lungs ached as she began to run out of air, and she grasped Nick's hand tighter. She reached out blindly with her other hand, desperate for the clean air of her basement, but felt only the thickening goo around her.

She opened her mouth to scream but the viscous substance

filled her mouth. The light began to dim as she choked and gagged.

Suddenly Nick's hand was ripped from hers; then she felt a violent shove and her body lurched toward the other side of the portal.

A hand was on her arm. Then another. Someone was pulling her into the light. With a final heave, Josie flew out of the portal onto the basement floor.

"Where's Nick?" she gasped.

Josie's dad knelt down by her side. "Jo Jo, he didn't make it."

Josie's body went numb. "What?"

"He pushed you through," her mom said. "He let go and shoved you toward us."

Her dad stroked her hair. "Then Penelope and I grabbed you and pulled you free."

Nick was gone. He'd died trying to come with her, swallowed up by the suffocating substance of the portal. She'd lost him again, this time for good.

Josie clasped the necklace in her hands, and cried.

FIFTY-FIVE

7:10 A.M.

JOSIE'S DAD TURNED AROUND FROM THE DRIVER'S seat with a look of concern on his face. "Are you sure you want to do this?"

Josie glanced out the car window. The brick façade of Bowie Prep loomed above her, familiar and yet different. It was her school in her universe, and yet nothing about it was the same as it had been a week ago. Josie's hand strayed to the necklace that rested against her chest. Or more precisely, *she* wasn't the same. After all that she'd been through, the idea of facing Madison and Nick and a school full of people who still gossiped about her in the halls as she walked past suddenly seemed unimportant.

"Josie?" Her mom leaned around the front passenger seat. "You don't have to go. We don't want to rush you into this."

Out of the corner of her eye, Josie saw her dad reach out, take her mom's hand, and squeeze it affectionately. Despite her own sorrow, she was so relieved her parents had found each other again.

Josie stared out the window. She couldn't just sit at home. Every time she stopped doing something, every time she closed her eyes, she thought of Nick, and the sorrow of losing him washed over her afresh. No, she had to go back to school. It was the only way she could keep going.

"I'm ready." She opened the door and slid out of the car. "Penelope will be there. I'll be fine. I promise."

Bowie Prep felt strange as Josie slowly made her way upstairs to her second-floor locker. She remembered her first day at school in Jo's world, the excitement and anticipation she felt, combing the hallways for a glimpse of Nick. She'd expected to find a boyfriend with whom she could make amends for the mistakes in her own relationship, but instead she'd found something else.

Love.

She was no longer afraid to face Madison and Nick in the hallway at school. She was no longer afraid of the whispers and rumors. None of it mattered. Nick was gone, she would never see him again, and her love would live with her forever, a dull ache that would never go away.

She rounded a corner, lost in her own painful memories, and ran straight into her ex-boyfriend.

"Josie!" Nick said, a look of relief on his face. "I've been looking for you."

She thought she'd prepared herself for this, to see her ex-boyfriend who was the identical twin of the love she had lost, but her heart clenched at the sight of him and it took every ounce of her strength and self-control to keep the tears at bay.

"Hey," she said. It was all she could manage.

"Hey?" he said with a playful grin. "That's all you've got for me?" Nick leaned down, his lips reaching for hers.

"What the hell?" Josie dodged his attempt, her stomach instantly sick at the idea of kissing him.

Nick reared back as if he'd been slapped. "What? Come on, after the other day I thought we worked this all out. Madison and I are done, I swear. Just like I texted you."

"You broke up?"

"Yeah, gorgeous," Nick said, slipping back into their old routine. "I told you—you're the only girl for me."

Josie curled her lip. A week ago she'd have killed to hear this Nick say those words to her again, but now? Now she just felt sorry for him.

"Sorry, Nick," Josie said, shaking her head. "I don't know what you thought, but I'm not interested."

"Huh?"

She reached to her neck and wrapped her fingers delicately around the necklace. A strange sense of calm washed over her as she turned her back on Nick forever, and walked down the hallway. "Go back to Madison. You two were made for each other."

3:59 A.M.

"Are you sure?" Nick says.

Jo nods. "It's the least I can do."

Nick's face is anxious. "And she'll see it?"

Jo shrugs. "She should. She's seen everything else." She glances at her watch. *Only fifty-five seconds until four o'clock.* "Hurry up."

Nick looks into the mirror in Jo's bedroom. Jo follows his gaze, even though she knows what he'll see: her room. Just her room. A regular reflection of a regular room, not another room like hers, with a girl who looks like her but isn't.

Josie used to wish she lived Jo's life. Now it's the other way around.

Nick sighs and turns back to her. "I'm ready."

"Go ahead."

"Josie," he says, staring straight at Jo but without seeing her at all. "I'm here. I'm okay. Dr. Byrne pulled me out of the portal."

Jo clears her throat.

"Dr. Byrne and Jo pulled me out of the portal."

"You're welcome," Jo says.

"I never got to say it the other night." He runs his hands through his thick hair. "But I . . ."

Nick's voice trails off and a look of sadness sweeps over his face. Jo knows how he feels, the dull, endless ache of a love that can't be. She knows it only too well.

She looks at her watch to hide the emotion she's feeling. "Thirty seconds."

Nick nods and takes a deep breath. "Josie, I don't even know if you can see me. I may never know. But I had to tell you at least once: I love you. I love you so much it feels like a piece of my heart has been cut away at losing you."

Nick takes a step closer and Jo catches her breath. "Ten seconds," she whispers.

"I swear this, Josie. I swear on my life I will never stop, never give up until I find a way back to you. I promise."

Jo fights to keep her eyes on Nick's face.

"I love you, Josie," he says again. "Never forget."

Josie's eyes flew open.

Her cheeks were wet with tears that came while she was sleeping, immersed in the most beautiful dream. She was sad, and yet she was smiling, so big and so real she thought her heart might burst. Nick was alive, and he loved her.

She sat up and stared at the remnants of the mirror. The glass had been shattered, the last of its shards removed and melted down at the lab by her mom. But her dad had built a stand for the empty gilt frame and positioned it in the corner of her room, where she could look at it every day. A remembrance. A memento.

A promise that she'd never forget.

Josie slowly lay back down in bed, her fingers tracing the loops of the hearts that hung around her neck. Nick's face still danced before her eyes; his words lingered in her ears.

"I love you too," she said out loud. "Never forget."

ACKNOWLEDGMENTS

Some books practically write themselves; others are a struggle. *3:59* was the latter. The people below made this book happen. Without them, I'd still be curled up under my desk in the fetal position.

To my darling John Griffin, who literally held my hand throughout this process. He gave me strength, encouragement, and unwavering support, and a hug whenever I needed it.

To Roy Firestone, who, as always, listened to every complaint, rant, whine, tirade, and breakdown with calm sympathy.

To Ginger Clark. I refer to her as "my rock star" for a reason. She's not just an agent, she's a partner in crime.

To Kristin Daly Rens, who worked as diligently as I did to whip this book into shape. She saw the kernel of a fantastic story, then made sure I saw it, too.

To the amazing folks at Curtis Brown: Holly Frederick, Dave Barbor, Jonathan Lyons, and Kerry D'Agostino.

To my Balzer + Bray family: Donna Bray, Alessandra Balzer, and Sara Sargent, as well as the ridiculously talented HarperCollins team, including Emilie Polster, Stefanie Hoffman, Caroline Sun, Ray Shappell, and Kathryn Silsand.

To Carrie Harris and Laurel Hoctor Jones, whose astute critiques and timely brainstorming saved this book.

To my Bacon sisters: Jessi Kirby, Stasia Kehoe, Elana Johnson, and Carrie Harris (again). I'm only sane because of you.

To Deb Shapiro, publicist extraordinaire, who did not get a thank you in *Ten*.

To Amber Sweeney, who generously did all the legwork and design on the Army of Ten promotion—http://armyoften.blogspot.com—and who has been a tireless advocate and ally.

To the Generals in the Army of Ten, the best street team in the history of street teams: Alisha Blanchard, Sophia Candrilli, Danielle DeVor, Jennifer Halligan from A Book and a Latte, and Jen Runkle.

To my mom, as always. My little red caboose.

Turn the page for a sneak peek at

GET EVEN,

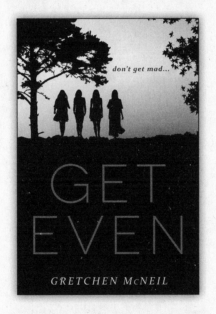

the next book by Gretchen McNeil!

ONE

BREE SAT BACK AGAINST THE CHAIN-LINK FENCE, BOUNCING her tennis racket lightly against the toe of her black Converse. "Why do we still have physical education in school?"

John snatched the racket out of her hand. "It's a political conspiracy to repress the youth of America through enforced humiliation."

A quartet of diligent tennis players trotted past Bree and John to the last empty court and began to hit the ball back and forth over the net with enthusiastic, if not particularly accurate, strokes. They looked lame in their white skirts and sneakers, glistening in the fierce afternoon sun, as they bounced and swayed like Maria Sharapova in a Grand Slam final.

"You'd think," Bree said, pulling her knees up to her chin, "that a fancy prep school like Bishop DuMaine would have some kind of virtual phys ed. This *is* Silicon Valley. Shouldn't we be high-tech?"

A whistle blared from the other side of the courts. "Deringer! Baggott!" Coach Sampson pointed at them with her racket. "This isn't break time."

Bree scanned the occupied courts. "We've got next," she shouted, accompanied by an overly enthusiastic thumbs-up.

Coach Sampson slowly shook her head in disgust as she turned her attention to a mixed doubles team.

"First week of school and I already hate phys ed." John tossed Bree's racket onto the court. "Can't your dad get us out of this?"

Bree arched a brow. "Can't your mom?"

"What's the point of having a state senator as my best friend's dad if we don't get any perks?"

"What's the point of having the school secretary as my best friend's mom," Bree mocked, "if we don't get any perks?"

John ran his fingers through his black hair, dyed the only color not verboten by Bishop DuMaine's strict dress code. "At least I'm not afraid to ask."

"I'm not afraid," Bree said sharply.

"You will be." John hunched his shoulders and employed his crackly-voiced Yoda impression. "You. Will. Be."

Bree rolled her eyes. Most days, John's geeky insistence that there was a *Star Wars* quote for every occasion was relatively entertaining, but today it was about as welcome as a raging case of the herps. All she could think about was tomorrow's supposedly surprise school assembly.

"Did you hear about the special assembly tomorrow?" John said out of the blue.

Bree inhaled sharply. Was he reading her mind? "There's an assembly tomorrow?" she asked, trying to sound indifferent.

John nodded. "Called by Father Uberti himself. Overheard him talking to my mom about it in the office this morning."

Bree smoothed down her thick bangs and avoided John's eyes. "Why is he calling an assembly?"

"Duh." John turned to face her. "It's gotta be about DGM."

"DGM is going down," a voice boomed from behind them.

Bree craned her neck and found Rex Cavanaugh, flanked by his wingmen Tyler Brodsky and Kyle Tanner, on the other side of the chain-link fence. They stood shoulder-to-shoulder with tree-trunk arms folded across overly broad chests. All three wore matching royal blue polo shirts sporting the words "'Maine Men," with the Bishop DuMaine crest emblazoned over their hearts.

Part club, part school-sanctioned goon squad, the 'Maine Men had been created by Father Uberti in response to the school-wide wave of humiliating revenge pranks perpetrated by an anonymous group known only as DGM. In an amazing, ironic move, old F.U. had recruited the school's top tier of bullies, poseurs, and power-hungry egomaniacs—the same people DGM targeted—and tasked them with ferreting out the students behind the group.

Much to Bree's delight, the 'Maine Men had been a total bust. In the last year and a half, the score was: DGM—6, 'Maine Men—0.

And she hoped it stayed that way. At least for one more day.

"Did you hear me?" Rex barked.

Bree squinted into the sunshine. "Aren't you a little short for a Stormtrooper?" Next to her, John snorted.

"Huh?" Rex asked.

"What do you want?" Bree said slowly, articulating each word.

"DGM is going down," Rex repeated. Apparently, that was his

only talking point. "Once and for all."

"Right," Bree said, narrowing her eyes. "Because you've done such a fantastic job of that so far."

Rex shoved his sweaty face against the fence, so close that Bree could differentiate the individually clogged pores across the bridge of his nose. "We know you're involved, Deringer. Just wait till tomorrow. Even your daddy won't be able to save you."

John was on his feet in an instant, wedging his body between Bree and the fence. "Lay off, Cavanaugh."

Rex shook the chain link back and forth like a caged gorilla. "Maybe you want to be next, Baggott the Faggot?"

Bree threw back her head in a mock laugh. "Ha. Ha, ha. Cuz that joke's never not funny."

"Rex!" A sandy-haired guy with a horrific case of acne trotted up. Bree had never seen him before, but judging by the creases down the front of his blue 'Maine Men shirt, it had recently been removed from its packaging. A new recruit. "Rex, you've got to see this."

"Who are you?" Rex said, his eyes still fixed on John.

"Ronny DeStefano?" the new guy said.

Rex shook his head. "Who?"

Ronny's forehead bunched up in confusion. "We met at Jezebel's house party last week."

Rex pursed his lips as if trying to force his Neanderthal brain to recall the booze-soaked party. "You new here?"

"Yeah," Ronny huffed. "We have a mutual friend, remember? From junior high?" He looked at Rex pointedly. "We both had a weird experience with—"

"Right!" Rex said quickly. "Ronny. What's up?"

Ronny nodded toward the soccer field. "There's some shit going down with Coach Creed. I thought you should—"

"Let's roll," Rex said, cutting him off. He stormed away, Tyler and Kyle close behind, leaving Ronny to scamper after them like a puppy.

Bree looked at John. "Any idea what that was all about?"

"Dunno." John stared over her head toward the soccer field, where a crowd was gathering. "But I have a feeling we're about to find out."

Olivia swept out of the girls' locker room, racket in hand, and straightened her designer tennis dress.

"That outfit looks amazing on you," Amber said, gliding up beside her. "I'm glad you don't mind wearing last season's line."

"Not at all," Olivia said. Half of her wardrobe consisted of hand-me-down items Amber had deemed "last season."

Peanut fitted a baseball cap onto her head, pulling her long ponytail through the back. "Too bad Donté's basketball practice is in the gym," she said absently. "If he saw you in that dress, you'd have him eating out of your hand."

Olivia stiffened. "Why would I care what Donté thinks?"

Peanut's eyes grew wide. "Didn't you tell me last week that you were going to get back together with him?"

That was supposed to be a secret, Peanut.

Amber arched an eyebrow. "Liv, sweetie. We talked about this. You need someone . . ."

"Richer," Jezebel said, lumbering up behind them. She pulled a white hoodie on over her beefy shoulders and shook her head. "*You* broke up with *him*, remember?"

Olivia bit her lip. "Um, yeah."

"If you try to reboot," Amber added, "you'll look pathetic."

"I can't believe we have to wait until Monday to find out what the fall production's going to be," Olivia said, changing the subject. The last thing she wanted was another conversation with Amber about Donté Greene. "The anticipation is killing me."

"*I* can't believe Mr. Cunningham is missing the first week of school," Jezebel said, with a shake of her head. "What kind of teacher does that?"

Amber fished a tube of gloss out of the pocket of her new designer tennis dress and lacquered her lips sans mirror. "I'm still putting my money on Mamet."

Olivia smiled. Amber would be the last person to have inside information on the drama department.

"Whatever it is," Peanut said, "there will be a perfect role for you, Livvie."

"You never know." Olivia ran a hand through her pixie cut and laughed. "Maybe with my hair this short, he'll want to cast me as a boy."

Jezebel sighed dramatically. "Only you would shave your hair for a role and have it grow back looking like a supermodel."

The role of crotchety cancer patient Vivian Bearing in *Wit* last spring had been Olivia's crowning achievement. Mr. Cunningham had offered her a bald cap for the performance, but Olivia had shocked everyone by shaving off her strawberry blond curls for opening night. It was a decision she never regretted—every performance was sold out, and she got at least three curtain calls each night.

"Guess we'll just have to wait and see," Amber said with a toss of her brown mane. "Come on, ladies. Tennis awai . . ."

Her voice trailed off as she caught sight of something on the other side of the yard. Olivia turned and saw Rex blazing across the blacktop at a breakneck pace. He was bookended by Tyler and Kyle, with some skinny guy Olivia had never seen before trailing in their wake.

"Hi, baby!" Amber cooed at Rex. She turned to the side and posed provocatively in her barely-there outfit.

"Not now!" Rex shouted, flashing his palm.

Amber's jaw dropped as Rex and his buddies broke into a jog. "What the fuck?"

"What's that all about?" Peanut asked.

"No idea." Olivia eyed the large group of students gathering at the top the hill above the soccer field, as Rex and his 'Maine Men buddies pushed their way into the throng. That couldn't be good.

Amber sniffed at the air. Like a shark with blood in the water, she could sense gossip-worthy drama from a mile away. A sly smile broke the corners of her mouth.

"I think gym class just got significantly more interesting."

If Kitty had ever doubted that Coach Creed needed his ass handed to him, he was making it real easy for her to get over it.

"Move it, Baranski!" Coach Creed's bark drifted across the

all-weather track where Kitty was leading the Bishop DuMaine varsity girls' volleyball team in a warm-up run before practice.

Kitty paused. Below her, students dotted the hillside that stretched down to the soccer field. Clad in their blue-and-gold gym uniforms, they were frozen in various stages of hill charges, eyes fixed on the bottom of the slope and the chubby, panting figure of Theo Baranski.

Coach Creed towered over him, hands on hips, flexing his pecs like an MMA fighter. "It's the first week of school, Baranski, and you're already falling behind."

Theo's face was beet red, and slick with either sweat or tears. Maybe both. He stared up at the steep hillside, his eyes reflecting a mixture of fear and shame. Deep inside Kitty, a memory stirred, so close and so real it was as if she was back in sixth-grade math class, where the numbers and symbols of pre-algebra swam before her eyes, as meaningless to her as hieroglyphics.

Kitty squeezed her eyes shut. The shame of not knowing the right answer. The fear that Ms. Turlow would call on her . . .

How can you be the only Asian kid on the planet who isn't good at math?

"How can you be the only kid on the planet," Coach Creed continued, "who can't haul his ass up that hill?"

Mika jogged up behind her. "That poor kid's got enough problems without Creed jumping down his throat every day."

"I know," Kitty said quietly. Theo had transferred to Bishop DuMaine last spring, and Coach Creed had been on his case since day one.

Mika pulled off her headband and patted her tight black curls in place. "Theo's going to have a heart attack if he tries to charge up that hill one more time. We should do something."

We already have.

As much as Kitty wanted to step in and help, her hands were tied. She'd been hoping Coach Creed would lay off Theo the first week of school, giving DGM enough time to put their plan into motion. No such luck.

"You know," Mika said slowly. "The volleyball team could really use a manager. Do you think I should talk to Coach about bringing Theo on board?"

Kitty smiled. "That's an awesome idea."

A commotion rippled through the gathering crowd, as Amber Stevens pushed her way to the front, smiling gleefully in Theo's direction. "What a pig!"

"Great," Mika muttered. "The Supreme Bitch has arrived."

Amber straightened her neck with the regality of a queen and addressed her subjects. "I mean, have a little self-respect. Back away from the double cheeseburger, fat ass."

"Move it!" Coach Creed roared. The gathered audience was fueling his rage. "I don't care if it kills you. Haul your ass up that hill."

Without warning, John Baggott emerged from the mass of students. "Screw this," he said, and marched down the hill.

Margot paused midway up the hill, sticky and uncomfortable in her oversize sweats, and gulped huge mouthfuls of air as she tried to calm herself down. Beneath the layers of cotton and microfiber, her heart pounded in her chest, not from the physical exertion of hill charges, but from outrage as she witnessed Coach Creed's latest assault on Theodore Baranski.

"I said, move it!" Coach Creed growled. "Everyone's waiting for you."

Margot understood the degradation, the knowledge that every set of eyes was on him, judging his overweight body, murmuring "fat ass" under their breath while they tacitly assumed the obesity was his fault. Without thinking, Margot touched her forearm through the sleeve of her sweatshirt. She desperately wanted to help Theo, but how could she without ruining DGM's plan?

Suddenly, the tall, lithe figure of John Baggott ambled over to Coach Creed.

"'Scuse me!" he said, his voice light and his angular face all smiles. "Don't mean to interrupt, but are you Theo Baranski?"

Margot started. What was John doing? Why didn't Bree stop him?

Coach Creed whirled around. "What do you want, Baggott?"

John coolly met Coach Creed's glare. "I came from the office," he said, still smiling. "Father Uberti asked me to fetch Theo from gym class. Some kind of emergency."

The idea that Father Uberti had personally requested an errand from John Baggott was ridiculous to the point of being farcical, but short of calling John a liar, Coach Creed had little recourse.

"An emergency," Coach Creed repeated.

"Yep," John said with an affable grin. He patted Theo on the shoulder. "We should hurry."

Coach Creed shook his head in disgust as John led Theo up the hill. "You're pathetic, Baranski," he called out. "You too, Baggott. I'm not done with either of you."

Margot stood rooted in place long after Coach Creed had stormed off across the field and the rest of sixth-period gym class had filtered back to their assignments. It took her a moment to realize that three figures still ringed the top of the hillside, silhouetted against the bright afternoon sunshine: Kitty Wei, Bree Deringer, and Olivia Hayes.

They looked at one another, shifting their glances as if they were all thinking the same thing. An hour ago, a revenge plot against Coach Creed would have generated no obvious suspects. But now, Bree's best friend would be at the top of Father Uberti's list. One degree of separation from an actual DGM member was too close for comfort. Should they abort or not?

All eyes drifted to Kitty. She'd know what to do.

Without hesitation, Kitty drew her hand across her chest, from her left shoulder to her right, giving the signal, then dropped her arm to her side and strode away.

Margot let out a slow breath. The message was clear: their plan against Coach Creed was a go.

More spine-tingling reads from
GRETCHEN McNEIL

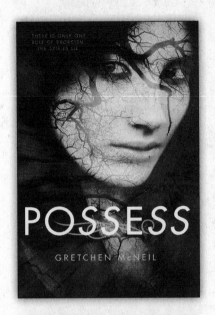

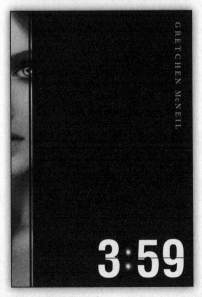

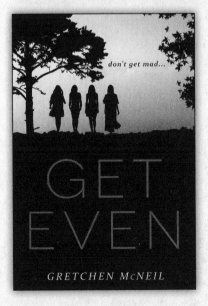